THE DEPTHS OF THE SEA

THE DEPTHS OF THE SEA

Jamie Metzl

ST. MARTIN'S PRESS ≈ NEW YORK

www.stmartins.com

Book design by Nick Wunder

First Edition: May 2004

Library of Congress Cataloging-in-Publication Data

Metzl, Jamie Frederic.
    The depths of the sea / Jamie Metzl.—1st ed.
        p.   cm.
    ISBN 0-312-32202-X
    EAN 978-0312-32202-1
    1. Americans—Cambodia—Fiction. 2. Americans—
Thailand—Fiction. 3. Intelligence officers–Fiction. 4. Fathers
and sons—Fiction. 5. Missing persons—Fiction. 6. Refugee
camps—Fiction. 7. Cambodia—Fiction. 8. Thailand—
Fiction. 9. Adoptees—Fiction. I. Title.

PS3613.E895D47 2004
813'.6–dc22

                                          2003069718

10   9   8   7   6   5   4   3   2   1

For my family

ACKNOWLEDGMENTS

I have benefited enormously from the love, support, and editorial advice of my family and friends in the seven years it took me to write this book. Three friends in particular—Rakhi Varma, Ben Brown, and Gayle Weiswasser—played an especially important role in helping me tighten my prose and further develop my characters. I am enormously grateful to each of them for their help, and for the friendship that their assistance symbolized. Other friends and family members, including Elizabeth Wang, Rebecca Bond, Ming Chen, Jonathan, Jordan, and Joshua Metzl, and my parents, Marilyn and Kurt Metzl, also read the manuscript and provided excellent comments. Bob Abbot kept me from making mistakes about the life of a CIA operations officer, and my dear friend Rasmey Nhek reviewed the manuscript with great care and helped correct and systematize my transliteration from Khmer. Many others helped introduce me to Thailand and Cambodia during my two and a half years living in Southeast Asia. I am particularly grateful to Jim and Ginny DiCrocco in Bangkok, who treated me as their second son, even though they already had a son named Jamie. Finally, I would like to thank Linda McFall, my wonderful editor at St. Martin's Press. This is a better book because of her warm encouragement and thoughtful advice.

PROLOGUE

The first hint of the rising orange sun drew the jungle toward life from its mournful darkness. Insects chirped their indifference. Leaves rustled in the wind.

The three black-pajama-clad Cambodian soldiers seemed to be almost enjoying the march. In front of them, the decrepit prisoner struggled to keep the pace. His arms tied tightly behind him with a rope extending to one of the soldiers' left hand, the prisoner hobbled forward like a wounded dog on a leash. Blood seeped from his bruised and contorted face.

"New khang mok bantec teat mean kanlang del knyom chol chet," I have a favorite spot up ahead, sneered one of the soldiers wearing a thick, green canvas belt.

"Min bach oy os kraub kampleung ter," No sense wasting a bullet, replied another soldier carrying a hoe over his shoulder.

The soldier holding the rope looked almost disappointed. He pointed the AK-47 in his right hand at the prisoner's head. "Oh just one? I think the people will understand."

The prisoner stumbled on, his every step increasingly less sure. His head bobbed forward as if suspended from a spring.

They entered a valley where damp marshland languished beside a small lake of two concentric circles.

"Just a little more and the new grass will grow," said the man with the green belt.

Suddenly, the weight of the journey seemed to overcome the exhausted prisoner. His left leg gave way sending him stumbling face down into the wet marsh. The soldier holding tight to the prisoner's rope jolted forward from the weight of the falling body then planted his feet to catch himself. Murky water closed over the prisoner's unmoving head like the ocean claiming a sinking ship.

The soldier with the rope pressed his sandaled left foot on the back of the prisoner's head and pointed his AK-47 at the prisoner's heart. Pressuring the trigger with his right index finger, he turned his eyes to the man with the green belt for authorization. A smirk came across the commander's face. He'd been waiting for this.

It happened in the briefest of moments.

Like a hooked fish jumping from its first encounter with land, the prisoner jerked upward. The force of the prisoner's body yanked the soldier with the rope off his feet and sent him stumbling into the marsh. The prisoner slithered one hand out of the knot behind him then looped the rope around the soldier's head. Pulling the rope to the right with one hand, he jammed the soldier's head to the left. The sound of snapping vertebrae marked two seconds like the beat of a metronome.

The hoe was already off the second soldier's shoulder. Jumping left, the prisoner felt the slice of the hoe missing his skull by a hair. He drove his head deep into the stomach of the man with the hoe, knocking him back. His karate chop landed on the second soldier's trachea with trained precision. The soldier gasped. The prisoner reached around the man's head to complete the kill.

But the prisoner knew there were three men, and in these few seconds he had only accounted for two.

He turned and saw the third soldier reaching behind his green belt. The third soldier's hand was cool, methodical. The prisoner crouched. Hatred and rage pumped adrenaline through his depleted body. His toes dug into the dirt as he leaned into a desperate lunge at the third man.

Time had run out.

The bullet entered through the prisoner's forehead. His muscles held him up for a fraction of a second until his uncomprehending eyes descended from the third man's face, to his waist, to his feet, and then, the dirt.

The insects chirped on. The hue of the orange sun shifted toward yellow.

1

Streaking through the Berkshire Hills Conservancy in Manassas, Virginia, Morgan O'Reilly waited, prayed even, for the click. The crunch of his step on pine needles, the ebb and flow of his breath, the musical chirping of birds, formed a symphony of sound, a facade of harmony.

The click, the shift into overdrive. More than a second wind or a runner's high, it was the wind filling his sail of being. The hope of reaching it drove Morgan's thirty-five-year-old legs along the nine-mile trail, even now that time and experience had taken their toll on his wiry body. The click, the escape from the ghosts, from the nightmares.

Morgan's nightmares weren't triggered by the swirl of helicopter blades or the crackle of fireworks like the other vets. Smells wafting from Asian restaurants brought him back, smells carrying memories of meals simmering in clay pots over charcoal. *Samlaa m'chou, nyoem moen*—was it tamarind or curry? or was his mind playing tricks on him, drawing him back like a siren to a sunken reef? Seeing children in the grocery store, watching them think that they were separated from their parents—their eyes desperately searching the empty aisles for familiar faces. Could the pampered American children ever understand how it would feel to never see their parents again?

Their faces were with him, in his dreams, on his runs, in the dark spaces of the forest. Six of them, streetwise, rambunctious, remarkably precocious. Cambodian orphans lost in Phnom Penh. His job had been an impossible one. It was '71, just eight years before, and the Khmer Rouge communists were already beating Lon Nol's army. America's help wasn't turning the tide. Everybody knew that the KR were stirring up trouble in Phnom Penh. Everybody knew that the communists had infiltrated every level of Cambodian society—the US-backed Lon Nol army, the government, the press. How to get them out was anybody's guess.

Morgan's boss hit upon the idea when he'd realized his wallet had been lifted by the unassuming Cambodian shoeshine boy working just outside the gates of the American embassy. He had hardly noticed the kid was there. Who ever noticed the ragged children eking out a living on the desperate streets of Phnom Penh? Colonel Bauer didn't know if the Agency had ever done anything like this before, but what chance did Lon Nol have if the CIA station chief couldn't muster a little creativity?

Morgan first thought Bauer's assignment was a joke.

"An intelligence unit of orphans? You've got to be kidding."

Bauer wasn't kidding, and he had picked his man carefully. Bauer had once been concerned that O'Reilly was "going native," getting even too comfortable in his operating environment. The moment he'd hatched the idea, however, Bauer knew that this liability was what made O'Reilly perfect for the job.

Morgan hit the streets of wartime Phnom Penh with a vengeance. The street kids he was looking for lurked in the dark alleys of the city, in the refugee camps just outside. They lived in cardboard boxes, lived by their wits—stealing, charming, cajoling, surviving. He patiently observed the tiny details of life on the streets that most people missed, looking for some special signal, a divine spark that showed through even the direst of circumstances. He selected them one by one.

He found Phim in a dark alley forging government ID cards with an unwavering attention to detail. From the shadows he watched Vuth surreptitiously remove thirteen pairs of brake-light covers from cars parked at the Norodom hotel. He saw Rithy transfer three loads of fish from the submerged net of a fisherman on the Tonle Sap river to his own burlap sack without ever being noticed. Sophal, the invisible shoeshine boy who'd lifted Colonel Bauer's wallet, it turned out, was supporting twelve other street kids with the forty-seven wallets he'd stolen thus far. Morgan's was the forty-eighth. Sophal opened it that night to find a photograph of himself on the make with a long note written in stilted but readable Khmer. The children proved the ultimate secret weapon. Who would ever suspect that these pestering street children were undercover agents?

But they became more than that to O'Reilly. Morgan hadn't been born such a careful observer of human nature. He'd learned it by necessity. How else was the quiet child to know when his father would explode from silent brooding to explosive rage? How else was he to know when to stay away as his mother locked herself away in busy isolation? Morgan had never imagined that this was even a skill before he left the marines and the CIA sent him to Phnom Penh. He had never imagined how much he would find once he got there.

There was something about the children that felt so empowering to Morgan. Some of them were dreamers, others con men of the highest order. Given half a chance, they could have all been doctors or businessmen, certainly great actors. But what Morgan offered them was still better than what they had. It was a way out, a purpose, a team. They would no longer face the elements alone. None of them would. They could fight for their country, not just passively suffer its destruction. He wasn't offering them the world, that he knew. But it was much more than what they had.

The children seemed to have all been raising themselves during the war years. No matter how well they had done, they needed more. Morgan knew he had to be a leader, perhaps a parent. The small incentives drew the children in. Morgan gave them a place to stay, some decent and reliable food, the types of recruitment offerings described in the CIA field guide. But nowhere in Morgan's training had anyone ever mentioned sitting up with a young boy remembering his dead parents or fighting through a drug overdose. With patience, determination, and care, Morgan built a network, a unit, a team. At times he felt, against his professional judgment, a family.

Phim, the ID forger who had learned to fake perfectly a missing leg and a deformed shoulder, was the ultimate insider. He could work his way anywhere. Who in the Lon Nol army's strategic planning division would have suspected the reed-thin, disabled waif with the sunken cheeks begging at the gate? The colonel in the Lon Nol army passing war plans to the Khmer Rouge certainly didn't. That was his mistake. Vuth, the thief, could invisibly follow his target for hours. The Khmer Rouge spy walking through Phnom Penh's Central Market probably never knew that the orders he was to deliver had been taken from him and replaced with new ones by the little street urchin he'd hardly noticed. Rithy, who'd spent his first years in a floating fishing village on the Tonle Sap, could frolic on the waterfront for days at a time, recording the comings and goings of boats and men with uncanny reliability.

They were all special, but Sophal was somehow different. Though by Cambodian standards short and scrappy for his fourteen years when Morgan had recruited him, Sophal's indefatigable spirit burst through everything he did. How many other fourteen-year-olds would sneak into a Khmer Rouge safe house, handcuff the Khmer Rouge's sleeping leading spy to the bed, then hit play on the spy's cassette recorder as he climbed out the window? The gongs and chimes were still blaring as Lon Nol's secret police arrived a few moments later.

Sophal didn't become a leader in the group because of his mind or even his spirit, but by looking after the others. When the corrupt Cambodian police officer found Vuth, the indistinguishable delivery boy, rifling though his papers after returning from the toilet, it was Sophal's rock through the window that allowed Vuth to escape. Sophal had a sixth sense about when he was needed, and an uncanny ability to be there when he was.

Sophal also had a sense about Morgan. Though the powerful American seemed almost invincible to the other children, Sophal innately understood that Morgan was both more determined and more vulnerable than any of the others could know. Sophal was the child who understood the parent, who recognized that just as the children needed Morgan, Morgan needed the children. Though the others wouldn't have guessed that their leader needed teaching, Sophal quietly taught the older American the Cambodian power of silence, patience, and invisibility. He also taught him the ways of the street, Cambodian slang, and, with a fiendish wink, how to cheat at gambling.

So many memories, the planning, the execution, the celebration of successes—breaking the air force spy ring, foiling the bomb at the national assembly. The successes brought them together, drew them in from their solitary worlds apart. They were all orphans, Vanny, Phim, Sophal, Rithy, Choeun, Vuth. Sometimes, in a way, Morgan.

Morgan could still picture each of them vividly. Why is caring so painful, Morgan wondered. Hadn't childhood taught him to build a wall around himself? Seeing so much death in Vietnam and Cambodia had prepared Morgan to face the terrible things. But the good memories now seemed the most piercing. It was so much easier to be haunted by bad memories.

Morgan focused to try to clear his racing mind. The click, the wings to soar away from it all, blindly, deliriously, freely. Morgan longed for his body's simple chemistry to carry him away, even for just a moment. But the memories raced alongside Morgan, weighing him down, holding him to the haunted earth. Phnom Penh's defensive wall breaking down in '75, the earth shaking from the pounding of bombs, the Khmer Rouge moving closer, the panic, the chaos, the wailing in the streets, the incessant swirl of helicopter blades as the once proud Americans withdrew. It had been abundantly clear what the Khmer Rouge were planning to do. They had essentially announced it in advance. There would be no room for the old ways, the old people in the new Cambodia. Anyone perceived as an enemy of the state was in grave danger. The Khmer Rouge, everybody knew, had been killing off their enemies for years. Morgan knew they all had to get out, that he had to get them all out.

"Fuck your priority list!" Morgan screamed at the lance corporal handling the evacuation. "Where's Bauer?"

Morgan found the station chief frantically burning documents in the embassy compound.

"These kids have given everything they've got for this damn war. Don't give me goddamn bullshit priority list. We've got to get them out of here. You know what the Khmer Rouge are all about. You know what's going to happen!" Morgan's throat went dry.

"Hey, I'm sorry Morgan," Bauer said softly, "I'm really, really sorry. This whole war, the whole goddamn thing, breaks my heart. We've got a set number of people and a certain number of planes, and not a lot of time. You know as well as I that Lon Nol's top people—generals, the prime minister for Christ's sake—have much more to fear from the communists than a bunch of kids in a secret unit nobody even knows about. We're leaving some of the best people behind and I feel like shit about it. I'm sorry, Morgan."

"God dammit . . . Sir. That is unacceptable."

Bauer pursed his lips and looked Morgan in the eye.

"Sir . . . please." The desperation broke through Morgan's voice.

"I'm sorry, Morgan." The colonel's voice was barely audible.

Morgan's mind raced as he wandered the chaotic city in desperate thought. There was no way, no goddamn way, he was going to leave them behind. He'd read the intel reports from the countryside—peasants' heads sawed off with razor sharp banana leaves, forced labor, torture, executions—the KR wouldn't rest until they had tracked down everyone from the Lon Nol side and anyone who'd had too close a relation with the Americans or the old guard. All it took was one confession, one file left behind, and they would hunt them down.

A shiver ran down Morgan's spine.

He had to think—but what? Could he send them down the Mekong River to Saigon? Then what? A bunch of Cambodian orphans as that city falls. By land? Where could they go? The only place was Thailand, but that was two hundred and fifty miles though KR territory filled with angry soldiers and land mines. The idea hit him with the sad, humiliating realization that it was all he could think of. He raced back to the embassy grounds.

"Sir, I know you can't get my team out"—Morgan winced inwardly—"I accept that. But you have empty planes flying north to Battambang to pick people up. Just let me send my team up there on one of those planes."

"O'Reilly, that's madness," Bauer said, still tossing piles of papers into the fire. "Battambang's just as vulnerable as Phnom Penh. Why would you want to do that?"

"Battambang is sixty miles from the Thai border. At least there they'll have a fighting chance of getting out. Here they'll . . ." Morgan could not finish the sentence.

The colonel took a deep breath. He owed Morgan and he knew it. He too had once believed.

"OK, O'Reilly. It's a terrible idea, but OK."

"When's the last flight today?"

"If it can take off it'll be at 1700, but the airport is getting pounded pretty hard."

"We'll be there."

"Not you, O'Reilly." Bauer knew Morgan O'Reilly. "The plane won't fly if you're on it, period. There's nothing for you in Battambang."

Morgan hated to admit it, but the colonel was right. The kids' only chance was to work their way invisibly toward the Thai border. Morgan had once seen himself as their protector. Now proximity to him would mean their death.

"1700 then . . . sir." It was a fifth-rate plan. The kids deserved to fly the hell out of here in one of the hundred Huey helicopters dominating the Phnom Penh sky, not be thrown in the rapids and forced to swim.

Morgan worked his way to the meeting point in an alleyway near the Old Market. After everything they had been through together, how, he tortured himself, could he offer them so little? He felt his passport pressing against his chest in his shirt pocket. This random paper, the difference between life and . . . No. Focus Morgan, think. It was up to him to change the outcome—to do whatever it damn-well took to change the outcome. Could he give his passport away? The US army wouldn't leave a white American behind, passport or not. But an Asian with an American passport still had a fighting chance of getting on a helicopter. How could he save just one? How could he choose? His subconscious had long since made the choice.

He found all six of them at the meeting point. He'd never promised any of the kids that they'd be taken out of Cambodia, but Morgan had promised himself that he'd take care of them no matter what happened. A deep shame overcame him as he described the plan.

The six looked at Morgan blankly. They'd all been survivors before they'd met Morgan and their lives had changed so abruptly. They were still survivors, but they had begun to dream that life could be different. Hope had softened them. Now it was clear—there would be no California beach parties, not even the regular meals they had slowly become accustomed to. They would revert to the lives they had previously known, to the selves they had struggled so hard to overcome. What, after all, had they ever really expected?

Vuth turned down his face. His breathing became heavy. Morgan perceived a look of fear on Vuth's face he had never before seen.

Rithy, Choeun, and Vanny stared at Morgan with wide, uncomprehending eyes.

"So what do we do once we get to Battambang?" Phim asked, disappointment bubbling beneath the surface calm of his face.

"You work your way toward Poipet on the Thai border and cross into Thailand at Dalat Klong Luk. When you get there, tell the Thai army to contact the US embassy in Bangkok, and I'll be there." Morgan felt the hollowness of his words deeply. "I'll be there" had meant something a few weeks before.

Morgan brought out the maps he'd taken from the embassy and a stack of fifty dollar bills. They only had an hour to get to the airport, they'd plan on the way. The thunder cadence of dropping shells, the human panic pouring through the streets, made the drive impossibly hectic.

Sophal took the map of northwest Cambodia from Morgan and began charting different routes from Battambang to the border. From the Jeep's rearview minor, Morgan watched Sophal rising, once again, to take care of the others. He felt the passport in his pocket. Was he doing the right thing? He had built this family, how could he now take it apart? Flashing his ID at the nervous marine manning the airport's perimeter, Morgan raced the Jeep onto the runway.

"You O'Reilly?" The lieutenant shouted above the chaotic din of twirling helicopter blades.

"Yeah."

"Well get your fuckin' people on this bird 'fore we get shot to shit."

"Go," was all that Morgan could muster. He didn't want to make this any harder than it had to be. The emptiness was expanding within him. He placed his palms together before his face in the traditional Cambodian manner. The children looked at him with a mix of tenacity and fear in their faces. None of them moved. Sophal was the first to break the impasse. He placed his hands together in front of his forehead. The others, more hesitant, followed this show of respect.

"Move it, go, go, go," the lieutenant yelled.

"*Tos teu,*" Sophal said to the others with a flick of his head. Let's go.

Vuth nodded gravely and moved toward the plane.

The thud of a bomb hitting just beside the runway rocked the earth.

"Get on the goddamn plane!" the lieutenant barked frantically.

There seemed nowhere else for the kids to go. Another bomb hit so close nearby that they could feel its heat on their faces. Vanny, Choeun, and Rithy dashed toward the plane. Phim looked sadly at Morgan then walked behind them.

Morgan gulped. "Sophal, wait. We have one more mission to complete here. I need to send you on the next flight tomorrow morning."

Sophal looked up, stunned. His first reaction was to turn to his friends waiting in the cargo hold of the C-130. Phim and Rithy, Vuth, Vanny, and Choeun stared down at Sophal, incomprehension overtaking their faces.

Sophal felt a moment of panic. His place was with the others heading out for a final ride. But only he saw the desperate pleading in Morgan's eyes. He felt paralyzed.

Another bomb exploded just beside the runway.

"Close the damn door, close the damn door now!" the lieutenant yelled.

The plane's back flap lifted, blocking the five faces staring out from the cargo hold. The flap locked into place. The C-130 rolled down the runway and lifted its wide body into the air.

Morgan and Sophal stood watching the plane recede into oblivion until the dropping shells came so close they could feel the wind of the blasts and the earth giving beneath their feet. As they ran for cover, Morgan handed Sophal the blue passport. Sophal opened it to see his picture and the name Paul Ly.

"Tell them you work for Emerson Catering. I think it should be OK." Morgan's eyes pleaded with Sophal to accept this humble gift.

Sophal looked down in shame. His fate was with the others whirring toward Battambang, but his life, he sensed, was now linked to this small blue book. He should be with them, but he also had to be with Morgan. Somewhere deep within him, Sophal understood that he had to let Morgan save him so that he could save Morgan. He lifted his head and looked into Morgan's eyes. Sophal nodded slightly.

In a day, Sophal would be on the USS Hancock in the South China Sea. Three months later he would land at Dulles Airport in Virginia.

When the Khmer Rouge took control of Cambodia and announced the total evacuation of Cambodia's cities, Morgan could guess where his Cambodian friends were going—to uninhabited parts of the country, to holes in the ground to fertilize the communists' utopian rice crop. Morgan knew he should have left the country with the other Americans, but somehow he couldn't bring himself to cut and run leaving so much of what he now valued in life behind. He cased the back alleys he knew so well, not knowing where he was going but unwilling to beg his way into the French embassy compound, the final receptacle of foreigners no longer useful to the Cambodian nation. Even Morgan, with his perfect Khmer, was nothing less than a hundred percent conspicuous. There was no place for foreigners in the new Cambodia.

The fierce look of hatred in the unflinching, adolescent eyes of the Khmer Rouge soldier foretold the end of his story. Morgan almost welcomed it. Perhaps Morgan did not deserve to leave when the kids had no choice but to stay. But Khmer Rouge orders were not negotiable and the foreign swine, the polluters of Cambodian culture, the imperialists who had brought the Cambodian people to their knees, were to be thrown into the French embassy. They pushed Morgan through the gate as if tossing garbage into a pile.

Most of the three hundred foreigners crammed in the French embassy complained that food was running out. It didn't bother Morgan much. He had little desire to eat. What was going on in the world outside the high concrete and steel embassy walls once built to keep people out? Morgan wanted to be on the other side. The Khmer Rouge had other plans. Two weeks later the foreigners were all on bus convoys crossing the Thai border. The French sang the *Marseillaise* as they passed the fortified frontier post. Morgan was silent. What was he outside of this place, apart from the people who had trusted him, from the only family he had ever truly known?

Afterward, it was the silence that killed him. Six months on the Thai side of the border and nothing. Only a trickle of stories—mass executions, the country as a vast work camp, ceaseless interrogations, the hunting down of Lon Nol soldiers and collaborators by the Khmer Rouge—each a dagger draining Morgan of his lifeblood. The kids were survivors, but being a good swimmer didn't help when going over a waterfall. After six months Morgan's CIA manager decided that enough was enough. It was time to bring him back to Langley. The war was over.

The memories of all that he had left behind—the children, himself— were with Morgan in the forest, in his dreams, everywhere. They haunted him, devoured him, seeped into every aspect of his life back in America. All he could hope for was—ahh, there it was . . . the click.

His legs transformed into wheels, rolling smoothly along the trail. His heartbeat, the circulation of his blood, his thoughts, his arms and legs, his skin, all unified in the harmonious rhythm. His body became a perfect instrument of motion. He glided his last three miles toward his house—at one with the forest, at peace with his now distant self.

2

If furtive stares were bullets, Tom Dillon thought, both men would now be dead. Tensions had been rising between National Security Advisor Witkowski and Secretary of State Bohlen for the past year. Sitting across from each other in the coral-blue Cabinet Room in the West Wing of the White House, their dignified hostility seemed almost a presence at the long, oval mahogany table. President Carter's anger did little to calm things down.

"This is getting way out of hand. I'll tell you this. I'll be damned if I'm going to go down in history as the president who lost the Vietnam war a second time."

Witkowski, Bohlen, and the other National Security cabinet officers tried to match the president's intensity with the determined focus of their eyes. Each of them was a king everywhere but in this room. Here, they were courtiers. It was eight o'clock in the morning. None dared touch the pitchers of coffee set before them.

"Look at this." Carter held up the clipping. "Now"—he allowed the pause to sink in—"what the hell are we going to do about it?"

The president put on his glasses with a deliberate slowness.

"*New York Times,* March 28, 1979," he said for effect, as if the courtiers didn't know the date, as if any courtier would dare show up to a meeting with the president without being fully briefed on the morning's papers. He read the headline he had already committed to memory. "Soviets Move into Cam Ranh Bay, Worst War Fears Realized."

The public opinion buzzards, they had all learned, could be deadly, waiting to swoop in on real or perceived weakness. It amazed Dillon how quickly fortunes in Washington could turn. A few months ago, this untested farmer from Georgia was being hailed as a foreign policy mastermind— Camp David, normalizing relations with China. Now, just three short months after the glory of the China normalization, the tide seemed to be turning, and the president was going to do whatever it took to turn it back. Each of the two titans of the foreign policy team was determined to harness this energy and store it as power.

Witkowski was the first to speak. A wave of silver hair curled from his furrowed head like a salute. His sharp, green eyes held a disarming, penetrating depth.

"These activities are an outrage," he declared in his accented but precise English. "It is abundantly clear that the Soviets are behind Vietnam's invasion of Cambodia three months ago and now are behind Vietnam's push toward the Thai border. The Soviets are turning Vietnam into a client, the Vietnamese are making trouble in Cambodia, and we've got a serious problem, Mr. President."

Perfect, Dillon thought, his temples a barometer of the pressure in the room. Set the scene and move on.

Witkowski looked at Carter then fired a quick glance at Bohlen.

"As I see it, we have one and only one interest in Indochina, and that is to keep the Soviets out. The Soviet move into Cam Ranh Bay completely undermines our credibility in Asia. Our Thai allies are petrified the Vietnamese might even make a move on Bangkok. God only knows what the Chinese would do if they see the Soviets moving in on their southern border. We're arming the Thais, but that's not enough. We've been completely out of Vietnam for four years now, but that doesn't mean we can let the Soviets and their Vietnamese puppets do whatever they like. Mr. President, we need to show our Asian allies as well as Peking and Moscow that we're serious."

"What do you propose we do, Felix?"

"Mr. President, we need to oppose the Vietnamese and Soviet move in every way possible—diplomatically, through assistance programs to our allies, by supporting those who are fighting against the Vietnamese aggression."

Dillon was pleased that Witkowski was following the strategy they had together conceived. Keep going, Felix, he thought to himself.

"And who might that be, Felix?" Despite the gentlemanly manner of its expression, Bohlen's question was neither curious nor neutral. Bohlen seemed totally at ease, a posture Dillon recognized as the familiar product of breeding.

Though he had spent his entire life in three isolated enclaves— Cambridge, Massachusetts, Wall Street, and downtown Washington, DC— Secretary of State Perseus Bohlen had somewhere developed a keen sense of domestic politics that Carter trusted.

The Secretary of State's golden hair rested gracefully above his long face. Only the wrinkles around his eyes betrayed Bohlen's sixty-one years. The rest of his face clung to the promise of youth, to the boyish glow of thirty years of six A.M. tennis matches. Bohlen hadn't clawed his way from nothing like Witkowski, but he had been born with power and a keen sense of responsibility about how to use it.

Dillon pressed his toes against the soles of his shoes and inhaled deeply. He felt as if his own fate was being determined alongside Cambodia's.

Jerry Graves looked to Witkowski, as if for permission to speak on his behalf. The national security advisor nodded almost imperceptibly.

Pencil thin and six and a half feet tall, until recently president of the California Institute of Technology, Graves should have been more confident than he appeared. The newly appointed director of Central Intelligence seemed more sure of the facts than comfortable with his responsibilities.

"We've been trying to monitor events on the Thai-Cambodian border over the past months. All kinds of Cambodians are coming out of the woodwork on the Thai side of the border claiming to lead the resistance against the Vietnamese. There are old generals from the deposed Lon Nol regime, officials returning from exile in France, smugglers and bandits who operated on the border during the Khmer Rouge years. The Thais are putting the refugees streaming across the border into camps, and different leaders are claiming to control them. It doesn't look like these guys are doing much fighting against the Vietnamese, but it's early. There's not a lot of food, and the situation is still pretty chaotic. The Vietnamese pushed the KR to the border three months ago, but they still haven't finished them off. The KR are holding out in a zone on the Cambodian side of the border. It looks like they're still getting guns from China."

"What kind of condition are the refugees in?" asked Carter, now in a more reflective mood.

"They're in pretty bad shape, Mr. President. I think you've seen our report on the Khmer Rouge years in Cambodia?"

The President nodded gravely. They had all seen the gruesome pictures of putrefying dead bodies.

With a lift of his eyebrows, the president signaled for Graves to continue.

"Well there wasn't much food then and there's certainly less now. The KR areas on the border are some of the worst—nowhere to grow rice, malaria, mines. Still, the Khmer Rouge are probably the only ones fighting the Vietnamese at all."

Bohlen's frown cast a shadow over the room. The secretary might be a gentleman, Dillon thought, but he had not risen this far by being stupid. Bohlen was probably sharp enough to know when a "spontaneous" discussion had been precooked and to understand that Graves's analysis was supporting Witkowski's position. Everyone in the room knew that Bohlen was becoming increasingly annoyed by Witkowski's never-ending power games and one-upmanship, and ever more determined to hold his own. Bohlen shifted in his brown leather chair.

"With your permission, Mr. President." The phrase was not a question, merely a statement akin to "may it please the court." Bohlen spoke quietly yet firmly. "Nobody underestimates the threat that this blatant Vietnamese aggression poses to our allies and interests in Southeast Asia and the world. However things may have changed since the end of the war, the basic fact remains that we fought for ten years to hold back the Vietnamese communists, and now, for whatever reason, Vietnam, with Soviet backing, has taken the offensive. I make no excuses for Vietnam's aggression, but I have to put a stop to all of these not so subtle hints that we ought to be aiding the Khmer Rouge to fight them."

Carter nodded pensively.

Witkowski raised his head from its resting place in his palm with a subtle, dismissive frown. He was impressed with the secretary's insight, but that hadn't been exactly what he'd had in mind.

Under his calm exterior, Dillon felt a momentary fright. What if Bohlen pulled it off? What if the discussion stopped here?

The secretary continued.

"For three and a half years we've been condemning the Khmer Rouge as, in your words, Mr. President, 'the worst violator of human rights in the world.' These people are murderers, probably genocidal murderers. Neither history nor the American public will look kindly on any activities to support them. If you'll excuse me for saying this, Mr. President, one of the reasons the American people sent us here was because they were sick and tired of behind-the-scenes intrigues in Southeast Asia." Bohlen glanced passingly at Witkowski. "I can only imagine the harm that public disclosure of any activities to aid the Khmer Rouge might do. Aiding the Khmer Rouge is just not what we're here to do, Mr. President."

Like his boss Witkowski, Tom Dillon despised this kind of posturing. Nobody had mentioned a plan to aid the Khmer Rouge. Bohlen was trying to push them into a corner. Million dollar corporate lawyers like Bohlen could afford to argue human rights and morality straight up. Dillon knew their world intimately. It was easy for people like Bohlen to be pure, but life for everyone else just became more and more complicated.

Dillon could feel Bohlen's words moving the President. Carter nodded his head, half in agreement, half in thought. Perhaps Carter was picturing the headlines in his mind—"Human Rights President Aids Khmer Rouge

Killers." The tide was turning away. The power of Dillon's confidence overtook his deep appreciation of the stakes of failure. He had worked this room before, yet felt more nervous than ever. He scribbled a quick note and passed it from his seat against the wall to his boss Witkowski at the table. The national security advisor read the note and nodded.

"Mr. President," Witkowski interjected, "with your permission, I'd like to ask Tom Dillon to say a few words."

It was hardly protocol for anyone other than the cabinet officers to speak at such high-level meetings. Although Dillon was the most powerful deputy in Washington, the arrangement of the chairs made it perfectly clear who was a cabinet officer and who was not. Bohlen thought about objecting but decided to hold his tongue. On the books at least, Dillon was still a State Department officer, but he'd developed a power base far beyond the department in his six years at the White House.

As Dillon stood, it was clear to all in the room that something about Dillon commanded a presence far beyond his age and even his position. Dillon's angular good looks and nonchalant wisp of parted auburn hair with the first hint of gray showing at his temples gave him the aura of a gracefully aging college athlete. Though a decade or two younger than everyone else, Dillon's focused mind, they all knew, was the perfect complement to Witkowski's grand vision, and it was sometimes difficult to tell where the one man's thoughts ended and the other's began. The scion of the great Dillon-Reed investment bank who had heeded the call and joined the foreign service, Dillon and his elegant wife Meredith had entertained most of them at their palatial McLean, Virginia home. Dillon scanned the room for a brief moment and then spoke.

"There has been a lot said this morning that makes good sense. Clearly, aiding the Khmer Rouge would be tough for us to do politically. But the alternatives aren't limited to tacitly accepting Vietnamese aggression."

Dillon noticed the president slightly nodding his head. He continued.

"No matter what our feelings about the Khmer Rouge might be, the fact of the matter is that the Vietnamese invasion violates international law. It also hurts our interests. The Thais are scared that they are going to be

Hanoi's next target. They're also extremely concerned because they don't see us taking decisive enough action to support them.

"The Chinese see Moscow behind all of this and want to be certain we're on their side. Even minimal gestures of support would be looked on very favorably by Peking, would enhance our strategic interests with the Vietnamese and the Soviets, would reassure the Thais, and would produce almost no political fallout domestically."

A few heads perked up, Bohlen's not among them.

"What I have in mind is this. First, I don't think we can recognize the new Cambodian government installed by the Vietnamese. No matter whom they kicked out, it's still Soviet-backed aggression. Second, I suggest that we neither comment on nor interfere with Chinese and Thai attempts to aid the Khmer Rouge in whatever ways they see fit. We wouldn't get any benefit from stopping them, even if we could. My third proposal may amount to nothing, but I think it's worth discussing."

Dillon hoped he was sounding natural. He felt the growing pressure on his forehead. He fought to empty his mind of the tremendous weight of this moment, of all that was personally at stake, of everything but the suggestion he was about to make.

"As Director Graves mentioned, there's a lot of activity by opposition groups along the Thai-Cambodian border. Some of it is legitimate and other parts are just smuggling operations, but we don't know enough about what's what. If some of the groups organize, and I think they will, this could be the germ of a third force that would be neither Khmer Rouge nor the Vietnamese-installed government. I think supporting these groups, some of whom we know from the past, is at least worth a look."

"What kind of look?" Secretary Bohlen asked suspiciously. He could feel himself being pushed toward a compromise he did not want but feared he could not escape. He held back his resentment at being out-maneuvered by the shifty Witkowski and his arrogant underling. Meetings with the president were only rarely the time for overt bureaucratic battles, and those opportunities needed to be selected wisely.

"Well, sir, first, just a political assessment of whether what they are putting together has any potential. Second, a needs assessment of what kind of aid they might need to become viable. And third, if appropriate, aid itself."

Bohlen opened his mouth to speak but was cut off by the president.

"Now that's operational." Carter seemed relieved by the reasonable compromise, unwilling to be implicated by any of the details to follow, and ready to move on. The courtiers would take care of the rest.

The secretary took off his glasses and placed them on the table.

"I think that sounds about right," the president continued. "Unless there's any disagreement, I'll give you the go ahead. But," Carter added, looking apologetically at Bohlen, "I just want to make one thing clear—no aid to the Khmer Rouge."

Dillon's heart was pounding. He tried not to look as relieved as he felt. Relaxing his grip on his pen, he only now recognized the deep imprint the cap had made on his tightly clenched hand. He quietly poured himself a cup of coffee and leaned back in his chair. He had done it.

3

"Chapter 7, verse 19 from the Prophet Micah commands us to 'cast thy sins into the depths of the sea . . .' The depths of the sea." The young rabbi paused to let the significance of the phrase sink in. Wind blew his chestnut hair. "What does it mean that today, on the first day of *Rosh Hashanah,* the new year, we empty the contents of our pockets into the water? It is not only the contents of our pockets that we purge. No, it is the contents of our souls." He paused again. "Our transgressions, our failure to follow our ideals, our imperfections that keep us from doing what is right and sometimes lead us to do what is wrong. But in expelling these sins, in casting them 'to the depths of the sea,' we also seek renewal, the chance to start over, to be forgiven for our sins against God as we face the next chapter of our lives. When we truly understand our failures and our sins, when we promise from our hearts that we will not remain as before, our sins drift away with the flowing current. We become ready to face the new year with hope . . ."

Jonathon Cohane stood with his parents at the stream's edge. The sounds of the current and of children playing nearby floated in the cool wind. Autumn leaves painted the world in amber and crimson.

How could this all seem so calm? Jonathon wondered. How could it feel so comfortable while all of *that* was going on? Like a tiny spark starting a massive fire, a word was taking hold of Jonathon. He could not seem to shake it.

He had heard it so many times before—over and over, at home, at school, in his parent's tale of Poland, of Auschwitz. But somehow this felt different. This time it seemed demanding.

The starving child's eyes bulging from his emaciated, insect-like head had stared at Jonathon as he'd surreptitiously leafed through his copy of *Newsweek* during a lull in his advanced contracts class at the University of Chicago Law School a month before. Is this what my family had looked like? he asked himself. The names repeated to abstraction at Passover Seders— Cousin Jacob, Catherine, Hilda—came alive through the Cambodian child's eyes. Could there be another "Holocaust"? Maybe these types of realizations did not await opportune moments. Maybe they grabbed you and held on until they changed your life forever.

> *Western intelligence reports suggest that up to three million people have been killed in the last three years under Khmer Rouge rule. If reports of famine are correct, it is feared that 2.25 million Cambodians face immediate death and that the Cambodians face extinction as a people.*

Extinction as a people. Those words could not simply settle into Jonathon like a pebble tossed in a stream.

Didn't the other students around him read the papers? Jonathon knew he could be like them. He could turn the page of his *Newsweek* past the Cambodian child, could step onto the escalator of life that his law degree would provide, and move away from the overpowering realization he was fast approaching.

The idea of doing something drastic frightened him. Yet somehow he had never been like the others. He had always felt more intense, more relentless than most of the people around him. Every science fair project or research paper was an opportunity to delve deeper into the wonders of the universe. But seeking knowledge was a solitary act. With his books, and his

ideas, and his solitude, Jonathon had understood. And when you understand . . .

"Mr. Cohane." Jonathon was almost too lost in thought to hear his name
being called. "Can you please describe the development of *caveat emptor*
doctrine in common law jurisprudence?"

Jonathon sat silent before the question. The contrast was so great. The
sixty-four students camouflaging their preprofessional eagerness behind
tie-dyed shirts in Professor Marsten's ten-thirty contracts class, the past
deans looking down from the oil paintings in front of the classroom like
medieval knights of legality, the framed photographs of graduating classes
of past years, all seemed superfluous. They beckoned him to the halls of
the blind. *Caveat emptor,* buyer beware, beware of becoming stultified in
legal inevitability.

"I'd like to pass, sir."

The class held its collective breath. There were some classes in which
passing was an option. This was not one.

Jonathon waited for the next salvo from Professor Marsten. It was all
seeming to matter less. The class photos did not pause for 1942, '43, '44,
or '45. Jonathon could just sit and answer the question. He could be a distant dot in the class of '81 photo less than two years from now. Or he
could stand and face 2.25 million Cambodians, face 6 million victims of
the Holocaust, face himself.

"Mr. Cohane, can you please explain to me the holding of *Chandelor v.
Lopus?*"

Jonathon felt 128 eyes boring into him.

"I'm sorry, sir. Excuse me." As if from a distance, he watched himself
stack his papers and move out the door. Could a person give up so much so
quickly, so impulsively? The thought of a single moment transforming his
life seemed both terrifying and exhilarating. What was he doing? He had
worked so hard to get here. His heart pounded. Could he simply step off
the life he knew into a vast unknown?

Jonathon left the building and sat dizzily on a bench beside a massive ginkgo tree. He read the *Newsweek* article slowly and carefully, as if dictating to his soul. Could he do it?

> *As refugees pour across the border, an international consortium of relief agencies, aided by a ragtag group of international volunteers, including backpackers whisked from budget youth hostels in Bangkok, have begun the impossible task of assistance.*

People were doing something, people like him, who saw, who cared, who risked. Auschwitz had also been far away. That was no excuse. Jonathon had lived in the shadow of his parents' experience. Now, he knew he had to face it, had to see that past for what it was, for what it compelled him to do. Facing the real world, he was coming to believe, was facing the vast darkness with a spark of light.

Jonathon spent his next day in the university library. He found the names and addresses of aid organizations working on the border and sent off nine letters. The response from a Christian aid agency called Mercy Relief had arrived just three days before *Rosh Hashanah*. "We need all the help we can get. Please stop by our office at 273a Sukhumvit Soi 42 when you arrive in Bangkok." "We need all the help we can get," Jonathon repeated to himself. Maybe one person can make a difference. Sukhumvit Road, Bangkok, the border—all seemed far away. But who would he be if he did not go?

The final step toward making it all real was here, at the Heller Nature Preserve in Highland Park, Illinois. The rabbi finished speaking. The twelve men and six women read the three paragraphs to themselves and then turned their pockets inside out. They threw bits of lint and some pebbles into the stream. The rabbi chanted a few verses in Hebrew.

Jonathon held his parents' prayer books for them as they fulfilled their ritual obligation. His parents seemed more frail than the year before. It should not have been surprising that they were aging, he thought. The Warsaw ghetto, Auschwitz, the displaced persons camp, the struggle to build a life in America, had earned them the right. Where would he be for next year's *Rosh Hashanah?* Who would carry their prayer books to the park?

But maybe, Jonathon wondered, *Taschlich* was about striving to not have to do *Taschlich*. It was a nice idea to empty your pockets, your sins, into the river. It was nice to forget, to start over. But Jonathon's mind was becoming obsessed with something higher, with living a life so devoted to doing what was right that there would be nothing to throw into the stream and abandon for the fish.

He had agonized over how to tell his parents. How would they take the news that their only son was going so far away, to a place they didn't understand? He didn't fully understand it himself.

Maybe there would never be a perfect moment, but *Taschlich* might be as close as he could hope for. What were the sins they were throwing into the river? They were sins of commission, the bad things people had done directly to others. But they were also sins of omission, of not doing what needed to be done, not doing what there was a moral imperative to do. How many times had his parents described Auschwitz to him? Jonathon had imagined rings of guilt surrounding the camps. In the innermost rings were the Nazis, the murderers, the perpetrators. Then, there were the little people, the helpers, the clerks, the Jewish kapos who did the Nazis' bidding. The third ring now intrigued him. The third ring were those who knew what was going on, who had to know, but who didn't respond. It was the University of Chicago Law School graduating class of 1944 posing on the law school steps. What river could accept their sins?

As they strolled past the small red brick homes, past the impeccable lawns fed by the ebb and flow of sprinklers, Jonathon looked toward the sidewalk and asked his question.

"Mom, Dad, what did it feel like to be in the camp? Did you wonder where everyone else in the world was?"

His mother looked at Jonathon thoughtfully. She paused for a moment to consider the question. A look of pain came across her face. Jonathon wondered if he was doing the right thing.

"Most of the time we were so focused on surviving," she said in broken

English, "on getting anything to eat, on keeping from freezing to death, dat we almost forgot de rest of the world was there. But every once on a while, I would look up at the moon at night and I would wonder if this could be de same moon that people all around the world were looking at, if people who were out for a walk or sitting on their porch were looking at de moon and thinking how beautiful it was. And I would cry. Could it be de same moon? Where was everyone who was looking at this moon? Where was the world? I felt so alone. Like no one cared. Like I was forgotten."

Jonathon reached out and took his mother's hand. He had known she would say this. He'd heard it before and it chilled him every time. He felt almost guilty for turning her words on her, but was he not honoring them by what he was about to say?

"Mom, Dad, I have something I need to talk with you about. I hope you can understand. We've always talked about the Holocaust. We've always said 'never again,' but now . . . it's happening."

Jonathon's parents didn't seem to comprehend his words.

"It's happening in Cambodia."

They had seen a few stories in the *Tribune,* but were not sure how this place related to their son.

"Two and a quarter million people look like they're going to die by the end of the year. The Cambodians face extinction as a people. We've talked about the Holocaust, about other people's responsibilities for us."

His parents stared at Jonathon. They knew their intense son. They had seen him lock onto ideas before, but this somehow seemed different.

"We . . . I . . . have a responsibility. It's not just words. I have a responsibility to do what I can, to stand and be counted. I've been thinking so much about it. I wrote to a refugee agency in Thailand about going to help the Cambodians. I don't know how else to say this, I hope you understand . . . I, I've decided . . ."

Jonathon hesitated. Somehow saying it made it finally irreversible. Life up to this point seemed so easy. He had worked hard, but had he ever really been tested? The words flowed like a stream springing from within him.

"I've decided to go out to Thailand to help the refugees."

His parents had stopped walking. Tears welled in his mother's eyes. She knew her son, knew this voice, knew his determination. Asia was a fleeting image on the TV news, not a place for her only child.

"But what about law school, your plans, all your work?"

Jonathon had no answer. He had taken a leave of absence and could always go back, but that was starting to seem like a different life. His life was turning elsewhere.

"Cambodia? It's so far away. What can you do?"

"Mom," Jonathon said with a quiet determination, "can't you see? That's just what they said about us." He squeezed her hand. The look of sadness in her eyes gave him a pit in his stomach.

"No, Jonathon, don't go. How can you possibly know?"

His father covered his eyes with his hand, as if shielding them from the face of God at morning prayers.

His mother looked at her son and knew that all the words she and her husband would expend over the next days would be in vain.

4

As the door to his West Wing office swung shut, National Security Advisor Witkowski could not help but give Tom Dillon a stiff pat on the shoulder.

"Well done, Thomas," Witkowski chortled. "A few more doses of that Bohlen moralism and who knows how many Nicaraguas we'd have on our hands."

Witkowski opened a small drawer set in the wall behind his desk and took out a crystal stopper. He poured two shots of Polish vodka.

"Thank you sir." Dillon took a small sip. He'd learned in Vietnam that good intentions alone were rarely sufficient and often dangerous. "It did look as if Bohlen lost the game."

"Perhaps," Witkowski said thoughtfully. He knew better than to underestimate someone like Bohlen. "But we still have a set and a match to go."

"Well the ball is clearly in our court." Dillon wondered if he was being too cute.

Witkowski laughed. The tennis metaphor was beginning to sound absurd. He recited the words Bohlen had written for the Carter inaugural.

"Today my administration pledges that by honesty, sincerity, and optimism, by providing food to the hungry and hope to the downtrodden, will the principles of human rights to which we pledge ourselves, the principles of this great nation, be fulfilled."

Both men smiled until a sudden seriousness came over Witkowski. He looked at the ceiling in thought.

"We do have to fulfill those promises. I pledged this when I came here fleeing the Nazis. What Bohlen doesn't understand is that an army of Gandhis is no match for one Hitler."

Dillon did not miss his cue. "That's why we need to move quickly."

"Yes," Witkowski said, drawing out the vowel. "Tell me what you have in mind."

"Sir, I spent two years in our embassy in Saigon and I've been closely tracking events in Vietnam and Cambodia for the six years since I left Vietnam. There's a lot we don't know, but we know as much or more than anyone else."

"Yes," again cautiously.

"As you know, if anyone finds out that we're doing anything in Indochina they might mistakenly think suspicious, there are going to be problems."

Witkowski nodded. He thought of Bohlen. Those kinds of problems were the last thing he needed.

Dillon tried not to sound anxious.

"Our first priority has to be assessment. We need to know who is on the border and what their capabilities are. But if we ever want to build on that in the future, we need to be careful that nobody gets wind of what we're doing. Nobody. Not the press, certainly not Bohlen. The only way I see doing this is by keeping a tight lid on what's going on, who's involved, and who knows about it. Even the usual channels are probably risky. Felix"—— Dillon rarely ever used his boss's first name but needed to make his personal commitment clear—"I'd like to report only to you."

"And the CIA?"

"We're going to need them, but they've been extremely leaky. I want to bring them in on a need-to-know basis only."

Witkowski focused his eyes on an elevated middle distance as he considered Dillon's proposal. It was risky, but he hadn't fought so hard to get here to be cautious. Did he trust Dillon that much? He'd worked with

Dillon for two years now and had become ever more impressed with his deputy's ability to subtly wield power to drive results. Dillon could sink him if he screwed up. Witkowski's distant gaze transferred to Dillon's face, then locked on his blue eyes. He did.

"I'll want you to keep me fully informed."

"Of course, sir." Dillon tried not to let on that his heart was pumping as powerfully as it was.

"I'll talk to Graves."

"Thank you, sir."

"Let's see what you can do."

Dillon turned to leave.

"And Thomas?"

"Yes, sir?"

Witkowski spoke to himself as much as to Dillon.

"I've given my word to the president. Stay away from the Khmer Rouge."

5

Jonathon Cohane had never heard the Beatles' "Yesterday" sung quite the same way.

Twenty-four hours of continuous flying had brought him halfway around the world and ever farther from home. When he switched to his Thai Airways flight from Tokyo to Bangkok he realized immediately that for the first time in his life he had become both white and truly foreign.

The British pilot's announcement that the plane was entering Thai airspace brought a surge of excitement and a twinge of apprehension. The American-made Boeing 727 was a small capsule of a world he knew entering a world he did not. He thought of the old pictures of paratroopers sitting anxiously as their planes approached Normandy on D-Day. Was he ready? He felt nervous. One step at a time, his idea was becoming a reality—telling his parents, leaving law school, arriving. What awaited him in the fog below?

The cavernous exit hall felt more like an open-air market than an airport. Families lounged on straw mats on the floor, tossing orange peels into haphazard piles. Old women sat with vast baskets pulled closed with thick twine. There were few chairs. Lights flickered. The mass of brown faces perched above the steel retaining wall seemed to look past Jonathon. To his relief, he read his name under the words "Heavenly Gate Hotel" on a placard near the end of the corral. The rotund, middle-aged Thai man, adorned in an elaborate white safari suit, did not look excited.

"I am Jonathon Cohane," Jonathon said eagerly.

The man bowed his head slightly.

"Welcome to Thailand, sir. I get your bags?"

"Oh, I only have this backpack."

"You please, sir."

"No, no, I can carry it myself.

"Sir?"

"I can do it, thank you very much."

The man stepped back and led Jonathon away toward the exit.

As the electric door slid open, the hot air rolled over Jonathon. Touch and smell were the first of his senses to arrive. A dank humidity pressed on his skin. The air smelled of overripe fruit.

The man led him to a white van, opened the door, and handed Jonathon a perfumed washcloth wrapped in plastic. Jonathon rubbed it on his hands as the van rolled onto the highway. It was almost midnight, but cars sped by as if everyone were late for an appointment. An endless stream of neon signs flashed advertisements. Beyond them, small dots of dim light spread over the distance like stars in the night sky. What was the story behind each of the dots? Was a family eating dinner under a kerosene lamp? a fisherman sitting beside a pond? There was a new universe to discover.

When he finally arrived at the hotel, Jonathon was too excited to sleep. He went down to the hotel lobby for a look around. Crawling with boisterous Taiwanese tourists, the Heavenly Gate hotel was not the type of place he would have chosen for himself. But his mother had insisted on making the booking through her travel agent in Highland Park. If Jonathon was heading off the known map, at least he'd have a clean bed when he arrived. A plump Thai woman he guessed to be in her mid thirties stepped from the bar entryway and took him by the arm.

"Monsieur, you come in?"

Jonathon did not resist as she showed him to a table.

"Yesterday, ah my truh-buhs sim so fah away," the Asian nightclub performer crooned. It amused Jonathon that something so familiar could sound so strange. He sat down.

"Hey, I sit with you?" a young voice asked. Jonathon knew she couldn't be more than fifteen. Her long, velvet hair flowed down beside her smooth, round face. Her red silk dress followed the contours of her girlish form, kissing the floor just beside her feet.

"I'm sorry?" Jonathon asked, giving himself a moment to think.

"I sit with you mister?"

"Well . . . OK."

"Where you from?"

"I'm from Chicago."

"Chi-ca-go," she said, introducing her faint recognition of the name as a point of conversation.

"Where you from?" Jonathon asked.

"I from Thai-land," she said. "You come Thailand how long?"

"I don't know. I'm not sure. Maybe long time." Jonathan wondered why he was talking like an Indian in a cowboy movie.

She smiled, and in her smile Jonathon saw the first glimmer of connection. He relaxed.

"Thailand is a beautiful country." He hadn't seen much of it, yet sensed he was not lying.

"What you do Thailand?"

"I work with Cambodians, Cambodian people."

She nodded blankly.

"Cambodia, Kampuchea . . . no food, you know? No food." He held his hand to his stomach.

She nodded neutrally. "You buy me drink?"

"I'm sorry?"

"You buy me drink?"

"No, thank you."

A pudgy girl in blue jeans with a boyish face and close-cropped hair walked over.

"You no buy drink, she no sit with you."

THE DEPTHS OF THE SEA

"She can sit with me if she likes."

"You buy drink?"

"No, I'm sorry."

"You very rich."

"Oh no, no, I am student." The words didn't make much of an impression.

The pudgy one led the slighter girl away.

"Now I need a place to hide away . . ."

Jonathon listened to a few songs then returned to his room.

Up at six the next morning, he took a quick shower and headed down to breakfast.

The buffet seemed to Jonathon arranged along a spectrum of most to least familiar. On one end were Frosted Flakes, milk, pancakes, bacon, bright yellow scrambled eggs, french toast, hash browns, and blueberry muffins. At the other end were different kinds of fried rice, hot noodles with spiced vegetables and peanuts, various curries, and other dishes he didn't recognize. He started at the exotic end, eagerly ingesting each new taste. Some were delicious, some odd, some disgusting. After his meal, he asked the concierge for directions to the Grand Palace and set out with his map. He was supposed to be at the Mercy Relief office at 3:00 in the afternoon. He had the day to explore.

The streets of Bangkok attacked Jonathon's senses. The pungent and intermittent smells of garlic, spices, fried meats, excrement, garbage, and mold were alternately overwhelming and intoxicating. Every inch of the city brimmed with activity and commerce.

An endless stream of cars, motorcycles, bicycles, and three-wheeled taxis raced in all directions. Dilapidated buses rolled by packed so full that a few men dangled from the outside of windows, their legs swinging over the open road. Ratty dogs lounged beside the dusty street. Small wooden huts suspended on stilts stood cautiously over chemical-green water languishing below. Modern high rise apartment buildings rose from the middle of slums.

Vendors in small, wheeled machines looking like miniature tollgates on wheels sold fluorescent yellow corn, sliced fruits in clear plastic bags, tiny orange pancakes with dollops of tapioca, steaming soup with fish balls and chicken's feet, grilled sticks of beef, and a multitude of items Jonathon could not classify to a throng of passersby.

Jonathon watched the pedaling of an old man's bicycle and the footsteps of saffron-robed monks walking door to door carrying silver bowls. School children in white and blue uniforms sauntered along arm in arm, swinging their school bags back and forth.

Jonathon tracked the red arrows the concierge had drawn on his map, stopping to drop a few coins in the cups of limbless beggars or filthy women lying on the ground with sleeping children. Bangkok was like nothing he had ever seen before.

The golden peaked domes of the Grand Palace reminded Jonathon of the hulls of ships. The tall, rectangular palaces seemed to pull with the wind as if floating toward another world, their gold pediments glistening in the bright sun. Mythical birds in blues and reds peered down from above. Jonathon knelt before the sacred Emerald Buddha inside the main building. The small, green statue perched atop a multilayered platform of gold. The smoky mist of red incense sticks wreathed the room in mystery.

Mimicking the Thai visitors, he held his hands together in front of his face with his thumbs pointing inward. He thought of his parents in Highland Park, prayed for them even. What was happening in Chicago right now? Jonathon felt a momentary pang of loneliness.

Jonathon's guidebook told him that the palace contained a miniature replica of Cambodia's Angkor Wat temple. He headed over for some glimpse of the world he had come to help. The wooden model's five spires looked like elongated beehives. Long terraces spread from them in three directions. Mysterious faces covered the tower walls on one of the temples. What was his connection to this place, this culture? He had no answer. But his path to it was the number 8 bus down Sukhumvit Road to the Mercy Relief Bangkok headquarters.

The office was a small, simple wooden house tucked away on a side street off Sukhumvit Road. An elderly Thai gentleman tending the flower garden nodded at Jonathon as he walked by. A large wooden cross hung above the open front door.

"I'm Jonathon Cohane," he announced hesitantly. "I wrote from the United States?"

"Yeah, how you going, mate?" an effusive Australian beamed back. "Come on in and have a seat."

Jonathon entered.

"I'm Bob McCah-thy and this is Silimband Pandipatra."

"You call me Pat. Please have seat."

Jonathon sat down.

"So, you want to go to the border do ya?" McCarthy asked.

"Yes."

"When can you go?"

"As soon as possible, I guess." Jonathon wondered why he was sounding tentative.

"We've got a car going out tomorrow morning. Can ya make it?"

"Sure." He was determined to overcome his initial caution.

"Well that settles it then. Meet here at seven tomorrow morning."

"Do I need to fill out any forms or anything?"

The two men laughed. "That won't be necessary. They'll take care of everything when you get the-ya."

"Is there a place for me to stay?"

"Right now people are staying in a guest house in Aranyaprathet. We'll pick up the tab. They'll fill you in when you get the-ya."

"Is there anything else?" Jonathon felt that there ought to be.

"Just come back tomorrow at seven."

Jonathon paused for a moment as if waiting for some more complicated process.

McCarthy smiled and nodded his head.

"See you tomorrow then," Jonathon said as he stood up. That was surprisingly easy, he thought to himself as he hesitantly stepped out the door.

6

Maria Esquevera loved the sound of bells. Ever since her childhood on the Philippine island of Mindanao, Maria had associated the sound of bells with the sublime. Bells announced when to wake up and put on her dress for church. Bells proclaimed the start of mass. The village in its finery would parade to the majestic cathedral's gates. When her parents fought, when the rice crop was bad and there wasn't enough to eat, Maria sat quietly in the corner waiting for the bells to ring. The bells led her to the church choir, where she sang with messianic fervor. Sister Susan, the American head nun, even once told Maria that her soprano voice rang with the clarity of a bell.

Recognizing the girl's devotion, Sister Susan offered Maria free lessons in English, music, and scripture. Everyone assumed that Maria would eventually take her vows. But Maria had become friends with a quiet and intense schoolmate named Fidel. They would walk out in the rice fields by the hour. When Fidel expressed his love for her, Maria didn't know how to respond. Fidel was her special friend, but what of everything Sister Susan had said? What would it be like to kiss a boy? It was nice, like nothing she had ever experienced. It was pure and clean, soft. Her body sang with hypnotic joy. She felt lost in a new song, floating outside of herself. She hardly knew what was happening. When she did, when the "no" escaped her throat like a wheeze, it was too late, too terribly, life-changingly late.

Sister Susan sensed there was something wrong, so there was no use hiding it. Her look of disappointment cut Maria deeply. Maria kept reading her Bible, kept singing in the choir, but the bells faded. The heights of the world had been lowered and Maria felt herself sinking toward the depths. Colors seemed less vibrant, songs less joyous. Life began to feel less worth living.

Sister Susan drew Maria to her in a strong, protective hug. Maria burst into uncontrollable tears, burying her face in Sister Susan's shoulder. The Sister did not say a word as she held Maria. When the tears began to subside, Sister Susan finally spoke.

"Maria, I've just received a cable from Father Romero in Manila. It seems there's a scholarship available for the University of Santo Tomas. I told him all about you and, well, it's yours if you want it."

Maria could not believe her ears. It was as if God was extending a hand to her, inviting her to climb back, maybe not completely, but certainly at least partway. Her tears of sadness became tears of gratitude. Maybe she wouldn't be a nun, but she would be something. She threw herself at her university studies, perfecting her English and receiving top grades in American literature, her major. She joined the university choir and became treasurer of the Catholic Student Missions Society. When a recruiter came to gather students to distribute aid during the summer vacation to the drought-stricken farmers of a northern Philippine island, Maria volunteered immediately. Handing rice to the grateful peasants, she realized that she didn't need to be a nun to do the Lord's work.

As her final year at the university neared its end, the scrap of paper called to her from the university job board.

CATHOLIC CHARITIES SEEKING AID WORKER TO ADMINISTER DISTRIBUTION OF FOOD AID TO CAMBODIAN REFUGEES IN THAILAND.

Maria knew immediately what she was supposed to do. She had never left the Philippines before, but trusting the voice within her, she was learning, was the path away from desperation. She prayed for two days to be sure. Two months later, just after graduation, she boarded the Philippine Airlines flight to Bangkok en route to the Thai-Cambodian border.

7

"It's so awful. I thought I could do it but I can't," the young British woman in her leather sandals and tie-dyed shirt wept. "It's just too much."

Tim Anderson, the American field director for Mercy Relief, nodded understandingly.

"I know, I know, Penny. Nothing can prepare you for it."

"I thought I was ready, but I saw three children die today, one in my arms as I was trying to feed her." Penny's sobs overcame her words.

From his rustic wooden chair on the side of the single story, open-air shop now transformed into the Mercy Relief office, Jonathon tried to lock his eyes with Penny's. He wanted to share his hope with her, to understand what she had seen. She didn't seem to notice. She looked downward breathing heavily.

"There are a lot of things people can do to help around here. Maybe you could give us a hand around the office. Others can do distribution. We got these two new volunteers in today." Tim motioned in the direction of Jonathon and the other volunteer. "Things aren't as tight as they were a month ago."

Tears gradually became sniffles. Penny began to sit up in her chair.

"I can take your place," Jonathon's voice interjected from the side of the room. Whatever it was she had seen, that was why he was there. That was the darkness he had come to face.

Tim picked up on Jonathon's offer.

"Yeah, that would be perfect. Penny, if you start working here in the office, that will free up a space on distribution, and you, what was your name?"

"Jonathon."

"Jonathon can go on distribution. As a matter of fact, could you start working in the office now? We really need you."

"Yeah . . . sure," Penny said, pulling herself together.

Tim opened the door.

"Suchinda, Penny is going to be working with you in the office. Would you mind showing her how the record system works?"

Suchinda, a boyish-looking Thai woman in her early twenties, giggled, "You come?"

Tim turned to address the two new volunteers.

"Quite an introduction. I guess we need a waiting room. It's tough here." He added the last phrase almost as an afterthought, as if to address what had just happened without calling too much attention to it. "Anyway, a thousand thanks for coming. We can really use the help. Your names?"

"Jonathon Cohane, from Chicago."

"And you?"

"Evan Pritchard from Sydney," said the second man, a wiry, pale Australian who seemed to be in his early thirties.

"Welcome. We've made arrangements for the two of you to share a room in the Sunny Garden guest house. It's not much but there isn't much around here. What do you all know about the camps?"

"Just what I read in the newspapers in America," Jonathon said.

"I met some travelers from Bangkok who had been here for a while. They told me what they saw. Pretty horrific," Evan chimed in. "I thought I'd come have a look."

"I'm glad you did. Things have gotten pretty crazy around here these past months. The number of refugees crossing from Cambodia has gone way up since the Vietnamese started pushing toward the Thai border. There's no food over there in Cambodia, their side of the border's full of mines—it's hell. The stories we hear from the refugees about what the Khmer Rouge did—suffocating people with plastic bags, smashing their heads with hoes, cutting fetuses out of pregnant women—make you sick. Things are getting a bit better, though. A few months ago, the Thais weren't letting the refugees cross. They even pushed a big group of them back over a ravine in Preah Vihear. God only knows what happened to them—the mines, Jesus. Now they're letting them cross. I guess the Thais want to be sure there are at least a few Cambodians left to fight the Vietnamese. Press coverage is also helping. Finally there's some money. Everyone needs food. Our job is just to give as much as we can. You know what they say—he who saves a single life, it's as though he saved the entire world. That's what we're trying to do. We go out at seven in the morning. So why don't you get settled in, get to know Aran, and we'll head out tomorrow morning. Just be here at seven."

Jonathon and Evan dropped their bags at the guest house and wandered the streets of Aranyaprathet.

Wooden huts lined the wide dirt streets. Dust blew. Thai school children with white shirts and blue shorts rode women's bicycles five sizes too big, zigzagging down the sleepy streets. Chickens nervously pecked at a few kernels of rice along the road. Roosters crowed in the distance. The same type of scrawny dogs Jonathon had seen in Bangkok, scarred from head to tail, languished in front of houses they nominally protected.

"Except for the Thai signs," Jonathon said to Evan, "it almost looks like something out of America's Old West."

The two wandered to a noodle cart. They sat on the small plastic chairs.

"*Phad thai mee mai kap?*" Evan stated.

"Hey, that sounds pretty good," Jonathon noted.

"Yeah, I picked up a few words in Bangkok. *Song phad thai kap.*"

"What was that?"

"Oh, I just ordered us some dinner."

"Very good. What do you do, Evan?"

"Oh, not much. Little of this little of that."

Evan seemed aimless to Jonathon. What was someone like that doing here? How else could someone arrive at this god-forsaken place if not by deep conviction?

"How about you, mate?"

"Well I was a law student in Chicago until I read about everything that was happening over here. So I jumped on a plane, and here I am."

"Oh, a dropout do-gooder are ya, mate?"

The question troubled Jonathon.

"I guess I think of myself as a drop in do-gooder."

"Yeah, sure mate, whatever you say."

The Thai woman had now assembled her ingredients and began cooking. The chimes of the steel spoon on the wok, the sizzling oil, and the steam rising from the noodles combined into an exotic music. Jonathon wanted to savor these new tastes, the noodles, Aran, Thailand, the adventure unfolding before him, this new place he was beginning to make his own.

8

The first sight of the royal-blue Lincoln Mercury put an instant end to Morgan's reverie as his elongated stride carried him, once again, over the final hill.

The click, this time, had come later than Morgan had hoped. Perhaps the ghosts were catching up with him. He'd been only two miles from home when it had come, but that was enough. He'd been free, at peace, gliding. Then he saw them.

The two men leaning against the car dropped their cigarettes when they saw Morgan. They stomped them out with the soles of their shoes and walked toward him.

"O'Reilly, we were wondering where you'd gone. Looks like I guessed right," said Bill Jeffrey, chief of the CIA Directorate of Operations East Asia Division.

"Hi," Morgan said impassively. He recognized the second man, but didn't want to make introductions any easier than they had to be.

"O'Reilly, this is Tom Dillon, deputy national security advisor."
Morgan nodded.

"Sorry to barge in on you at home like this. May we come in?" Dillon asked.

Morgan opened the door. These were the kinds of visits that changed a person's life. Morgan knew they were going to ask him to do something he didn't want to do. Why else would the deputy national security advisor be here? Why else would they come on a Sunday? Why else would they apologize for coming?

"I'm not going to beat around the bush with you, O'Reilly. It's about Cambodia, and"—Jeffrey paused—"it's about Sophal."

The words hit Morgan like a blow. It had to be Sophal—Morgan's one point of hope, the one fragile success of his life.

"Tell me now, Bill. Tell me. What's happened to Sophal?"

"Dammit, Morgan, you know what Sophal does, don't act so surprised."

Morgan wondered, for a moment, if he even had a right to be surprised. Wasn't he the one responsible? Sophal hadn't known anything when he'd arrived in America. Morgan could have steered him in any direction. But how could he have gotten him a job with a newspaper, or as some kind of businessman? Morgan didn't have the connections. Morgan got him the one job he knew.

And Sophal had done brilliantly. First at the CIA field school, then analyzing Khmer Rouge radio broadcasts, and finally working the Thai-Cambodian border. Morgan didn't know much about what exactly Sophal was doing. Not much about Cambodia passed through the Directorate of Intelligence's Africa division, where Morgan now showed up from eight-forty-five in the morning to five-fifteen in the evening Monday to Friday as a little-noticed policy analyst. But what was the deputy national security advisor doing here? Morgan felt a pounding need to know.

"We don't need to go into the background with you about the Khmer Rouge, the Vietnamese invasion," Dillon asserted dryly. "I'm sure you've read the news reports. There's a bit more in the cables. Not much, but we'll get it to you. It's the same story—Khmer Rouge on the Cambodian side of the border, the Vietnamese trying to starve them out, a few new noncommunist groups forming on the Thai side to fight the Vietnamese."

"What about Sophal!" Morgan was uninterested in Dillon's sophomoric analysis.

Dillon sensed this would be a tough sell. The Morgan O'Reilly in front of him seemed tougher and more wiry than the photograph in the file had suggested. Though O'Reilly was only five foot nine, he didn't seem at all short to Dillon. Morgan's icy reserve worried Dillon for a moment, but the file in his hand gave Dillon a deep confidence.

"The president authorized a survey mission to assess the situation on the border," Dillon said. "There's a huge amount of activity there right now. The Vietnamese have pushed a lot of refugees into Thailand, and different groups are organizing themselves to fight back. We're working together on this one and I . . . we, sent in an officer, Heng Sophal, to contact the new groups, see what their needs are, and assess the situation. We were getting some pretty good stuff. But all of a sudden, it stopped. Nothing. Nothing from Sophal, and your guys in Bangkok can't seem to find anything either."

Morgan felt the pang deep inside him. The thought was unbearable, impossible. Dammit. Sophal. Out of contact? Missing? Morgan tried to stay calm. He couldn't tell how much of the blood surging through his heart came from his run and how much from this devastating news.

"Do you have any idea what's happened?"

"No."

"Any idea where he was or where he was going when you lost contact?"

"No, nothing."

"What the hell . . ." The sorrow seeped through Morgan's hardened eyes. Dillon lowered his voice. He had anticipated this response. It was time to move in.

"We know the two of you were close, that you got him out of Cambodia four years ago."

Morgan didn't need to be reminded. "Then I'm sure you know about the others," he responded dryly.

"Yeah, we know," Dillon said. "There are a lot of things we feel sorry about, O'Reilly. But whatever our regrets, Sophal is there. We know that he made contact with someone he knew in the camps. We're not sure, but we think it might have been a member of your former unit."

Morgan's eyes widened. Could it be? He had buried them all in his mind, and so much of his hope with them. What chance would they have had?

"Who was it?"

"We don't know."

"Do you know where he found them?"

"No. He didn't tell us."

Morgan felt his world becoming unglued. Could he reopen his entire history, reopen a wound he had so methodically dressed for four painful years, just on this one man's word?

Now, Dillon thought to himself.

"O'Reilly, we have this one lead and not a lot more. It's not much, but anybody else wouldn't even have that. You know the language, you know the people, you know Sophal and his world. I'll lay it on the line." Dillon was going for broke. "We need you. We need you to find Sophal, see what happened to him, and bring him back if you can. You're our best chance, O'Reilly. You're Sophal's best chance."

Dillon opened the file in his hand. "I know it's a hell of a thing to ask any of us to go back. There are a lot of memories there. I know you're an ex-marine. It's not just the marines, none of us want to leave our people behind."

The absurdity of those hollow words struck Morgan. He turned to face Dillon.

"We did," Morgan shot back, as much in anger as confusion.

Dillon looked Morgan straight in the eye.

"We were wrong, and we're not going to do it again. That's what this mission is about. It's about not leaving someone behind."

Dillon felt the nauseous truth of this statement. He interpreted Morgan's expectant pause as an early hint of consent.

"I spoke with Marc Solomon at the Africa division in the Directorate of Intelligence," Bill Jeffrey continued. "He's agreed to let you go . . . if, of course, you're interested. You're too good to be pushing paper, O'Reilly. Our country doesn't need our Medal of Merit winners slogging away at desks."

The sales push had gone far enough. Dillon sensed it was time to back off. "Take your time to think about it. Just don't talk about it. It's top secret code-word."

"Why don't you come to my office and read the cables traffic," Jeffrey chimed in.

Dillon placed his hands on Morgan's shoulder and again looked him in the eye. "Just let me know by the end of the week," he said almost empathetically. Dillon knew more than to look triumphant at a critical time like this.

Jeffrey followed Dillon out the door.

In his shorts and singlet, Morgan watched the blue car pull away. Sophal, where are you? One of the kids—alive? Going back to the field, Cambodia, the border. The thoughts ricocheted through his mind. The click seemed far off. The ghosts were coming to get him.

9

The barren plateau stretched for miles under Jonathon's gaze.

The endless series of blue rectangles massed one beside the other created a pointillist landscape of blue on dusty beige. As his truck in the thirty-strong aid convoy crept down the hill and toward the barbed wire gate, Jonathon made out the twisted sticks and boards holding up the blue plastic tarps stretched to become slapdash huts of no particular order on the sun-baked plane.

After all it had taken to get here, he had finally, actually, surprisingly arrived. The abstraction of coming to the border was now becoming real. He felt a nervous excitement.

Perhaps, Jonathon thought, this was his reunion, turning to face his own past. It was a past his parents had so narrowly escaped in Europe, a legacy, a responsibility he now faced in the name of those left behind.

Perched on the back of Mercy Relief's flatbed truck, Jonathon surveyed the world unfolding beneath him. Wind blew the baked earth around the simple bamboo offices lining the clearing inside the gate. A slow, steady wind muffled the voices of the anxious refugees huddling near the trucks. Armed Cambodian men in worn, mismatched fatigues stationed themselves clumsily around the clearing, creating a perimeter the refugees did not seem to challenge. Refugees stared blankly at the convoy. The silence was disarming.

"A bit startling at first, isn't it? It's better than it was. Couple of months ago we were losing twenty or thirty people a day. A lot better now. Excuse me a second." Tim walked back near the trucks where three refugees in olive beach hats were talking with relief officials. He shook hands with the men. Everything seemed to be in order. Tim approached the two volunteers.

"Who are those guys?" Jonathon asked.

"Those are Rongrit's men."

"Rongrit?"

"Prince Rongrit's the leader of this camp, the Cambodian part of it, anyhow. Says he's a relative of Prince Sihanouk. Nobody knows for sure, but I don't think too many people are gonna question him. Tough guy. Says the Buddha sent him to lead the Cambodian people and expel the Vietnamese. A bit of a nut. Our main concern is getting the rice distributed. For that, he seems to be doing an OK job. We deliver the rice to each quarter, and then Rongrit's people take it from there to each section, block, and then family. Works pretty well."

"How many people are here?"

"Rongrit says about a hundred eighty thousand. It's hard to check, but that seems about right. Come on, let me show you around."

Tim led Jonathon and Evan down the meandering roads of parched dirt lined with impromptu drainage ditches. Refugees bobbed down the crack-ridden paths with wooden sticks balanced precariously over their shoulders, a bucket on each end. Little children dressed in rags looked up at Jonathon with wide eyes, sunken cheek bones, and what seemed like thousand-year-old faces. Naked infants played in rancid puddles and drainage ditches along the road. Young girls, not more than ten or eleven themselves, stood cradling naked infants on their side, leaning away from the infants to support the weight on their tiny frames. Men with deep, dark wrinkles lining their faces hobbled toward the trucks, supporting with long walking sticks the space where a knotted empty pant leg betrayed the memory of loss. Jonathon was stunned to see so many amputees, so many naked, forlorn children in such a concentrated space. The tragic history of Cambodia seemed engraved on this theater of faces.

But Jonathon's mind struggled not with shock, but with the surprising normalcy of life in the camp. Silence hovered over the camp's pathways like a ghost. There were no cars, no horns or bells, few shouts. There were no dogs in front of the huts, no chickens pecking to and fro, there were no exuberant yells of children coming home from school—only silence, a hollow, mysterious silence. Life quietly went on in the camp. What else, he now wondered, had he expected?

"This is the medical zone," Tim stated authoritatively as they entered an enclosure covered by an impromptu thatch and bamboo awning. "In the beginning, a lot of the camp was like this, but now things are improving. We've tried to separate out these people so they won't infect the others. We can also treat them better here."

The cadaverous patients looked up at them from straw mats on the ground. The children's expressionless eyes bulged from their faces, staring into an unknown space, a twilight zone Jonathon could only imagine. Men and women lay on their backs, sores covering their reed-thin arms and legs. A low, incessant rumble of coughing and the stench of excrement and rubbing alcohol permeated the air. Jonathon felt a surge of emotion—fear, compassion, confusion—welling within him. This was the face of suffering. He was surprised by the calm of it all.

"Well it's better than it was, least we can say that," a lanky British doctor in a white coat, blue jeans, and sandals said as he approached them. "Andrew Brownlie. Welcome. Drugs starting to come in. Isn't always what we need, but a little press coverage seems to be working wonders."

Evan took out his camera and took a few shots.

"You guys new here?"

"Yeah, first day."

"Pretty grim." Brownlie nodded pensively. Jonathon sensed the young doctor's anxiousness to categorize the macabre scene. "I've seen it all here, things I never thought I'd see. Of course the usual, what you'd expect— malaria, cholera, TB, dysentery, but strange stuff," he lowered his voice, "cerebral malaria, liver flukes, Japanese encephalitis—a whole textbook of infectious diseases. Just wish we could do more."

"How long have you been here?"

"About three months. Seems like forever."

"Do you have much help?"

"Yeah, got five nurses. Mission gave us Maria to keep records in the office. Then we got some refugee workers who help out. Course, families always hanging around trying traditional remedies and the like, helping with the feeding. When there's enough food and a little peace, things do get better. Where will the two of you be working?"

"I think I'll have them do just a bread distribution at the orphanage for the first day," Tim said. "Tomorrow they'll start working the regular distributions."

"Well good luck. See y'all around."

"See you," Jonathon said warmly.

"I won't take you too close." Tim led them toward the northeast corner of the camp, an open area of stripped trees and dense undergrowth. "They call this place the minefield. At first the foreigners were pretty afraid to go over there. We'd all heard the stories of the millions of mines along the border. I think it was the flies that tipped us off. Turns out Cambodians don't like to go to the bathroom where somebody else has gone. So much for latrines I guess. We dug the damn things, but after a few times people stopped using them. First they'd go near the latrines. When that area was covered, they started moving farther and farther out. Pretty soon the whole thing was covered, a regular minefield. Some days we wish it were the real thing, at least they don't stink. I probably shouldn't joke."

The smell was beginning to hit them, as was the growing chorus of flies.

"That oughta be close enough," Evan suggested.

"I'll show you the market then."

The stench of rotten fruits and vegetables announced that they'd arrived. Sellers of all ages sat with paltry goods laid on small straw mats before them—Thai sandals and soaps, gnarled vegetables, plastic bottles of cooking oil, T-shirts and piles of used clothing, cigarettes, Cambodian scarves, and an endless array of seemingly worthless items. Old women sat with small scales in front of them weighing tiny pieces of gold and jewelry.

Hundreds of refugees jostled in an endless flow, a whirlwind going everywhere and nowhere.

"Incredible," Jonathon muttered. He didn't know what to make of the scene. It seemed so alive in this place where everyone was supposed to be dead.

"Yeah, it's amazing what comes though here. It's like Cambodia is being emptied out and replaced by little pieces of Thailand. Cigarettes and gold are the main commodities, but they'll trade anything." The three stood gazing at the spectacle. "You'll be seeing more of the camp than you ever wanted to. Why don't we get you guys started with work."

Tim led them to the orphanage, an open awning similar to the infirmary. The hundred or so children appeared lost and neglected. A few wrestled with each other. Most just lay on the ground listlessly. Jonathon could feel the tears pushing toward the front of his head. Where were their parents? Where were the games? They should have been in blue and white school uniforms laughing their way home. He implored himself not to cry. He was here to act.

The children wandered over curiously.

"Poor devils," Evan said.

The children didn't touch the men, didn't smile. Approaching like scientists examining a specimen, they had clearly learned to keep their distance.

"The Red Cross is trying to figure out whether any of their parents are alive. Probably most of them aren't, but it's a tough job," Tim said. "They live on rice and vegetables, a piece of dried fish now and again. A bakery in town donated a hundred loaves of bread, so we thought you guys could distribute them today. Tomorrow we'll get you going on the main distribution. I just wanted to let you settle in. Just have the kids line up."

"And the bread?" Jonathon asked.

"Yeah, I'm going to head back to the trucks. I'll have them bring the baskets over."

Tim left, and the enormous wicker baskets arrived a few minutes later. Rasady, a refugee interpreter in his early twenties assigned to the group, came along as well. His slight frame was overwhelmed by the enormous, faded orange bowling shirt he was wearing, the name Joe embroidered on its chest.

"Could you please ask them to line up in three lines," Jonathon said to Rasady. Jonathon remembered a similar drill he'd carried out as a Chicago Jewish Community Center summer camp counselor a few years before. Rasady nodded and spoke to the children in Cambodian. The children did not seem to respond.

"Muey, pii, bey," one, two, three. Rasady pointed as he counted. He picked up a small boy and placed him in a line, then another behind him and another. Slowly, the children got the hang of it. After about five minutes of strenuous effort, the lines were in place. Maybe, Jonathon thought, there wasn't such a difference between the two camps. Children were children.

The plan was for each child to receive his or her bread and then walk behind the volunteers. A young girl shyly stepped up, hesitated for a moment, then quickly snapped the bread and was pushed on. A few others followed. The plan seemed to be working.

After six or seven of the children had passed each line, the volunteers began to relax.

Jonathon looked behind him. All of the children had vanished. He saw the little girl reentering the line at the other end of the hall, a small bulge in her shirt.

"That little girl has already gotten hers. Rasady, can you please explain to her that we only have one loaf for each child?"

Rasady went up to the girl, lifted her up, and began to carry her to the side. The quiet girl erupted, kicking and screaming. Rasady held her at arm's length as he carried her away.

"That one too, over there," Jonathan said.

The other children watched as distribution ceased while Rasady and Jonathon dealt with the problem. A nervous look came over many of their faces. Were kids being taken out of line? they seemed to wonder. Am I going to get one?

A hand reached around Evan's leg into his basket and grabbed a loaf. Evan noticed and swung his arm down to catch the thief. He was too slow. As he grabbed for the escaping child, two other hands reached in from the other side. The lines so painstakingly formed a few moments before began to crumble. The children circled hesitantly but determinedly toward the baskets.

"Everybody back in line," Jonathon said, looking to Rasady to interpret. He began gently lifting them up and placing them back. Rasady's words seemed to have little impact. The children took a few steps closer in. A few nervous boys in the front twitched.

As if on cue, the children in front dove for the baskets. Evan and Jonathon tried to pull their baskets back, but were halted by the weight of the children. Loaves of bread flew in the air as chaos broke loose in the orphanage. Children plunged for the baskets, grabbing each other and whatever else came in their way. Jonathon felt his shirt rip.

"Back, you little bastards . . . Ah, the hell with it," he heard Evan saying.

Jonathon lifted the basket above his head to free it from the children's reach. From above him, a small head appeared from the basket as the remaining loaves tumbled to the waiting hands of the children. Realizing the futility of his struggle, he laid the basket down and scrambled toward Evan.

"Everybody, sit." He knew they didn't understand. He sounded to himself as if he were giving commands to a dog. What had happened to these kids? Jonathon could feel his heart pounding. He panted from the exertion.

"The little shits," Evan said, "don't they know we're here to help them?"

Jonathon didn't know what to say. How could they have known? How could they not have known?

With nothing more to do in the orphanage, they returned to the camp gate.

"What happened back there?" Tim asked frantically as he rushed to meet them.

"I don't know. Maybe we did something wrong. We tried to feed them but they attacked. Aren't they fed?" Jonathon was searching for an explanation.

Tim shook his head. "These kids have been through a hell of a lot," he tried to explain. "War and refugee camps don't tend to bring out the best in people. But, Jesus, what do they think we were doing, stealing from them? Maybe we just need a better system. What a mess. What a damn mess. You don't look all that good. Why don't you sit in the van on the way back to town. We'll talk more when we get there."

Calming himself, Jonathon walked to the van and got in. He rested his face in his hands and took a deep, exhausted breath.

When Jonathon lifted his head a few moments later, he was startled by what he saw. In the row of seats in front of him, her head turned to face him, was a woman of about his own age. Thick black hair flowed past her shoulders like silk. Her face angled down from her large, brown eyes past her delicate nose, her aquiline mouth, to her thin, soft chin which almost seemed to vanish toward her throat. Something drew Jonathon toward her, a quiet magnetism. Was it her eyes? They stared at him, warm and kind, with such forgiveness. Her half smile reminded Jonathon of the face on the replica of Angkor Wat he'd seen at the Grand Palace in Bangkok. A large silver cross dangled low from her necklace. Halting their unconscious wandering toward the cross, he consciously pulled his eyes upward.

"Are you OK?" she asked, rolling her "r" and unfurling the vowel tail of her "you."

"I'm OK."

"I hope so. Very difficult day, yes?"

"Yeah, a bit tough."

She tilted her head slightly. "My name is Maria, I'm from the Philippines."

Jonathan summoned a tired smile. Something about this woman radiated a warmth he craved.

"I'm Jonathon. It's nice to meet you." His eyes locked with hers for a moment before looking away.

10

Maria Esquevera felt ready for whatever the Thai-Cambodian border could throw her way.

Getting to the border was easier than Maria had expected. Everything had been taken care of by the mission. Two Thai nuns met her at the airport, made sure that everything was OK during her brief stay at the monastery in Bangkok, and put her on the bus for Aranyaprathet. Father Pierre, the head of the border delegation, had been waiting to greet her when the bus arrived in Aran. She arrived just in time for the evening prayer session. The twelve brothers and sisters at the mission home, mostly nuns, priests, and lay Catholics in their forties and fifties, welcomed Maria. They sat in a circle, an unbreakable bond, praying for peace, for the health of the refugees, and for personal strength.

The group had rented a large house with a wooden upper story over a cement base. A tall coconut palm adorned the small front lawn. The furnishings were simple, with only a few basic wooden chairs, tables, and beds. In the evenings, they took turns preparing dinner for the group and their Thai staff. The meals were nothing elaborate—stir-fried vegetables, a few simple Thai dishes, spaghetti when the noodles were available. On her third night in Aran, the night before her first visit to the Nong Chan camp, Maria insisted on preparing *pansit,* her favorite Filipino dish. The dish, and

Maria's enthusiasm pulling it together, were a hit. A tall, middle-aged Canadian nurse named Donna with a sharp nose and puffy cheeks put her arm around Maria and told her how welcome she was. Donna's warm smile curled up toward her cheeks.

Maria returned that night to her small room on the second floor basking in her praise and the warmth she had found in her new home. She had listened to her voice. She had been right. She knelt before the cross Sister Susan had sent her as a departing gift. "I know you'll be strong, Maria, the Lord will be with you," Sister Susan had written. Maria lay on her bed and slept with the words.

But working in the camp proved tough. Maria had seen malnutrition and dysentery in the Philippines, but nothing like this. The tiny legs, the children's faces like the ancient death masks from the outer Philippine islands. Had not Jesus tended to the lepers, to those others wouldn't touch? It was so tragic, but faith was strength. The refugees were God's children. And Maria knew she had been called.

Her assignment was to keep the medical records for the infirmary. Though the refugees sometimes seemed to some of the other aid workers to be a coughing, malnourished, diseased horde, everyone had an individual identity in the Lord's kingdom. Maria carefully tracked which medicines each refugee was on and what treatment they were receiving. Every file, like every individual, was important. None could be lost. From the chaos of scribbles and scraps that had been the infirmary office, she fashioned an efficient, clean, orderly system.

There were times when her personal system was challenged. A feisty twelve-year-old girl missing two front teeth named Virak was battling cerebral malaria. Maria had prayed for her every evening before bed. Maria arrived one morning to see Virak's bulging, rolled-up straw mat being carried away over her father's shoulder. Maria closed her eyes as she cried. She prayed for strength. She pushed herself to go on, throwing herself ever more fervently into her office duties. There were moments when Maria felt her faith tested, but the answer was to pray harder, to remember Sister Susan's words. She stayed up later into the night kneeling intently before her cross.

There were times when Maria's persistent faith delivered her to heights she had never before known. A middle-aged former school teacher from Battambang City in northern Cambodia came to the infirmary lost in herself. Her husband and her three children had been killed by the Khmer Rouge. Her face had become grief and she had lost her sight. A pitying neighbor brought her to the infirmary. After the doctor's antibiotics produced no results, they released her. Nowhere to go, she dragged her straw mat to a corner of the infirmary which became her home.

"Hello?" Maria said, seating herself beside the woman during an afternoon break.

The woman lifted her head to trace the sound. She repeated back her one word of English. "Hello," she said in a weak monotone.

"I am Maria."

The woman did not seem to understand.

Maria took the woman's hand, folding in all but one finger, which she pointed at herself.

"Maria," Maria said.

The woman nodded and almost smiled.

"Maria," the woman repeated.

The woman pointed the same finger at herself. "Neang . . . Neang."

"Sousdey, Neang," hello, Neang, Maria said with her few words of Cambodian.

"Sousdey bong srey Maria," hello, Sister Maria, the woman answered with the distant hope of a smile.

Every day for the next month, Maria brought Neang different objects to feel—a bandage, a bag of IV fluid, anything to activate her touch. She put Neang to work tearing paper into fourths for the doctor's prescription pads and sharpening pencils. She brought Neang a pillow from Aran. Neang's grief seemed to recede slightly, her face almost to relax.

One day, Maria was in her office when she heard a scream. She ran out to see the box of pencils strewn across the dirt floor. Neang had perceived light through her eyes. The two women held each other's hands and cried. For a moment, it all made so much sense.

And yet there were times when Maria felt caught between these moments of faith and her doubts about life in the camps. These were the most difficult. They were outside of any system, any sense of order, unfilable. If God could reveal himself through Neang's eyes, she couldn't help asking herself, where was he for Virak and the others? She would wake with these feelings unexpectedly in the night, then summon her faith in search of an answer.

In those moments, Maria felt a loneliness. There was no Sister Susan to give her a hug, to understand, no church bell to ring its announcement that the world was OK, just silence. It was an empty silence punctuated by the rhythmic chirping of crickets. By morning, she'd pushed these thoughts aside to face the new day. There were a thousand files to look after, a thousand details demanding her energy and devotion.

There were often visitors to the infirmary—dignitaries, aid workers, UN officials—but something about this visitor spoke to Maria. Something about him seemed different. He crouched down to look at the refugees with such intense, compassionate eyes—eyes that saw, eyes not hardened like the others. His shoulders slumped, his face dropped. Not particularly tall for a Westerner, his slightly messy parted brown hair, the gentle lankiness of his movements, the freshness of his hazel eyes against his white skin, and the earnestness of his demeanor gave him a boyish quality she felt somehow drawn to. She stood behind a door in the office and watched him move through the infirmary.

On the van back to town, the same man had entered and sat behind her. He looked worn and haggard. His shirt was torn. His eyes seemed somehow duller than earlier in the day. Maybe this was her chance to offer the gift that Sister Susan had offered her. She looked at him and smiled.

"I'm Maria," she said, giving through her eyes as much as she could give.

11

"Mr. Dillon. Morgan O'Reilly," the tall, silver-haired secretary announced in her patrician Virginia accent.

From his neatly ordered desk, Tom Dillon bounced to his feet.

"Mr. O'Reilly, Morgan, I'm glad you're here. I haven't yet received word from Bill Jeffrey. I'm hoping you're here to say yes."

"I'm not sure what I'm here to say, Mr. Dillon," Morgan said softly.

"Please, it's Tom."

Morgan had agonized for a week. Everything he had fought for since coming back to America was on the line. Dillon's offer was pulling him back toward a life he thought he had left forever.

"I read the cables you suggested. They'd been sent 'eyes only' to you?"

Dillon sensed Morgan's suspicion.

"Yes, that was for security. They're code-word documents. I passed them all on to Jeffrey."

There was a pause. Dillon realized he needed to say more.

"O'Reilly, I don't need to tell you how secret this all is. We're working under the president's directive. Witkowski and Graves are behind it as well, but we still need this to be secret. No matter what the merits, this sort of thing could give us a lot of trouble. You know that. We just need to be careful. Right or wrong, the Thai-Cambodian border is political quicksand. But we have friends there. You know better than anybody who some of those people are. I've read your file, Morgan. All of our hearts were broken in Vietnam. We've all left so much in that part of the world." Dillon looked reflectively out the window.

"Sophal was on the border making a political assessment. But," Dillon continued, "he was also seeing if any of our people were still around. We all feel terrible about what happened, but that doesn't mean we can just close our eyes and forget the whole thing, that we can just walk further and further away. At some point, we need to take a stand again. Things are changing fast over there. This is our chance just to begin to make amends. We have no idea who may still be alive." Dillon winced inwardly. "We don't know what's happened to Sophal, but you know as well as I do that we can't just leave him there, wherever he is."

Another pause. Dillon rushed to fill the silence.

"It's been two months since we've had any contact with Sophal. We thought about doing this differently. I know it's tough for you . . . going back to Asia. O'Reilly, you know that you're the only one who can find Sophal—not just because you speak Cambodian, but because you know the same people he does. You're the one who can find them, you're the one they're going to trust. And when you find him, you're the one who can get him out of there and bring him home." Dillon's heart was pounding, his exterior polished marble.

"And the others . . . if there are any?"

Dillon approached Morgan and stared him sharply in the eye. Something about O'Reilly seemed vaguely familiar to Dillon, as if he were meeting a lesser version of himself. "I'll give you my word on this, O'Reilly. If you see any members of your unit and you can get them out, I will take personal responsibility for getting them back here. No INS, no nothing. You just get them together and I'll do it for you. Anyone who's been compromised by their contacts with Sophal, anyone, you get them out. The last thing we want is for more people to get killed." A pause. "Do we have a deal?"

"I have a few more questions. You're the one running the show. Were you the one running Sophal? What were his orders?"

"He was to make contact with the border opposition forces and assess their viability to fight the Vietnamese."

"Any opposition, including the Khmer Rouge?"

"The Khmer Rouge is a delicate issue. We don't forget they're murderers, but right now, they're the main opposition in town. They're the only ones with even the prospect of challenging the Vietnamese invasion. But that's not really relevant here. Priority number one is finding out what happened to Sophal and anybody with him. Sophal did not have instructions to contact the KR."

"And it was all on the border?"

"Yes, of course. His orders were to stay in Thailand, not to cross into Cambodia."

"Not to commit suicide, you mean," Morgan said cynically.

"Those were his orders. We haven't heard a thing for two months. We don't know where he is. We're counting on you to find him. The president wants this to happen." Dillon wondered if he was making a mistake by appealing beyond the information he'd read in Morgan's file.

Morgan stared past Dillon and out the window at the clear view of the national mall. Abraham Lincoln sat in judgment, the Washington Monument pointed its threatening finger at the heavens. These images he had fought for. What did they mean? He thought of Vuth and Rithy, of Phim, Vanny, and Choeun. Were any still alive? How could they be—after everything Morgan had heard and read? Two million, three million dead in the last four years, a quarter of the population. And Sophal—was he trapped somewhere in need of help? Morgan had pieced his new life together in tiny pieces. Could he destroy it all in one word?

But hope, once awakened, could not be put to rest. Even if the chance was small, could he just leave them? He could never even entertain the idea that Sophal might be dead. Sophal was lost and Morgan would find him. After everything, despite everything, he was, in his heart, a marine.

"OK."

Dillon nodded slowly, cautiously, breathing in Morgan's reply. "We'll start making preparations right away then." He reached out and took Morgan's hand. "We're all counting on you."

Morgan, somehow, didn't feel like shaking hands.

Dillon ushered Morgan to the door, closing it behind him. Only then did he throw himself into his chair, tilt his head as far back as it would go, and exhale all the excess oxygen he had accumulated during the excruciating meeting.

1 2

To Jonathon's left, the rising orange sun proclaimed the new day as he rode in the convoy out to the Nong Chan camp. To his right, the sun's rays radiated off the shimmering Thai rice fields. The Thai workers bent low in the ankle-deep water, picking at rice stalks in the glorious green paddies like chickens pecking at corn. It had only been two weeks, but this faraway world was already becoming less exotic. Every day, the rhythms of life in Thailand, Aranyaprathet, the ride through the vast fields toward Nong Chan, the descent to the camp's plateau, were becoming the natural rhythms of his own life.

Even the seething, misery-filled camp had become part of Jonathon's routine. The aid workers would arrive and then divide the trucks into four groups, each heading to one of the camp's quadrants. These trucks were then divided by section, and Rongrit's men arranged for distribution from there to block leaders, families, and individuals. The system brought a rough order to the bubbling chaos of the camp.

The level of activity at Nong Chan was fast increasing. Watch and bicycle repair shops opened, little more than small stools with signs. A dentist's office declared itself with a frightening drawing of a gnarled tooth on its door. Small cafes offered hot tea and noodles. Little boys with Styrofoam coolers wandered about selling popsicles shouting *"Cah-rem, cah-rem."*

There was nowhere to go, but so many people going nowhere.

The market, Jonathon soon discovered, wasn't just the place Tim had shown him on his first day, it was the entire camp. All of life in the camp was a market. Anything was tradable. Everything had a price—a piece of food or jewelry, a service, a person's life to give through medicine or take with a bullet.

The stories he heard reminded Jonathon of his parents' stories from Auschwitz. Jews in the camps traded bread rations for spoons, a few beans for a rag to put in your shoes, a scrap of discarded metal, a shoelace. The bar of life could be set high or low, but wherever it rested, people fought to survive.

"Where is it all coming from?" Jonathon asked Rasady. "What's fueling all of the commerce?"

Rasady nodded. "Gold."

People had buried their gold, hidden it in the hollows of trees, or sewn it into their clothes during the Khmer Rouge years when money had been abolished and the possession of private property punishable by death. When the Khmer Rouge had fled the Vietnamese, the world of money returned to Cambodia and the border with a vengeance. Gold flowed from the refugees desperate for just about everything. The goods poured in, supplied by Thai traders who prized the cheap gold and knew that the refugees would take whatever they were given. Cambodian traders braved the minefields and the bandits to snake their way back into the country, bringing cigarettes, sandals, shampoo, just about anything into Cambodia. With the gold they brought back, they bought more consumer goods and made the same trip back. Those not blown to pieces by mines, arrested, robbed, beaten, mutilated, or raped, amassed small fortunes.

Jonathon had first assumed that the rice deliveries were essential. Rice was the staple. The Khmer Rouge, as Jonathon learned from Rasady, had sought to turn the entire country into one enormous rice paddy, a fertile, green land whose abundance would not only feed the Cambodian people but support the modernization of Cambodia from the inside with no help from foreigners. The results had been tragic, but who could deny the premise? Rice was life. But something nagged at Jonathon. If people had the money to buy what they needed in the market, why did they need the international community to give them rice for free? Couldn't they just buy it on their own?

The camp seemed difficult to understand. It was a strange environment run by stranger men. The camp leader Rongrit dressed in army fatigues and a green beach hat and occasionally sported rouge and lipstick. He walked with a swagger that suggested to Jonathon part man with a gun and the willingness to use it, part transvestite. He sped up and down the camp on his Honda Dream motorcycle decorated by flashing Christmas lights, his booming cassette player leaving a noisy trail behind him. He and his men, a motley crew of smugglers, cross-dressers, and others who would only have been classified as ne'er-do-wells in any organized society, hardly inspired confidence. But how else would rice be distributed but through them? What choice did the relief agencies have? The aid workers left the camp each day at 4:30 P.M. Who were they to determine who controlled the camp at night, when the foreigners were gone and the old rules returned?

Each morning, Rongrit's men met Jonathon and the others at the clearing near the camp's entrance. Each day, they divided and subdivided the rice. Yet something still made Jonathon uneasy. He couldn't put his finger on it. Was it that most of the refugees never seemed happy to see him and the others? That they didn't seem grateful for the gift being bestowed? Was it the gruff way that Rongrit's men treated the other refugees loitering around the distribution site? Something just didn't seem right. It nagged at Jonathon.

During breaks at the hottest times of the day, Jonathon would walk around his quarter playing linguistic charades as he tried to converse with the refugees. They often looked at him blankly. An old man approached Jonathon.

"*Miss-yuh, miss-yuh.*"

"*Oui,*" Jonathon answered, recalling his high school French.

"*Ma, ma grah fee.*" He pointed at the small girl he was pushing forward. "*Eh, eh, vous enseignez, eh, Anglais? See vous pleh.*"

"*Oui, oui,* I teach her, OK." Jonathon began his first lesson. "Hello, heh-lo," he nodded at the girl.

"Hellow." She turned beet red and ran off.

For the next four days, the man and his granddaughter seemed to appear miraculously as Jonathon would begin his daily outing.

"Hollow, how do yoo do. My name ih Tee-dah." It wasn't much after four lessons, but there was no mistaking progress.

After a few words of the lesson, the old man gently nudged Jonathon into a ramshackle hut. His eyes darted from side to side. He whispered frantically.

"Monsieur . . . I afraid . . . Don't tell I talk you. We, we people, rice very little, very very little." He made an eating motion with his fingers. "You rice big. Rongrit rice big. People very little." He made the hand signal again.

"Do they give you the rice? Give, give, they give rice?"

"No," the old man whispered frantically. "They give little, little. They sell Thailand."

Jonathon and the others had known that Rongrit's men were profiting from the camp. Everybody knew that the traders sneaking in and out had to pay protection money. Though they claimed to be a resistance force, Rongrit's men rarely, if ever, engaged the Vietnamese. Everything was taxed. Refugees watched what they said. But were Rongrit's men stealing food from their own people? Jonathan thought of the drunken transvestite warriors stumbling down the camp's streets. It would not be a surprise.

"You give them," the old man whispered, "they sell Thailand, Thailand sell you."

Was that it? Are they selling the donated rice to the Thai merchants we're buying the rice from? Jonathon felt sick.

"You no say I talk you, OK? No say." The man drew his finger across his throat.

Jonathon nodded as the man ushered him out. Why hadn't the man let on he knew English in front of the others? What was really going on in the camp?

Jonathon repeated everything to Tim on the way back to town.

"Yeah, I know," Tim said with a sigh, "I've heard it before. It's a big problem and we don't really know what to do about it. We don't have the people to distribute the rice. They've got the guns, they're in control of the camps. On top of that, Rongrit knows how to play the press and make it look like we're doing a bad job, and then our donors kill us. We try to track where it all goes but it's hard. All rice looks like rice and it's almost impossible to figure out if it's rice we've bought before or not. Take it out of the bag and who could tell one piece from another. To be honest with you, Jonathon, one of our main concerns is that if we lose Rongrit's help, how else are we even going to get rice circulating in the camps? They're loonies, we know, but anyone who tries to go around them in the camps is not going to last very long. I'm not sure if we have a choice."

"So you knew that this was going on?"

"Well, kind of. The border is a tough place, Jonathon, and sometimes you have to make tough choices to do the right thing. But now that you mention it, maybe there is something you can do to help us with this. Would you be willing to try something different?"

"Definitely," Jonathon said enthusiastically.

"Well, this camp's been growing every day since it opened. People seem to pour across the border, sometimes two, three, four thousand a day. They come and stay for a while, they cross into other camps. We don't really know how many refugees there are here. At first, Rongrit told us there were sixty thousand. That seemed about right. A month later it doubled. Now he's saying there are three hundred thousand. We've got the food, but the least we can do is deliver the right amount."

"Have you tried counting?" Jonathon's question felt absurdly obvious.

"We tried by family registration, but some extended families of twenty people registered as one, and other families had everybody register individually just in case we were giving something away."

"Can I try to think of something?" Jonathon asked.

"Sure, we need all the help we can get." A person with a brain like Jonathon's was a rarity on the border, Tim thought.

Within a few hours, Jonathon had come up with a plan. Almost all of the houses used the blue, plastic sheets the UN had distributed for their roofs. This meant that all the houses were pretty much the same size.

"All we have to do is get an average number of people in each hut, count the number of huts, and multiply the two."

"Good idea. We can get the aerial shots from the Thais."

Jonathon spent the whole next day counting. He wandered through all the sections of the camp with Rasady, trying to figure out who lived where and how many people slept in each hut. Seven here, twelve there, eight here. At the end of the day, he added up the people and divided by the number of huts he had visited. The answer was nine.

Tim had also moved quickly, and that night Jonathon counted the blue rectangles in the photos with legal precision.

"So if there are 300,000 people in the camp, there are 32 people in each hut. No way. My generous number is 100,000, but it's probably not even that. That bastard Rongrit wants rice for 200,000 refugees who don't exist."

But how are we going to do it? Tim worried. How are we going to cut the distribution without starting a riot? No one takes a two-thirds cut sitting down. Wasn't it just easier to get rid of the rice and not have any problems? No one was starving anymore in the camps. Tim wondered whether unleashing Jonathon was such a good idea after all. The druggie backpacker volunteers were pretty useless on the border, he thought, but were the idealists dangerous?

"I guess we'll have to meet with Rongrit and tell him what we found." Tim was already dreading it. What was he getting himself into? "I'll ask the Thais to come with us just to be safe," he added unenthusiastically.

13

The thought always seemed to come to Tom Dillon when riding with Witkowski back to the White House from yet another congressional hearing.

Washington, Dillon innately understood, was a vast ecosystem. The rules of the jungle that had dominated life in Vietnam were no less at play in the surface gentility of the nation's capital. The idealistic crusaders, the cynical realists, the power hungry, and the desperate fought and clawed their way up and down the Washington food chain.

Today's Cambodia hearing of the House Committee on International Relations in the Rayburn House Office Building had been a short one. Prepared statements had been delivered in advance and were available to all in the room. The entire hearing could have been replaced by paper. Yet something had gone on in this austere hall far beyond what any paper would have shown.

The three US representatives sitting at the elevated table in front of the room had not attended the hearing to gain any particularly new insights. Their eager young staffers sitting behind them on the dais had taken care of that. They'd shown up to demonstrate that the people were in charge. Witkowski and Bohlen, the titans of the administration's foreign policy team sitting before them, would forget that at their own peril. Although the hearing had been brief, the congresspeople's message had been clear—

there would be no blank checks, no more Tonkin Gulf resolutions, now that Congress was back in charge.

Each representative couldn't help the officials much but they certainly had the power to inflict significant harm. And when an individual challenged that ecosystem, or did not internalize its delicate balance, then the lightning came crashing down upon him. Dillon had watched this force of equilibrium bring the mighty Richard Nixon to his knees six years before. He respected what it could do.

"And what guarantee do we have that this will be the case and that our aid won't be going to Khmer Rouge soldiers?" Representative Martina Samberg had asked.

"We are monitoring aid activities closely . . . The president has ordered it," Witkowski had replied. Sensing that Samberg was not convinced, he'd added a final phrase from outside his briefing book. "And I guarantee it personally."

Dillon had tried not to alter his cool demeanor despite his boss's unexpected comment.

Looking up from his papers in the back of the car, Witkowski's green eyes engaged Dillon.

"I've given you a lot of discretion on this, Thomas. I'm counting on you to keep it clean."

Dillon felt the weight of his boss's words.

"Yes, sir. I understand."

Witkowski held Thomas's gaze, weighing it.

"Good," he said with a slight nod.

Witkowski went back to his papers.

Dillon kept his eyes on Witkowski a moment longer, then shifted his head to look out the window.

14

General Prem Rantanikorn had developed his own little kingdom on the Thai-Cambodian border. Commander of the Royal Thai Army's eastern division, it was his job to stand up to the Vietnamese threat. But the general also knew a windfall when he saw it and wasn't going to let a couple of ignorant foreigners get in the way.

Jonathon and Tim sat humbly in their small, wooden chairs facing the impassive Thai general. Green felt and an overflowing bowl of tropical fruit decorated the long table between them. They came, they knew, as supplicants, hoping to enlist the general's grace while recognizing that everything in the camps—food, trade, life, death—lay within the general's omnipotent discretion. They had explained their accounting system and described their evidence of the massive overcount. The general nodded politely.

The small bands of Khmer Rouge guerrillas who crossed into Thai border towns in '76 and '77 wreaked all kinds of havoc. They stole whatever they could find, cut innocent villagers into bits, and caused others to flee for their lives. When he could find them, Prem had fought the elusive bastards. They were ruthless, but ultimately were a mere nuisance compared to the Vietnamese who had taken Cambodia and now stood on Thailand's eastern border—they were a threat.

Hanoi had the fourth largest army in the world. They'd honed their skills in ten years fighting the Americans. They had the fancy equipment the Americans had left behind. The Vietnamese had the power to push all the way to Bangkok, and Thailand didn't have much of a backup plan. The Saigon leadership had fled like bandits. That wasn't going to happen to the Thais.

The Thais couldn't beat the Vietnamese head to head, but Prem had learned his lesson growing up in a poor farming community in the north—you don't bring down a tiger with a machete, you pierce him with a tiny poison dart. You don't discipline an elephant with a club, you poke him with a small, sharp stick. He'd learned the lesson yet again fighting alongside the Americans in Vietnam. The Americans had been the elephant who fled suffering a thousand tiny wounds. Where were the Americans now? Sure the Khmer Rouge were sons of bitches, but the Khmer Rouge were the stick. Better the Khmer Rouge should fight the Vietnamese than should the Thais.

This was Prem's job. It was his patriotic duty. It was his duty to the king. And if a little money could be made in the process, then so much the better.

Prem had argued to Foreign Minister Upadit to keep the Cambodian civilian refugees out of Thailand. What can these people do for us? We're going to end up spending millions to keep them alive, and build targets for the Vietnamese to attack. But Foreign Minister Upadit, an honorable man, had been overcome with emotion as he saw the starving refugees. The UN, the Americans, and the world community breathing down his neck also helped his thinking along. Upadit knew that letting the refugees cross would be politically costly and expensive, but the alternative was worse. And maybe, just maybe, the refugees would be good for something—a bargaining chip to keep the Vietnamese from asserting their final dominance over Cambodia. Maybe the refugees could become a buffer between the Thais and Vietnamese.

Prem had not wanted the refugees. But now that they were here, he was not one to turn away the opportunity. The Cambodians controlled the interior of the camps. There was no need to get involved on that level. The Thais commanded the outside.

This division of labor was the germ of a thousand deals. The border was a money machine. Worthless plastic sandals and cheap medicines could be traded for Cambodian gold. Traders going in and out of the camps could be taxed. And the fifteen percent commission on all rice sales wasn't bad either. Especially when the same rice was being sold to the aid agencies, repurchased at a discount from the refugees, and sold once again to agencies.

And now these naïve foreigners are here to tell me that there aren't as many refugees as they thought, that too much rice is being sold. Shocking, the bored Prem joked with himself, absolutely shocking.

"I'm sorry Mr. Anderson, the Royal Thai Army is not involved with day-to-day running of camp. I'm sure you understand that our acceptance of camps, and of your activity, is solely humanitarian gesture. If you have problem with distribution, you should take matter up with Prince Rongrit inside Nong Chan camp."

"But if we had less rice to distribute, we could use the money in other ways. We could bring in medicines. There's a lot more we could do."

"I'm sure that true Mr. Anderson, but that not our business."

"The bastard," Tim said to Jonathon as they left the Thai military head-quarters. "He knows what's going on. All we needed was some support. Maybe we'll just have to talk to Rongrit alone."

What am I getting myself into? Tim wondered. Jonathon's eagerness was contagious.

15

The Ki Ki's scene, Jonathon knew, probably would have been good for him. After experiencing all the tension and misery of the camp each day, it probably was normal to kick back, have a few laughs, and grab a beer. But Jonathon had never been good at relaxing. He had never really spent much time in bars. A few of his friends had gone in high school and college, but it all had seemed so synthetic to Jonathon. Why pretend that he was like everybody else? Why pretend that issues aren't important or that idle chatter is? But how could he not go to the one gathering spot in all of Aranyaprathet?

Ki Ki's had sprung up to serve the rapid influx of young Western aid workers who had colonized the Thai border town almost overnight. Aran stood at the center of a web of spidery dirt roads leading to most of the camps on the Thai side of the border.

Jonathon's camp, Nong Chan, was a half hour away. Some of the other camps were much further. At some point between five and six each evening, the aid convoys rolled back in town and the thirsty workers descended. "Ki Ki," the Thai matron, did what she could to be hospitable. Large posters of scantily clad Asian women dancing with oversized bottles of Tiger beer adorned the walls. Ki Ki quickly mastered the art of water buffalo burger grilling. The aid workers would joke, laugh, and tell stories of the crazy and ridiculous things they had witnessed in the camps. Jonathon tried to join them. He sat with his Sprite and awful burger and a forced smile. How could they all let go so easily, as if they were not surrounded by this suffering? He tried his best, but Ki Ki's was not for him.

Jonathon wandered over to a noodle stand near the town market a few blocks away, and read a transcribed word from the food section of his Thai phrase book. He wasn't sure if he had made himself clear. The seller started placing different ingredients in her wok. The thick rice noodles and broccoli seemed to melt in the sweet garlic-soy sauce. The proud cook brought him a plastic cup of cold tea.

He looked up and saw her in the distance walking toward the market.

"Maria," he yelled.

She did not seem to hear him.

"Maria." He stood and waved.

She nodded in recognition and walked over.

"Hello, Jonathon."

"Will you join me?" Jonathon asked with an almost sheepish, slightly crooked smile.

Maria was about to say she had already eaten. Something held her back.

"Yes. Do you eat here a lot?"

"No actually, it's my first time. I tried Ki Ki's, but it's just not for me."

Maria didn't understand what he meant, but nodded politely.

"How are things going in the camp?" she asked.

"It's gotten a little better since that first day when you saw me on the bus. At least I'm not getting mobbed by a band of munchkins."

Maria had seen the movie in an English class at her university. She laughed, then made herself stop.

"And how's the infirmary?" Jonathon asked.

"It's always tough for the refugees, but we have hope."

"Can I order some noodles for you?"

"Oh. OK. Thank you."

Jonathon looked in his book.

"Song gwaytio rad nar kap." It didn't sound like anything the Thais were saying.

The woman reached into a glass box and pulled out a handful of noodles.

"Very impressive," Maria said, almost flirtatiously.

"Yeah, we'll see what we get," Jonathon said with a wink.

Jonathon felt the tension ease from his muscles. He'd had no idea how much he needed a friend. There was a short moment of silence.

"Do you like Thai food?" Jonathon chastised himself for making silly small talk.

Maria didn't hesitate.

"Oh I love it," she said. "How about you?"

Jonathon looked at Maria and smiled warmly. Maria returned the look for a brief, precious moment before turning her eyes downward.

16

Returning to that former life seemed so effortless. The Thai agent at the airport in his ridiculous hotel receptionist's uniform waved the sign THAI ORCHID HOTEL WELCOMES MR. MORGAN O'REILLY.

For four years Morgan had run from the ghosts. Now he was turning to face them on their home turf.

"I'm Morgan O'Reilly. What's the local time?"

"Oh I'm sorry sir, my watch is not working."

Who writes these stupid agency recognition sequences anyway?

In the van from the airport, Morgan took in the humid, musty, polluted, sinful, exhilarating Bangkok air. He remembered the first time he had inhaled the air that would fill his lungs and seep so deeply into his soul. He'd been just twenty-six. It had smelled wild and exotic. The war had taken him so close to death he could almost taste it. It had also brought him closer to life than he'd ever imagined he might come.

Bangkok was the entrepôt to the world he had fled. It was the passageway to the border, to everything the border connected. The wild, formless city of nonstop motion and ultimate human possibility was just how Morgan had remembered it. The road in from the airport was still lined with the same billboards. Tacky neon signs still flashed the hopes of desires they promised to fulfill. The Thais still drove like hell, he chuckled.

The back gate to the US embassy on Wireless Road slowly opened and the car slipped in. The embassy hummed with the same purpose that had once been Morgan's own. The same world opened its gates to him as if he had never left. Morgan wondered if he ever had.

"O'Reilly? Welcome to Bangkok. I'm Dan Hutchins."

Hutchins was the type of man Morgan would have expected doing this job. The Agency liked keeping its high-breds in control at the embassies. Let the Irish and the immigrants bust their asses in the field.

"They haven't told us much about your mission, other than that we're supposed to give you whatever support you need no questions asked," Hutchins said with a shrug. "So whatever you need, you just let us know."

"Right now I need some information."

"Go ahead."

"I know that Sophal, Heng Sophal, passed through here six months ago. What kind of contact did you have?"

"We had the same orders for him as we do for you. No questions, information on a need-to-know basis, give whatever help he asks for." Hutchins was clearly annoyed. "Sometimes I think it's almost too secret for our own good. We didn't have much contact with Sophal, but enough to know we don't have any now. Rips me up. Maybe we could have saved him."

Morgan shuddered. "So you think he's dead?"

"Hell, O'Reilly, that border's a pit, it's a death trap. If the Khmer Rouge don't get you, if you don't get robbed and killed, if you don't step on a land mine and get blown to shit, a little mosquito'll probably bite your ass and you'll shiver to death with cerebral malaria. You don't hear from a guy in three and a half months, what else can you think?"

O'Reilly did his best to ignore the provocation.

"What do you know about Sophal?"

"Not much."

"What did he ask you for?"

"First he asked us to get him a camp pass for all the camps. We had to go all the way to Prem to get it for him."

"Prem?"

"General Prem's head of the Thai army's eastern division. Runs the border like a fiefdom. So we know Sophal was heading out there. He touched base with our man in Aranyaprathet, but not much after that except for his cables. A Thai courier'd deliver them to our man in Aran who'd pass them here for us to send through. We'd get the answers back, send them to Aran, and the courier picked them up and apparently passed them on."

"Did you read the cables?"

"Couldn't. They were all encrypted. We could have tried to break the code I guess, but no sense spying on our own people."

"Where were the cables going?"

"I don't know. It was a different channel. I didn't recognize the code. They seemed to be going somewhere and answers seemed to be coming back. Weird. It was pretty regular, though. That's what alerted us when they stopped. Maybe he's communicating some other way. Maybe he doesn't need us anymore. The whole thing just doesn't seem right to me."

"Have you gone to the Thais?"

"We tried, but they don't seem to know much either."

"Aren't they running the show over there?"

"There's a lot of shit going on, O'Reilly. The Thais are scared to death of the Vietnamese. The Vietnamese could whip their butts in a second and everybody knows it. Thais feel like hostages. On one hand they don't want to piss the Vietnamese off too much so they're claiming neutrality, say that the problems between the Cambodians and the Vietnamese are not Thailand's business. On the other hand, they're doing whatever they can behind the scenes to fight back. They've got Chinese arms coming in. They want us to arm the KR against the Vietnamese—I don't think they understand the words 'congressional oversight.' They're insisting that food relief be given on the border, they're beefing up their defenses. The only problem is that if they want the Cambodians to fight, there aren't enough of them to do it. That's why they're pushing the food aid so strong. Pump some food into these refugees and turn them into soldiers. You'll see the camps. Right now the only ones with a hope of fighting are the Khmer Rouge."

"And you? What are you guys doing here?"

"The State Department people set up a unit called the Kampuchea Emergency Group to get aid to the border. It's pretty legit. They're calling for aid to all the people of Cambodia—'aid to both sides,' they call it. So they make some deliveries to Phnom Penh and pump the food to the border. Works pretty well for us. Hanoi's people in Phnom Penh are all pissed because we're giving food to the border. They say we're sucking people out of Cambodia and should only be feeding Cambodia through the capital. Our guys keep saying 'aid to both sides' and keep sending it to both places. Then Phnom Penh tells us they'd rather eat grass than accept our tainted rice. Makes them look like murderers. We hope they take the rice. God knows they need it."

"I'll need to get out to the border right away. They told me you'd arrange things."

"Yeah, it's all taken care of."

Hutchins pulled out a sealed manila envelope and sliced it open.

"Here is your ID card for Catholic Missions International. The story is that you're on a survey and oversight mission from the headquarters in Baltimore. They know you're coming. Our man in Aran is Kevin Conley. We arranged a car and driver to take you out to the border in the morning. Takes about five hours. We've also booked you into Jim's Lodge down the street. So why don't you go get some sleep. We'll have the driver there 7:30 tomorrow morning."

The smooth-faced bellboy in his undersized and wrinkled baby blue uniform laid Morgan's bag on his bed and smiled. He opened the shutter on the window and smiled. He turned on the television and smiled.

Oh god, I'm out of practice, Morgan said to himself, his hand fumbling in his pocket.

"Yes, of course."

He took out his wallet and handed the boy a crisp dollar bill. The boy accepted it suspiciously eyeing the strange currency.

Maybe four years is a long time, Morgan thought. A new generation of Thai kids raised to recognize their own money. The bellboy shrugged and left.

The Thai characters on TV, two men dressed like women going through some kind of comedy routine, were fast annoying Morgan. But as the sound vanished from the room, Morgan realized that turning off the television had been a mistake. Noise and activity had accompanied him ever since he had left Dulles Airport two days before. There were drinks served, the captain's announcements, arriving, playing the operations officer again like trying on an old, musty coat. Everybody seemed to think that the life of a CIA operations officer was like a James Bond movie, never a dull moment, always active and exciting. But what characterized this life was not the few moments of tension when your stomach pushed against your throat. It was the silence, waiting for things to happen, endless waiting that opened the gates and let the demons in. Morgan's jet-lagged body drew him toward his bed.

As he wrestled with fleeting sleep, fighting for a few moments of release, the memories came back with a new intensity. The faces came to him—Vuth, Phim, Rithy, Sophal, Vanny, Choeun. "We're in this together, we can't lose as long as we stick together," he saw himself telling the kids meeting in the abandoned railroad car in Takmau.

"Oh yes, we can't lose. Let's see . . . The Khmer Rouge control seventy-five percent of the country, our government is corrupt, and the fate of our country rests with the diaper patrol," Vuth had said.

The absurdity of the situation inspired nervous laughter.

"Diaper patrol, huh," Sophal had replied with a wink toward Morgan. "Well you sure seemed about to mess yourself when you almost got caught at the police station."

The children's laughter began to turn raucous.

Phim walked across the railcar, squeezing his knees together and scrunching his face in a comic caricature of Vuth. "Save me, save me. I can't hold it in much longer," he chortled in a comic tone.

Choeun and Vanny moved behind Phim creating a conga line of playful mockery.

Laughter rocked the musty abandoned railcar.

Joy filling his heart, Morgan felt astonished by what he had created. These children had once been the forlorn refuse of the Phnom Penh streets. Phim, whose parents had been killed in the war, had arrived in Phnom Penh desperate, frightened, and alone. Morgan had found him forging identity documents in a dark alley, but he was now a self-confident infiltrator who could almost assume the identities he was forging to devastating effect. Vuth had almost himself vanished from the drug addiction he'd had when Morgan recruited him, but he could now almost magically appear and disappear at will, leaving the Khmer Rouge targets disoriented and blaming themselves when key plans went missing. Rithy had been like driftwood moving aimlessly up and down the banks of the Tonle Sap. He could now keep his focused eye on the entire Phnom Penh bank of the Tonle Sap and Mekong rivers, watching and waiting with an increasingly mature patience. Sophal had come to Morgan with a natural ability to lead. Under Morgan's guidance and care, this natural ability was quickly becoming an art. As far as each of them had come individually, they had all come even farther together.

Walking around the railcar, Morgan placed his hand on each boy's shoulder as if to say through this subtle motion, "we are not alone." Now, six years later, as his conscious mind caught up with his reverie, that sentiment seemed so terribly false.

Morgan had hardly slept at all when his wake-up call came at five-thirty the next morning. He had prepared for his same routine. His running shoes rested beside his bed, his shorts, socks, and singlet folded neatly beside them. It took three minutes to put on the clothes, two more to splash water on his face and brush his teeth, a few minutes of stretching, and he was out the door. He headed for Lumpini Park three blocks away.

The smells accosted him as he lunged toward the park. The noodle shops and soup stalls preparing for the morning rush . . . how many times . . . No, stop. Focus. One foot in front of the other. Each step landing in turn, breathe, in, out, deeply. Your body is a machine. Do you feel pain, marine? No, sir. Can you do it? Yes, sir. One, two, one, two. Come on, come on, the click. Where are you?

He was still longing for the click as he rounded his final corner an hour later and stopped breathless in front of his hotel.

17

The meeting with Rongrit followed the same absurd formality that Tim and now Jonathon had come to expect. Though Rongrit roared his motorcycle up and down the camp's roads at all times of the day, the self-declared prince demanded that an appointment be made for discussions of any issues. First, a request needed to be made to Rongrit's assistant, a slim twenty-one-year-old whose red, patent leather belt lined with dangling hand grenades held up his oversized army fatigues. "Lieutenant Colonel," as the man liked to be called, would then return with word of whether Rongrit was available for the appointment. It was hard to imagine what else he had to do.

Even though Rongrit's headquarters were constructed of the same thatch and sticks of the other hovels, the space was not too basic to obviate the need for a waiting room. Two Cambodian girls in sarongs poured hot tea from a battered thermos.

"Mr. Anderson, Mr. Cohane, his highness will see you now," Lieutenant Colonel announced, vainly portraying a formality he had probably never before known.

After the twenty minutes of waiting and three weeks of holding back their anger that the international community was being bilked for rice to feed 200,000 nonexistent people, Tim and Jonathon were hardly in a mood for pleasantries.

They and their interpreter Rasady sat at the table. Small plates of fruit and new tea glasses were placed before them.

"Welcome to my headquarters," Rasady translated Rongrit's words. "It is my honor to host you here and to praise your excellent cooperation and support as we nurture and rehabilitate our people."

"Thank you, we feel the same," Tim said perfunctorily. "That's what we are here to talk with you about. As you know, we've worked closely together to provide food and rations to the people of this camp. We very much appreciate your efforts to help. Because so many people have been coming and going, it's been very difficult for us to determine how many people are in the camp. We have now developed a system to help figure that out."

Rongrit's eyes widened slightly as Rasady completed the translation. His face remained calm.

"Our system is simple," Tim continued. "We figured out the average number of people in each hut, and then multiplied this number by the number of huts we counted from an aerial photograph. We determined that there were an average of nine people in each hut and a total of a little under ten thousand huts. So the total is probably around 90,000, but we increased it to 100,000 just to be safe. As you know, these past few weeks, we've been distributing rice on the assumption that 300,000 people were in the camp. We work in other camps on the border as well, and our only reason for wanting to be as accurate as possible is so that we can then have more money and food to help other refugees in need. So we've come to let you know that we're committed to working together to feed the people of this camp, according to the distribution plan we agreed to. But we're sure you'll understand that we need to use our money and rice to help all the Cambodians in need, and so starting next week we're going to send two-thirds of the rice to help people in other camps."

Tim and Jonathon waited to see how Rongrit would respond. The prince did not seem much affected by the news. He refilled their tea glasses then his, then lifted his glass and took a small sip.

"Thank you very much for your careful analysis of the situation in my camp," Rongrit then waited for Rasady to translate. "My responsibility to care for my people I take very seriously. That's why I have ordered my associates to keep careful records of how many refugees are in the camp. These records are updated daily and list every person's name. As you know, people come and go from the camp, and what was 300,000 three weeks ago, may have sunk to 290,000 today. But I can assure you that these numbers are absolutely accurate, and that any reduction in aid will lead to widespread malnutrition and even death among the people of the camp. So I hope you'll reconsider. It would be most unfortunate if the people who've come here to help end up being the very ones who cut our lifeline."

The media threat, Tim thought to himself.

"But I know that proper accounting is important to you," Rongrit continued, "and for that reason, I am prepared to recheck our figures and possibly accept a reduction to 290,000."

"Thank you very much, Mr. . . . Prince Rongrit. We are very glad you see our side of the matter. But I hope you understand that if we are seen to be giving aid to refugees who don't exist, it could be very tough for us as well. We need to be responsible to our donors, or foreign governments will stop giving."

The conversation continued like this for ten more minutes, each side saying as politely as possible that it would not budge from its position. Tim had feared that things would get out of hand. Oddly, Rongrit seemed to behave as if he knew something Tim and Jonathon did not.

Rongrit stood up.

"Thank you for coming to share your concerns."

He left the room and Lieutenant Colonel escorted Tim and Jonathon out.

"What do you think that meant?" Tim later asked.

"Maybe he realizes that we have to get the aid where it's most needed. Maybe he doesn't want to piss off the donors." Jonathon didn't fully trust his own words.

"Maybe," Tim said, unconvinced.

For the rest of the week, Rongrit's men seemed on their best behavior. Rice funneled through the camp distribution points with a previously unseen efficiency.

The following Monday, however, the distribution crew prepared for the worst.

"Listen up everybody," Tim shouted before the trucks headed out from town. "As you all know, today's distribution is two-thirds smaller than what we've been giving out over the past three weeks. Some people are going to be pretty upset about this. So I want everyone to be real careful and calm today. If there are any problems, just have the trucks clear out."

As the trucks rolled past the camp gate, everything seemed just as it had been the day before. Rongrit's men took the rice and farmed it out to the far corners of the camp. The aid workers waited all day for a sign, a change in the camp's rhythm. It never came.

"Not bad. Maybe this is going to work," Jonathon told Tim as their convoy drove back to Aran at the end of the day.

Tim didn't respond.

But as the convoy approached Nong Chan the next morning, it was clear that something had changed dramatically.

The clearing just past the gate near the camp entrance was filled to the brim with refugees. The low rumble of voices, the quick movement of bodies, and the palpable anger registered on the multitude of faces announced the brewing crisis.

Jonathon had thought about this possibility but discounted it. Would Rongrit really have just stopped the distribution, held his own people hostage?

Tim and Jonathon walked into the camp. The shouting came from so many directions that the two could not have understood the words, even had they been in a language they knew. Jonathon felt almost like a criminal being marched out before his accusers.

Rasady rushed up to greet them.

"What is going on here?" Jonathon asked.

"Two-thirds of the camp didn't get any rice yesterday. Everybody thinks you ordered the rice stopped."

"What? Why do they think that?" Jonathon shouted.

"Because that's what they told them. And there's no rice."

"Who told them?" Jonathon felt foolish for asking such an obvious question.

"Rongrit's people."

"And they believe them?"

"Yes."

"Tell them it's not true, Rasady."

Rasady knew better than to translate.

"Where's Rongrit?" Tim's voice was barely discernible above the nervous hubbub.

"I don't know."

Just then, Lieutenant Colonel stepped up.

"Where the hell is Rongrit?" Tim barked.

"Would you like to make an appointment to see the prince?"

"Are you joking?" Tim's patience with this foolishness was running out.

"You tell Rongrit that we're leaving. We'll come back when this place is in order. You know damn well that there's enough rice for everybody."

"You no leave Mr. Anderson."

"What? We're here to help you people. We have rice to give. Look at these people—your people. Is this what you want? I'm sorry. We would love to help but there is just no damn way we can do it under these conditions."

Tim turned to walk away.

"Tim!" Jonathon yelled frantically.

Tim turned to see Lieutenant Colonel's gun pointing at his head. He froze.

"Bring the rice in." There was a coldness in Lieutenant Colonel's eyes that made it clear that his threat was not idle.

Tim's heavy breath expanded his chest outward. Fear, incredulity, and disgust measured equally on his face. Jonathon turned toward the nonchalant Thai guard manning the gate thirty feet away. With wide eyes, he pointed desperately at Lieutenant Colonel.

The Thai guard lifted his M16 and shouted a command in Thai. Lieutenant Colonel's gun slid back into his red belt. He vanished into the crowd.

Tim exhaled. Tears welled in Jonathon's eyes. The two jumped back on the trucks and waved the rice convoy back to Aranyaprathet.

Jonathon could not speak for the entire ride home. He felt as if black soot was darkening his heart. How could the very people he had come to help be blaming him when their own leaders were the ones holding them hostage? How could trying to do good feel so compromising?

18

To find Sophal, I must be Sophal, Morgan thought to himself as his car entered Aranyaprathet.

The Thai town was a window to the border, to the unknown expanse of Cambodia that lay so near. Aran was the border's link to the rest of the world. Aran led everywhere and nowhere. Finding someone on one side of the window or the other, among the half million people in the camps, the seven million in Cambodia, Morgan sensed, would not be an easy task. Morgan knew he would never find Sophal just by looking. His only chance was to go one step further. Only then could the field be narrowed, only then were the odds not seven and a half million to one.

Morgan and Sophal had always maintained a special link, an intuitive connection that bound them without words. Morgan had given Sophal his passport the day before the Khmer Rouge took control of Phnom Penh in 1975 because he wanted to get him out. Yet the act was so much more. Morgan was sharing his identity with Sophal just as Sophal had shared his world with Morgan.

And just as Sophal had made Morgan a Cambodian, Morgan had made Sophal an American. Morgan had pulled what strings he could to get Sophal a job with the agency, to rush his American citizenship. The agency tapped Sophal for the same job Morgan had been sent to do less than a decade before. Sophal, like Morgan before him, was a CIA operations officer among the Cambodians even if they were now in Thailand. In so many ways, Sophal had picked up where Morgan had left off. As Morgan had sunk into his postwar depression, Sophal had struggled to keep alive the flame of passion his older friend had once known. As Morgan had questioned his commitment to his country and his former ideals, Sophal had taken them up with a vengeance. First in his class at the CIA field school, Sophal became the rising star of the division of operations. He was a true believer in America's inextinguishable spirit, a spirit that matched his own.

Morgan thought back to when he had helped Sophal pick out his first car. Against Morgan's judgment, Sophal chose a used 1974 Chevy convertible. It wasn't a practical car for the Northern Virginia winters, but it was so much like Sophal to believe that the seasons ought to conform to his wishes, not vice versa. Morgan smiled at the memory of returning home from the car dealership to realize that his wallet had been stolen and replaced with a cheap wallet containing a picture of himself smiling during happier times in Phnom Penh. His old wallet showed up in the mail three days later.

Morgan had guided Sophal's career almost as a last vestige of a self who had once believed. But now Sophal was lost, and Morgan needed to find him. To do so, Morgan realized that he needed to rediscover the lost part of himself that had once been a little like Sophal.

19

Jonathon's memory was built upon a maze of stories. Auschwitz was a place, but in him it was a connector of tales. His aunt Marta's daughter Hilda torn from her mother's arms and sent to the gas chamber. His mother's pediatrician, Dr. Molinsky, jumping from the train to be killed by angry German shepherds. Cousin Albert beaten to death just outside the Lodz ghetto for sneaking out to steal bread. The stories, told and retold, woven into him, now wove him into the new stories of the nameless refugees slowly accruing names.

Despite the chaos in the camps, the distribution nightmares, and the perfidy of Rongrit and his men, Jonathon felt determined to hold on to his own humanity by not denying the Cambodians theirs. Even after the compromise had been reached with Rongrit and rice distributions had been decreased by a paltry twenty percent, Jonathon struggled to keep his anger at Rongrit and his deep frustrations with camp life from closing the wide eyes he hoped would help him truly see the refugees.

Bopha said she was thirteen, but looked not a day over ten. Jonathon had noticed her loitering around the distribution area. While the other children, even some of the more malnourished ones with their reddish hair and bulging bellies, jumped over sticks or long threads of tied rubber bands to pass the time, Bopha paced back and forth on her own eyeing the distribution. At first, Jonathon feared she was casing the distribution point, then chastised himself for being so distrustful.

Jonathon brought a bag of candies with him from Aran. During a break, he walked around giving one to each child. While the other children took the candy quietly and without expression, Bopha broke into an enormous grin. She put her hands together in front of her forehead. Jonathon smiled.

Bopha edged a little closer to the trucks in each of the following days. Soon, Jonathon deputized her as his official candy distributor. While the other children learned two English words, "OK, bye-bye," which they repeated ad infinitum, Bopha picked up "Good morning, how do you do." She shyly repeated the small phrase each morning before turning her face downward in embarrassed pleasure. Through Rasady, Jonathon asked her a few questions each day, trying to piece together her story.

She'd been born, she said, in Phnom Penh. Her father was the principal of an elementary school. When the Khmer Rouge took power, her parents had been killed, and she was put in a child brigade in Pursat province. Her job was to tend the vegetable garden. One of the starving children had stolen a green bean and put it in his pocket to eat secretly later. In a surprise inspection, the camp cadres found the bean and the boy was taken away. Bopha never saw him again. Bopha probably would have died like so many of the others had she not found a series of protectors.

One of the Khmer Rouge leaders, an old one-eyed soldier whose young daughter had been killed by an American bomb, passed Bopha a piece of potato here, a fish head there. Not much, but enough to keep her alive. Later, in the chaos of the Vietnamese invasion, when the Khmer Rouge themselves were running for their lives, Bopha had attached herself to a young widow whose husband had vanished in the Khmer Rouge killing fields. This woman had heard that there was food and safety on the Thai border, and joined a small group of starved former commune workers making their way there. About half hadn't made it, succumbing to malaria or being killed by land mines along the way. Bopha's protector had stepped on a mine just before reaching the camp. Bopha stumbled with the few remaining others into the Thai camp.

Rasady, the interpreter, explained to Jonathon that when the Khmer

Rouge took control of Cambodia, they emptied the cities and divided the population between the "new" people from the cities and the "old" people from the countryside. Rasady, a former English student, was a "new" person in the greatest danger. People like Bopha's father—educated people, people with access to foreign ideas, doctors, former government bureaucrats, soldiers from the losing army—had been systematically sought out. Those who couldn't hide their identities were often killed. Rasady had lived by trying to forget everything he had ever learned in school, to forget his family, to deprogram his mind and become a simple farmer. He couldn't let anybody know of his past life. He rubbed his hands together each night to develop the calluses that a lifetime of labor should have bestowed.

Jonathon met Rathana at one of the distribution sites in the camp. A former Lon Nol soldier, Rathana had been told to report to the Battambang airport in uniform to greet Prince Sihanouk after the Khmer Rouge took control in 1975. The nervous soldiers of the defeated regime did not dare refuse the order. As they waited at the airport, they began to suspect that the prince was not coming. The Khmer Rouge soldiers moved in. They tied Rathana and his colleagues' hands behind their backs and marched them through the jungle to a large clearing. The defeated soldiers sank to their knees begging for their lives. On cue, the Khmer Rouge soldiers descended in a wild fury, smashing the prisoners' heads with hoes, bayoneting the bound soldiers. The Khmer Rouge walked among the corpses picking off anything moving with Chinese hand pistols, each burst answered by a call of birds.

A bullet had passed through Rathana's head. Miraculously, it missed his brain. He lay under the pile of bodies half dead and feigning the other half. When the Khmer Rouge left, he crawled into the forest and nursed himself back to health eating bark and insects. Soon after he could walk, he limped toward the border. Three months later, dehydrated, malnourished, bruised, and torn, he crawled into Thailand.

Jonathon also met Mr. Im Sakhan, an elderly gentleman who had offered his useful logistical services to the Mercy Relief team. Sakhan had been a civil engineer during the Sihanouk and Lon Nol days, and had trained for a year at the University of Phoenix. He'd been working at the

ocean port of Sihanoukville in southern Cambodia when the Khmer Rouge
took over. At first, the new regime had needed experts like Sakhan to service the few ships coming in.

This had all changed when a new Khmer Rouge leader showed up in his
town. The new leader was suspicious of Sakhan, contemptuously calling
him a leech and a parasite. "It's people like you who have driven this country to ruin." Sakhan, quivering, looked down, nodding in agreement. This
outward show of penance was soon deemed insufficient. Sakhan was arrested as an enemy of the people. The local cadre had a quota of enemies
they had to fill. People like Sakhan were easy targets.

He was sent to the interrogation center of Tuol Sleng in Phnom Penh
and chained in a four-by-five-foot brick cubicle. Brutal interrogation was a
daily event. The Khmer Rouge guards pulled out his toenails and fingernails
one by one, they forced water down his throat with a hose and then jumped
on his stomach, they dipped his head in a well to get him to confess his sins.
He was an enemy of the people, a saboteur of the revolution. Against the
odds, he held to a glimmer of hope even as he heard his fellow inmates
wailing. It was even harder when the wailing stopped after the inmates had
been sent to the nearby killing fields of Cheung Ek.

Sakhan would have gone the same way had it not been for a single for-
tuity. Torturing inmates through the day and night required a determined
cadre of revolutionaries. That they had. It also took electricity—for lights,
for electric wires tied around men's testicles or inserted into women's
vaginas. The power station of Phnom Penh had shut down, and this electricity was provided by a generator.

One day, as Sakhan was being interrogated, the generator blew. For
two days, the uneducated cadres struggled to repair it without success.
Trembling with fear that his expression of expertise would prove he was
the elitist they claimed, Sakhan took a chance.

"If you please, sir. Only to serve you and serve the people . . . I think I
might be able to fix the generator."

The section leader, suspicious of the offer yet annoyed by the two days
without light or power, made a deal.

"If you can fix it in a day, go ahead. If you can't make it in that time, we'll have to reconsider everything."

The threat was not an empty one. It was Sakhan's only chance. Summoning forth everything he had once known, calling up all the energy in his mangled, malnourished body, he took the generator apart piece by piece. He laid each part out, mapping its original location with his trembling hand. He found the broken section and fashioned a rustic but workable replacement. Piece by piece, he rebuilt the machine. He added the oil and the gas. He pulled the cord. The machine sputtered, it choked. It glided into gear. Sakhan nearly fainted.

The section leader was pleased. Who knew when this thing was going to break again? It was impossible to get parts. Sakhan was put in charge of maintaining the generator. His worthless life now had value. He still slept chained, still haunted by the screams of the vanishing inmates passing through Tuol Sleng on their way to Cheung Ek.

When the Vietnamese took Phnom Penh on January 7, 1979, Sakhan, unlike the carefully recorded 16,232 inmates who had perished passing through Tuol Sleng, was among the seven who had survived. But there were too many ghosts in Cambodia. One night, he sneaked out and made his way to the border. Cambodia was for the dead. Phoenix was for the living.

Jonathon sat silently with Sakhan. These stories were terrifying, striking. They wove themselves into his family's stories that he had brought with him, stories that had brought him here.

But there were some aspects of camp life that Jonathon struggled to integrate into his narrative.

Jonathon hadn't known what the camps would be like before he'd arrived. He had been sure they would be awful. But he had never questioned whether what he would do there would be good. That had been a given. When he was distributing rice to the hungry and the infirm, when he was meeting with people like Rathana and Sakhan, he had little question that he was helping.

These experiences weighed in the balance against the increasing percentage of his time spent fighting off the refugees' greed. The refugees would accuse him and the others of shortchanging them, lie about whether distributions had been made, and would steal from each other. Fights routinely broke out at distribution sites, and hand grenades were occasionally rolled into huts as retribution. Refugees with desired goods like medicines forced others to sacrifice nearly all of their rice in trade. Much of Jonathon's time was spent not talking with people like Rathana and Sakhan, not giving candy to Bopha and the others, but designing systems to prevent stealing, trying to convince refugees that any shortcomings in rice were the fault of their leaders not the aid workers, and monitoring rice distributions ever more closely.

The system was designed to give life, but it made little emotional sense to do so by withholding rice, pulling the trucks out when things got out of hand, and treating the refugees as potential thieves. No matter how justified Jonathon and his colleagues felt when they pulled the trucks back, he could not help feeling like he was failing his ideals.

Jonathon returned from the camp each day tired both from the exhausting work and from the battle raging within him. Had he really thought about the refugees today, about each individual refugee? Had he instead seen them as a greedy, ungrateful horde trying to amass as much rice as possible without the slightest concern for one another?

His thoughts aroused the first pangs of guilt. If it was not goodness driving his actions, what was it? Did he simply want to make sense of the chaotic camps? He needed time and space to process all he was experiencing. There were a few others like him, but most everyone else was happy just to hang around Ki Ki's.

And then there was Maria—calm, sincere, understanding. Her silence reassured Jonathon. She seemed to accept him for what he was and value him for what he aspired to be. Their first dinner at the noodle stand had become a more regular event. The food stall owner learned their names and welcomed them when they arrived, wearing the Filipino bead Maria had given her on a string around her neck as she cooked. At first, Jonathon and Maria would look forward to describing their days to each other and learning each other's views. As time went on, each began to experience their time in the camp in some ways through the other's eyes.

Good-byes at the night's end seemed to take a little longer each night.

"Would you like to go for a walk?" he finally asked her at the end of one of those nights.

Maria blushed as she paused for a moment. They wouldn't miss her at the villa if she was quick.

"Well . . . OK."

They headed down a dirt road leading out of town. The faint glow of the distant moon revealed the placid glass of the dormant rice paddies. They shared the gentle silence, and from that silence deciphered words. He told of his feelings of guilt for fighting with the refugees.

"But you are trying so hard," Maria said.

Maria was slightly afraid but decided to take a risk. She told Jonathon about Fidel, her experiences with Sister Susan and about her family. "What matters is what's in your heart," Maria said.

Maria's words felt cleansing to Jonathon. She was so understanding, so appreciative of the parts of him about which he cared most. He told her about his parents in Chicago, the Holocaust, his reasons for coming to Thailand. Jonathon felt surprised by how comfortable he felt telling Maria things he hadn't told many others before. He felt drawn to her and wanted to touch her, but didn't dare jinx the world they were slowly creating.

Maria's life had been so different from his. He could only imagine her village in the Philippines. Could she picture Highland Park? Yet somehow they were building a bridge across their differences. She patiently described to Jonathon the rice planting cycle, the feeling of the seasons, and every detail of the festival of St. Antony, the patron saint of her village. Jonathon felt as if she was holding his hand and guiding him over that bridge.

Something had always prevented Jonathon from getting too close to people outside of his family. Yet Maria seemed so welcoming and open. It felt so nice, if but for a moment, to stop thinking and feel.

It was a quiet evening. The bright stars looked like holes punched in the night. He reached down to hold her hand. She paused for a moment, then slid her soft hand into his. They squeezed gently. Through their hands they could each feel the other's pulse.

20

Something about Evan Pritchard just didn't seem quite right to Jonathon. Jonathon had first been surprised by Evan's hostile words at the orphanage. Jonathon also noticed how many photographs Evan was casually taking in the camp. All of this was slightly odd, but there was so much to take in that he hadn't given it much attention.

The pieces gradually began to add up. Unlike the others, who were there each morning at seven, Evan missed work one, sometimes two days a week. Stomach problems, Evan said, some type of parasite he'd picked up. Jonathon was not convinced.

Evan's corner of the room was a mess. It smelled of cigarette smoke. He often did not return to the room until two or three in the morning. As Jonathon would dress to leave the following morning, Even lay flattened on his bed stinking of alcohol. When they'd return at the end of the day, Evan peppered them with questions. He hung around Ki Ki's greeting each newcomer. He interrogated people who visited the different camps. It was one of two things, Jonathon concluded. Evan was either a journalist or a spy. But how could he tell the difference? Either way, Evan was posing as something he wasn't.

Jonathon wondered if he should say something to Tim. But what would he say—that he didn't trust Evan? What if he was wrong and Evan was just lazy and curious? Jonathon could think of one way to find out.

"Evan, I want to talk to you."

"Sure, mate."

"What you do is your own business and I don't want to interfere with your private life. But it's hard not to notice things and those of us working in the camp might be compromised through our association with, well, with others."

"Sure." Evan did not seem on the verge of any confession.

"Well . . . you've been taking pictures around, you're asking lots of questions . . . and it just seems like more than curiosity. I mean, it seems professional. I'm sorry, but are you a spy?"

A laugh burst from Evan's stomach.

"Me mate, a spy? Who the hell would I spy for? Who'd want me?"

Jonathon's earnest expression curtailed Evan's humor. Evan stared at Jonathon for a moment, his face becoming more serious.

"OK. I'm not a spy. That's for sure."

The words did not placate Jonathon.

"If I tell you the truth are you going to turn me in?"

"I'll certainly do something if you don't tell me."

Evan sighed.

"OK, I'm a journalist. I work for Pacific Times News Service. It's a pretty small outfit based in LA. Well, I guess I kind of work for them. They pay me by the story. Now that the big guys are here—the *New York Times, FT,* the *Guardian*—there's not even much of that. Those guys are getting all the scoops and I don't have a chance. I just wait for big things to happen and get there fast. The camps are the story here and if I'm working here, I figure I'll get the big scoops when they come. At least it'll be something I can sell. Mercy Relief was asking for any help they could get, so I thought hell, anybody is anybody. Sorry, it's not a very exciting story. I'm no James Bond or anything."

Evan made his finger into a pistol and fired it in Jonathon's direction.

"I sold one story the whole time I've been here. Hardly pays for my beer. Doesn't make me much of a journalist."

"Does Tim know?"

"Jesus, man, of course not. And I would really, really appreciate it if you wouldn't tell him. I'm not hurting anybody. I'm just doing what you're doing. Come on man, give me a break. People gotta know about this stuff. Nothing wrong with information. It keeps the aid dollars coming, that's for sure. Where do you think the money to pay for all of this comes from?"

Jonathon's perplexed look gave Evan the impression he was winning. Evan kept silent, trying to maintain a trustworthy visage.

Jonathon took a deep breath and spoke.

"Well I'm certainly not going to promise you anything, but let's just see how things go."

A knock on the door interrupted the conversation.

"Jonathon, it's me."

"Yeah Maria, just one sec." He buttoned up his shirt and was gone.

Evan shook his head from side to side.

"Dumbshit," he muttered under his breath.

21

The heart of Christian love, Maria knew, was forgiveness. Jesus died for our sins not because he anticipated that a few of us would do terrible things, but because he understood that humans were imperfect by definition. No matter how hard we strove, we would do wrong. However fervent our belief, God's perfection would never be ours. Christian love was being good, was helping others to be good. It was helping Neang see the light through her pain-damaged eyes. But at its core, Christian love was forgiving all of us for falling short.

The Cambodian refugees to whom she had committed so much were far from perfect. They were survivors, people who had stayed alive because they were imperfect. They knew how to steal from each other, how to hide things, how to lie. When they reached the camps they were just a few months away from the hell that their country had been. Maria understood why they would steal from each other; she understood why medicines would go missing. Though it pained her, she even understood the attacks that happened at night as refugees settled old scores. But not all of the refugees were victims.

Everyone knew that former Khmer Rouge soldiers had made their way into the camp to evade the Vietnamese. These people had done terrible, unspeakable things. But perhaps because of that, it was they who most needed absolution. Sister Susan's hug was Maria's gift to share.

During breaks at work, she wandered out to the sick and dying refugees in the infirmary. Some lay motionless in trances halfway to another world. Men tossed and turned, they held their hands to their foreheads, perhaps trying to grasp the realization that they would live the rest of their lives with only one leg. Feverish patients moaned what seemed to Maria to be nightmares of past experiences. What had these men been doing two years ago? Were they working in the fields or ordering others at gunpoint into the dark jungle? Maria prayed for them all.

Faith, she knew, was transformative. It could accomplish miracles. But her faith could not save them. Her faith would spark theirs and inspire them to seek the path themselves. She would have to show them by example. Maria worked tirelessly to make the refugees' lives more bearable. She oversaw the little things—did they have enough water in their bottles? Did their families have enough cloth to keep them clean? She checked whether everyone was taking their pills at the right time.

Maria so wanted the refugees to recognize her inner calm, to ask her for the information she was so burning to share. If they would have faith, maybe their pain could be lessened and they could start new lives. She waited patiently, hopefully. The questions never came. Was it because she was Asian and not white? she wondered. The refugees addressed the white doctors and nurses with the highest honorific titles and the most respectful hand gestures. Was she imagining it or did the black American nurse and Maria never receive the same treatment as the others?

Or was it her? she asked herself. Was her faith not deep enough? Were her past failures weighing her down? Maria tried to banish such thoughts from her mind. They nagged at her search for purity, at her quest to overcome herself by overcoming the doubts within her.

Alongside these doubts, however, something new and pure was growing inside her. Her nighttime walks with Jonathon brought Maria a new serenity different from what she had experienced before. When he held her hand, her doubts, for a moment, seemed to float away. Jonathon was a pure soul, yet so tortured by his experiences in the camp. He was fighting to make the food delivery system work. The obstacles seemed so great, yet he too was a believer in a way, a troubled believer.

Jonathon was struggling as he strove to bring order to the camp. Maria had sensed from the beginning that setting such lofty goals for herself would have prevented her from meeting each individual refugee on his or her own terms, but still she tried to help Jonathon the best way she knew. She could accept him, could forgive him, inspire him.

After Jonathon's first touch, Maria had craved that physical connection. Should she hate herself for feeling this? Fidel had cost her so much so many years before. She had fought so hard, had come to the border even, to regain what she had lost. But even Jesus had a human body, had touch, and taste, and smell. Perhaps the senses were circuits through which she could pass her faith.

The rain had purified the air on the quiet, humid night. Maria could feel the evaporating moisture opening the pores of her skin. She stood motionless as he turned to face her. Jonathon leaned his head forward and brushed his lips gently across her cheek. She thought, for a moment, of Fidel, then banished the thought. This was different, so completely different. She tilted her head slightly, following the pressure of his lips. He touched her face with his open hand and leaned forward. His bottom lip slid between hers. She felt an energy rising from deep inside her. She closed her eyes and breathed in through her nose. The kiss deepened. Maria felt as if all of her being were focused through her mouth. His tongue passed her lips where she met it with hers.

A brief moment of panic. Was this right? The image of the stained glass window of the virgin mother at her church in the village flashed through her mind. She tasted his sweet kiss and swallowed its sweetness like a communion wafer.

2 2

Morgan was scheduled to meet with Conley at Catholic Missions International at 5:00, when Conley was due to return from the camp. That gave him three hours. Where would Sophal have gone when he'd first arrived in Aran? Obviously, he would have searched for clues about the others, but where? The only chance was that they were in a camp. But there were over thirty major camps, each with smaller satellites surrounding it. Populations moved in and out. How would he find the people he was looking for?

Refugee tracing was as likely a possibility as any. The Red Cross had set up an active presence in the camps to try to bring separated families together. Morgan wondered whether someone who had been through three and a half years of the Khmer Rouge, an orphan with no family, would put his name in with the Red Cross. Who would he think would claim him? But with so few options, anything was at least worth a try. Sophal, Morgan knew, would have covered all the angles.

Morgan found the white villa of the International Committee of the Red Cross Aran headquarters. The tracing officer was a young Swiss-French redhead who introduced herself as Claudine.

"*Bonjour,* may I help you?"

"Yeah," Morgan said, "I used to live in Cambodia and I have a group of, of friends. We lost contact in '75 but I've come to see if I can find any of them."

"OK. Do you have zeir names?"

"Yes, of course." Morgan wrote out the full names of the members of his former unit.

"We have ze list of refugees who've registered with us alphabetically, zis won't take a minute."

She scanned her long printout of names.

"No, I'm sorry. None of zem are on ze list. We get new ones all ze time. You might check back in."

"If I left the list with you, could you contact me if any of those names come through?"

"I can't promise anything. We're pretty busy. If you leave it with me and tell me how to contact you, I can do my best."

Morgan wrote his name and hotel on a piece of paper and handed it to her.

"Do you get many requests like this?"

"Not too many from outsiders. We're starting to get a trickle of Cambodians from France and America trying to find lost relatives."

"Do they leave the lists behind if they can't find the names?"

"Some of zem do."

"And what do you do with the lists?"

"We file zem. When I have time, I go through it to see if any of ze names have come up."

"Would it be possible for me to see that file?"

"Actually, zey are confidential. Why?"

"A friend of mine, I think, may have been here looking, and I wanted to know if maybe he had any luck."

"Well I can't show you ze list, but if you give me ze name of your friend, I can see if we have anything."

Morgan wrote it down. Claudine unlocked the metal cabinet.

"Heng Sophal, Heng Sophal? Yes, here. Zat is interesting. I shouldn't say it, but it seems to be ze same list as yours . . . I remember him. He came in dressed like a refugee, but his English was very good."

Morgan felt a twinge in his spine. Sophal had been here, in this place.

"When? When was he here?"

"Oh, I say about six or seven months ago."

"Did he leave his contact address?"

"No. He said he'd check by. He did once, but zat was it."

"Well thank you. If anything comes up you know how to contact me."

Sophal was looking for the unit, Morgan thought as he passed the spiked metal gate. He was not surprised. Sophal was dressed like a refugee and he had a camp pass, so he was definitely out visiting the camps. He also must have had some Thai links. How else would he have gotten the couriers to take his messages to the embassy?

It was three o'clock and Aran's streets were oppressively hot and dusty. He smiled at his realization about Sophal and his memories of their times together. It's hot, that bastard Sophal would have wanted a drink. He spotted a shabby looking Westerner in torn pants and asked him what the best place in town was for a beer. Morgan winked at him just as he knew Sophal would have done and got, he was sure, the right answer.

The man looked Morgan over and somehow decided he was OK.

"A lot of aid types go to Ki Ki's, but the real place is Madame Di's. It's two blocks up on the right. You gotta go through a little alleyway and there's a door marked '33'."

Morgan had often rebuked Sophal for his drinking and his careless attitude toward women. Maybe after years of being a street kid Sophal liked having money and wasn't shy about the various ways of using it. It wasn't Morgan's way, but Morgan's way wasn't going to get him any answers. Today, he was Sophal.

Madame Di's was the kind of sleazy bar he remembered from the war. No naked dancers slithering up and down poles like Bangkok and Saigon. Aran wasn't racy enough for that. But the same goods were available, that much was clear.

A young girl in a bright red miniskirt approached him.

"Hey mister, you buy me drink."

Some things never change. Morgan recognized the girl's accent and mannerisms right away.

"Niery chunchiet Khmai, boat?" You are Cambodian, yes? he asked.

"Chaa," she answered, acknowledging her identity as if by reflex before remembering that being Cambodian and not in the camps could mean big trouble. She tried to regain her composure.

"You buy me drink mister?" she said in English.

"Knyom som sor samnor muey." I'd like to ask you a question, he said in Cambodian.

She looked up.

"I no understand mister." She scurried away.

Morgan saw the back of a blond-haired man at the bar with his arm around the thin waist of a small girl. He recognized the Australian accent. Overcoming his initial revulsion, he reminded himself of his barroom identity.

"Tiger beer," Morgan said with a swagger as he approached the bar. He took a deep sip. He hadn't had a beer for a while and it soothed his dry throat.

"You been 'round here long?" Morgan asked. He looked up and was surprised to recognize the face. Who was this guy? He'd seen the parched face somewhere before, but where?

"Oh, not too long, in and out. What are you doin' here?"

"I'm . . ." Morgan was about to say he was visiting for Catholic Missions International, but that probably wouldn't look too good given the circumstances. "I'm just here looking for a friend," he said.

"Aren't we all, mate," the other man said. He patted the girl's hip suggestively.

Morgan was about to correct him but thought better of it.

"Many foreigners come in here?" Morgan asked.

"It's a good place to unwind a bit, experience the local culture." He rubbed the side of her leg. He seemed to enjoy the telling like an athlete in a locker room.

This kind of guy makes me sick, Morgan thought to himself. He knew that face from somewhere. Where was it? Was it Bangkok? Phnom Penh? Washington? No.

"You know, you look a bit familiar," the man said. "Haven't we met before? Yeah, we have. It was the embassy, the French embassy."

It came to Morgan. The filthy journos locked up with the others in the French embassy after the Khmer Rouge took Phnom Penh in '75. The Australian snapping pictures of the terrified Cambodian leaders being dragged by the French embassy officials out the door. The French said they had to hand them over to keep the Khmer Rouge from killing us all. The KR control Cambodia now and there's nothing we can do, they'd said. Morgan had argued fiercely to hold out. How could they so brazenly send these people to their deaths? The French bastards from the embassy only wanted to save their own skins. Morgan had stood erect in his powerless shame as they carried them out to the waiting KR. But this bastard, I remember him, this filthy bastard. He was in General Sak's face with his camera, as if the humiliation wasn't bad enough. He photographed Prime Minister Bora pissing in his pants as they dragged him away. This piece of shit, now he was here. Where was Sak, where was Bora?

"Yeah, I was there," Morgan said, still trying to rein in his indignation.

"Yeah, you were the bullet head trying to get us all killed, weren't you?"

The man was half drunk.

"And you're the journalist who stuck his camera in General Sak's face as they sent him out to die."

"Hey. You bastards made the problem. I just took a couple of pictures."

"Made the problem? Your damn pictures made the problem." Morgan chided himself as the words passed uncontrollably through his lips.

"Pull your head out, man. You can blame the messenger all you want. You know how fucked up things were there."

"Look at you. If you gave a shit you wouldn't be here." This was clearly not, he knew, what Sophal would have said.

"And where are you dumbass? I don't have to save the world. You bloody Yanks said you were doing that, and look what you did. Four years on, they're still cleaning up your fuckin' mess, and it's going to be a long time bloody coming."

Morgan felt the urge to punch this amoral son-of-a-bitch whoremonger. What the hell am I doing? he suddenly thought. Sophal would have been drunk and with his own girl by now. Keep on target, Morgan, focus.

Morgan chuckled, then laughed. The Australian looked at him, then slowly joined in.

"Hey, sorry, man," Morgan said. "Four years on and we're still fighting about the same old shit. You either laugh or you cry so you might as well laugh."

"I can't seem to tell the difference between the two these days."

"Morgan O'Reilly." Morgan put out his hand.

"Evan Pritchard."

They shook hands.

Morgan bought them another round of beer. His desire to find Sophal clearly tipped the scales against his disdain for Pritchard.

"I'm looking for a friend—Sophal, Heng Sophal. Do you know him?"

"No. Haven't been here long though. When was he here?"

"About five months ago or so."

"Sorry, can't say I know him."

"Here's his picture."

"No. Maybe the girls do. You know this guy darlin'?"

Evan's companion's face remained blank.

Morgan approached the Cambodian girl.

"Neary skual kort?"

She looked at him blankly.

"Skual, skual ter?" he pointed at the picture.

Still blank.

He sighed then took out a ten dollar bill and handed it to her.

"Knyom at skoal, pu," she answered in her native language. I don't know him uncle.

Morgan sat for a while with Evan making small talk about the old Phnom Penh. Evan told him he was working for Pacific Times News Service covering the border.

Morgan's watch reminded him it was almost five. "Hey, good to meet you pal. See you around," he said.

They shook hands, and Morgan bounced out the door. In the street, he rubbed his right hand on his pants and his smile transformed to a disgusted frown. The worthless son of a bitch. But Morgan's CIA training had instilled in him that no lead is ever lost. He filed it away and headed toward CMI for his appointment with Conley.

Kevin Conley, the head of Catholic Missions International's Aranyaprathet office, had the perfect cover. He could move in and out of the camps distributing aid and setting up services, and could meet with camp authorities and the Thais without rousing suspicion. It was more than a front, he was actually doing the relief work. All the agencies were getting money from the US government. He was just getting a little extra and doing a little more. Information cost something, and border accounting was flexible.

"You Conley?"

"Yeah."

"Morgan O'Reilly."

"Mr. O'Reilly," he said loudly. "We've been anxiously awaiting your arrival. Let me introduce you to our Thai staff. This is Sakthip and this is Warunee. Morgan O'Reilly from our Baltimore office. You'll join us for dinner won't you?"

"Of course."

"Let's not waste any time. Why don't you step into my office."

They entered and Conley locked the door behind them. He put a towel at the bottom of the door to cut the noise. "What can I do for you, O'Reilly?"

"I'm looking for Sophal. I understand you worked him through here?"

"I don't know if I can say I worked him. He asked for some things in the beginning—his camp pass, a motorcycle, not much. He asked us to pass on his cables."

"How'd you get 'em?"

"A Thai courier would drop them off and pick up the responses we'd get through Bangkok."

"Who was the courier?"

"I don't know. We never really had a chance to talk. I didn't want to snoop into Sophal's affairs either. The whole thing was coded. There was something they didn't want me, or us, to know."

"Did you ever talk to the messenger?"

"Just once. There weren't that many messages, only about, what was it, five going out and three coming in from the embassy. When he delivered the last message from Sophal, he gave a verbal message as well."

"What was it?"

"It didn't mean a damn thing to me. All he said was 'M-21.' Wouldn't answer any questions, wouldn't stay. Just said 'M-21' and left."

"What does it mean?"

"Haven't the foggiest, O'Reilly."

"Have you tried to locate Sophal?"

"Wouldn't know where to look. This whole border's a cloak and dagger operation. Can't trust the Thais working in my own office. A thousand things going on. Snoopier I am, more likely I am to blow my cover. Then we'd really be screwed. Imagine what would happen if the aid agencies told the press that the Agency is infiltrating the aid community, and a Catholic charity no less. Hell, I'm not going to do that."

"Do you know where the last message came from?"

"I don't know. Don't know if it was from one of the camps, from Cambodia. I don't even know what Sophal was looking for."

"You said he asked for supplies. Was there anything more he asked for?"

"Yeah, Fansidar and a motorcycle."

"Isn't Fansidar for malaria?"

"Yeah it is, but they don't have it in Thailand. We had to get it from Tokyo. Our orders are to get you guys whatever you need without asking questions, so that's what we've got to do."

"Why did he need it, the Fansidar?"

"Don't know. Really didn't know much, and he didn't change that at all."

"What kind of motorcycle was it?"

"Just an old, beat-up Suzuki 100 cc. Not much to look at, but it worked."

"Do you remember what it looked like?"

"It was an old thing, pieced together—faded olive, but the back fender, I remember, was red. They must have stolen it off something else."

"What kind of camp pass did he have?"

"We got him the best one we could, access to all the camps, except for the Khmer Rouge ones, of course."

"Why not them?"

"The KR control everything in their camps. Can't take a piss without permission. They're not going to accept anybody's pass but their own."

"Can you get me one?"

"For the Khmer Rouge?"

If Sophal was looking for the unit, Morgan thought, he wouldn't have gone to the Khmer Rouge camps. If they were living, our guys would have made their way to the Khmer Serei camps, the noncommunist resistance.

"No, just a regular camp pass. I don't think I'm going to need the Khmer Rouge."

Sophal, where the hell are you? Morgan wondered as he walked the streets of Aran that night. He could picture him. Sophal the goddamn cowboy on his motorcycle with the red fender heading out to fight the bad guys and save the world.

"Maan, that's nothin'," Sophal had probably been saying to himself, mimicking the black American GIs he had once mimed for a laugh when working the streets of wartime Phnom Penh.

Nothin', Sophal, then where the hell are you?

23

Jonathon was determined to make the food distribution system work. He had to make it work. Why else was he on the border?

The children in the camps had their whole lives ahead of them, they had a country to rebuild. A few kilos of rice would determine whether they would have the opportunity to do either. What had they done to deserve this fate? Nobody deserved it. The lucky ones made it through. Jonathon was determined to make more people lucky.

Conditions in Nong Chan seemed to be slowly improving. Was he getting accustomed to the signs of malnutrition, or were children's puffed bellies flattening? Were their arms and legs thickening, was their reddish hair returning to its natural black? There was no shortage of people in the clinic, but the whole camp was seeming less and less like a giant infirmary, and more like an endless open-air market.

It felt good to Jonathon to be part of this seeming resurrection. They had reported extinction as a people in the press, but these people were not moving toward extinction. There was still hunger. There was still even death. But after two months, the tide seemed to be turning.

Jonathon was too thoughtful to let it rest at that. He struggled to understand why the tide was turning. Was it the food aid or was it the trade? Was it donated rice or was it the gold pouring out from Cambodia? The refugees were getting rice, but if they were paying for it, why did Jonathon and his colleagues have to work so hard to give it away? If the refugees were bartering for their rice, then Jonathon and the others were not saints, just second-rate merchants.

Rongrit and his men were robbing the camp blind. This was now clear. They had fancy motorcycles. Their children were bedecked in gold necklaces, bracelets, anklets, and rings. The merchants showed signs of wealth as well. More and more TV antennas went up daily atop huts.

All this success made Jonathon and his colleagues sometimes feel extraneous, even ridiculous. Refugees were supposed to be refugees—poor, huddled, desperate masses. If they weren't, was aid just posturing? Yet there were still the children, the old, the infirm, the people who couldn't make it on their own in the Darwinian camp system. If there was any reason to be there, then surely it was getting aid to these people.

The doubts nagged at Jonathon. His reason to be in the camp, in Aranyaprathet, in Thailand at all, was to give aid. If the aid wasn't necessary, what was he doing here?

Jonathon and the others had worked hard to develop a system that could get aid to the people who needed it most. As they rode out on the morning convoy, there was a sense of nervous apprehension. They had always assumed that the aid agencies didn't have the manpower to carry out direct distributions in Nong Chan. The camp was just too big. There were too many people to keep track of. Distributing aid through Rongrit's men, however, had clearly proven a failure. Now that the Thai army had heeded the strong pressure from the aid agencies and restored order in the camps, maybe it was time to try something new.

If they couldn't bring the rice to the people, second best was bringing the people to the rice. Jonathon had suggested that if the soldiers were getting the rice first and the women and children last, then they should just reverse the order and make sure that the neediest would be in front of the line. It was a simple idea, but Jonathon knew that, like everything else, implementing it in the camp would not be easy. Getting Rongrit to control his men after Lieutenant Colonel had pulled the gun on Tim had been difficult enough.

Tim and Jonathon had gone in the day before and supervised the construction of vast corrals. Through Rasady, Tim announced on the camp PA system that food distribution would begin at 8:00 the following morning. Women should line up for distribution at that time. After each woman had received three kilos, distribution to older persons would follow. Orphans and nonattached men would report to a special distribution site at 10:00.

Would it work? Jonathon nervously wondered as the camp came into view. The refugees didn't seem to do well with new systems. Tim and the others had done what they could to explain, but people seemed nervous. But wouldn't they realize that they were getting the rice delivered straight to them? No interference, no siphoning off, no taxes. Did they trust the foreigners?

The long convoy rolled through the camp's gate and then fanned out to the distribution sites. As Jonathon's truck arrived in its designated open area, he saw the mass of people waiting. The stockades were up, but this attempt to impose order seemed to have had little impact on the chaos.

Tim stood on the edge of one of the trucks and shouted, "We'll need all women to line up beside this stick. Each woman will be given three kilos of rice. Your hand will then be marked with a red stamp, and you won't be able to come back for another distribution."

Rasady, bullhorn in hand, repeated the instructions.

"Som neary ning mieng om tang os teuv damrang chor pi kroy bangkol nis . . ."

There seemed to be little response. He tried again. When the people saw that the distribution was not going to begin until the incomprehensible foreigners were happy, they allowed themselves to be slowly moved to where the foreigners wanted them. The men and children were herded to the perimeter of the field, and the women were placed in eight lines, each demarcated by a bamboo corral. Nervousness filled the air. The distribution began.

The aid workers sliced open the one-hundred-pound bags, and carefully meted out three kilos of rice at a time. Each woman came with a Cambodian scarf folded in fourths, ingeniously transformed into a rice-carrying case, into which the Cambodian assistants emptied the allotted rice. A female assistant marked the recipient's hand as each woman passed. The system seemed to be working. One after the other, the process was repeated. Women passed through at an accelerating pace as the system's kinks worked themselves out. No matter how much rice was distributed, however, the line never seemed to grow shorter. How many women could there be? Jonathon asked himself as he helped keep the rice flowing.

Morning was giving way to day, and it was only getting hotter. The dirt baked on Jonathon's skin. The refugees were growing irritable. Vicious arguments broke out with increasing frequency. Women accused the Cambodian assistants of not giving the full three kilos. Women removed from the line for having traces of red ink on their hand barked back viciously. The men standing nearby were also becoming anxious. The women were taking so much time. Would there be enough rice for everybody? A few men made taunting catcalls at the distribution team. The Cambodian assistants became ever more flustered.

An old woman's rice bag dropped on the ground. Jonathon rushed over to see if he could help. The old woman, a forlorn look on her face, sunk to her knees and slowly, pitifully, gathered the rice with her forearms. Jonathon could see the specks of dried dirt mingling with the rice. After she shoveled most of the rice onto her scarf, she picked at the stubborn rice caught in cracks in the ground. Jonathon knelt down and helped the old woman. She did not seem to notice his assistance. Nor did either of them notice the shouts coming from the sidelines with ever greater velocity.

When Jonathon did notice, however, he could not understand the words. As he stood up to address this growing problem, he felt a sudden pang that he had not done enough to help the old woman. She was gathering her now filled scarf and beginning to shuffle away.

"Give me a bag with two kilos," Jonathon said to Rasady. Rasady looked at him blankly. Jonathon picked up a bag and scooped in what he thought to be the amount. He jumped off the truck and handed it to the old woman with a bow of his head.

In a flash, the crowd moved in on the truck. Hundreds of hands appeared outstretched as if demanding the same gift. Jonathon stood up and put his hands in the air.

"Everybody please return to the line," he said loudly, searching behind him for Rasady.

"Everybody, back in line." They certainly didn't understand the words, but his message was clear. It had no impact. Seeing movement in the areas closer to the trucks, those farther back surged forward, pressing the inner group closer and closer in. The noise level increased as the tension and excitement rose. Jonathon looked around for support, but the whole system seemed to be in chaos. There were no lines of people, only an endless sea of hands and arms.

A hand reached through a grate on the back of Jonathon's truck and pulled on one of the rice bags. It tore slightly and rice trickled out the side of the truck. Then another hand pulled and another. Refugees scrambled and fought to approach the trucks. Rice now poured through the side rails. The refugees on the outside surged in stronger than ever, pushing Jonathon against the truck, a mass of human body parts pressing against him.

"Please, everybody back," he pleaded, his words drowned by the forming riot.

Refugees dove onto the trucks to get at the rice. The trucks looked like Medusas of seething arms and legs. Enormous bags of rice came flying over the sides and were attacked by refugees below. People pushed and pulled and fought to get at the rice. The sound of yells was deafening.

"Stop! Everybody stop!" The futility of his shouts immediately struck Jonathon. He looked around for help and saw only Evan perched on the hood of the truck photographing the chaos.

"Let's get the hell out of here," Tim shouted to one of the drivers. One truck inched forward, inspiring the other drivers to start their engines and do the same. It would have been impossible to move had not the refugees moved away from the trucks after the entire rice supply had been emptied.

Jonathon climbed up the back of one of the trucks as it moved away. His shirt was torn, he was filthy. He looked, he thought, like a refugee. He knelt down, breathing heavily. Tears welled in his eyes.

"What happened, what happened?" Maria asked at the meeting point outside the camp gate. "Look at your shirt." She wanted to touch him, to hug him, but didn't dare with so many others around. She squeezed his arm. "Come, let's get you back to town."

On the road back to Aran, Jonathon searched his mind for some explanation, somewhere to file this experience without having it color everything. Why should I be surprised? he tried to reason with himself. Isn't this exactly what happened at the orphanage? Doesn't desperation make people desperate? He had hoped that the purity of his intentions would carry him through, yet at every turn he felt rejected, almost overwhelmed. He had to be tough, he knew, to follow his ideals, but he felt worried about what would be left of his idealism. He had calmed down a bit when Tim called him into his office soon after they arrived back in Aran.

"Are you all right?"

"Yeah, I'm OK. I'm almost getting used to it," Jonathon said with a crooked, unconvincing smile.

"This has really been tough for you. I'm sorry you've had so many bad experiences. I mean, it's not like we have these riots every day. You and I seem to get caught in the middle of most of them."

"Yeah, I know," Jonathon said. "It's just so frustrating. It's as if they think we're stealing from them. Like we're doing it for our own good. I feel like such a failure."

"I know. I really do know. I try to think of it like this. These people have been through hell. Their whole world's been turned upside down and they don't know who to trust. Sure, there's a lot of bad things going on, but the average refugee is just fighting to survive. I don't know if they're getting all the rice we're distributing, but there's rice there and it's coming from somewhere. At least when we drop it in the camp we know it's physically there. It's not a perfect system, but it's a system. Rongrit's a son of a bitch but we can't punish everyone for him, even though it sometimes feels like we should. It's getting aid to the people. That's why I want to ask you something Jonathon. Have a seat."

Jonathon followed the instruction.

"I've really been impressed with the work you've done here."

"Yeah, I've done great work. I've developed a real expertise in starting riots," Jonathon said sarcastically. He wondered where this newfound sarcasm was coming from.

"Seriously. It's been hard, but you've really given it your all. More than that, you're a thinker, and there aren't too many of those around here. Most of the others are happy to go out in the trucks and divide up the bags. You're thinking about things, processing things. Something's come up and I, I want to ask for your help. The refugees in the camp, some of them are good, some of them are not. Doesn't really matter to us. Our goal is to get rice to the people. Nobody deserves to starve to death. These ones are the lucky ones. Look at all the money pouring into these camps. The trucks, the rice, the infirmary—it's not free, somebody's paying for it. The situation in some of the other camps is a lot worse. There are camps up and down the border. The parts we know the least about are south of here."

"The Khmer Rouge area?" Jonathon asked.

"That's where the Khmer Rouge leaders control, but the refugees are pretty much like everyone else—women and kids like the ones here."

"Are they getting any aid?"

"Some, but not nearly the same level as the people up here."

"How are they getting it?"

"Well it's kind of complicated, Jonathon. As you know, most of our rice comes from the World Food Program. WFP is also supplying the Khmer Rouge."

"How?"

"The Thais seem to be delivering it from what I hear."

"The Thais?"

"Yeah, that was one of their conditions for letting us come here. All the refugees on the border get rice."

"Are the Thais distributing it?"

"Yes and no. WFP drives it to warehouses on the Thai side. The Thai military drives it to the border at night and it goes across."

"Who's paying for it?"

"The same people who are paying for ours."

"Jesus!"

"It's all aid to civilians, Jonathon. Can't blame the civilian populations, like you can't blame the people in Nong Chan for Rongrit. But now the donors are getting kind of scared. There have been a few reports that aid is going to Khmer Rouge soldiers, and they want to know if it's true."

"How are they going to do that?"

"Well . . . that's what I want to ask you about. After being such bastards for such a long time, the Khmer Rouge now want to be everyone's friend. They're praising the Western countries, say the aid effort is doing lots of good. They're pretty sensitive to the news reports because they know what can happen if their rice gets cut. It's their lifeline. They've got the Thais on their side but they're still worried."

"Yeah?"

"So when the reports came out, the donor countries complained to the Red Cross and UNICEF, who complained to the Khmer Rouge office in Bangkok. The KR denied the whole thing. Now they say they want to prove it."

"Prove what?"

"That their people are suffering, that the aid is going to civilians."

"So why are you telling me this?" Jonathon asked pensively.

"They want to prove it by inviting representatives from the Red Cross and UNICEF and the NGOs to cross the border and see for themselves."

"Go into the Khmer Rouge zone?" The Khmer Rouge zone was so close, yet seemed impossibly far away.

"I know it sounds surprising, but when you think of it, it makes sense. It's where hungry people are and our job is to feed them. But it has to be kept quiet. If the government in Phnom Penh hears about it they'll go nuts."

"How are they going to arrange the visit?"

"It's pretty simple really. There's a meeting point on the Thai side and then the KR say they'll take the whole crew with them across, guarantee their safety. The group will go visit the KR camps on the other side of the border and come back. I'd go myself, but if I'm out of here for three days, people are going to start asking where I am. Also, to be frank, I think you can do a better job of it than I can. And if it's all legit, we're going to need to start thinking about systems to get the rice there. That's somewhere you could really help. I know this is a tough request, Jonathon, but I want you to think about it."

Jonathon took a deep breath. He was flattered by the praise. Going to the Khmer Rouge camps? The Khmer Rouge? Even the name gave him shivers. But what was he doing here anyway if not to get food to the hungry wherever they were, to avenge the randomly allocated death sentences of so many innocent civilians? Maybe, he thought, this was where he could have an impact. Some of the people in Nong Chan were Khmer Rouge and that didn't seem to bother him. The women and children, the old people didn't do anything to be with the Khmer Rouge. They just happened to be in the wrong place at the wrong time.

Chance had sent those civilians into the Khmer Rouge zone. Should every civilian be condemned because they end up in the Khmer Rouge zone? Jonathon knew he had the skill to help them. No, not to help them, to see whether they need help. Crossing the border into Cambodia? It was risky, but that's what it was all about. Wasn't it? Taking risks to realize ideals. Why else was he here but to bring hope to the border, to bring a spark of light to challenge the darkness?

"Do you need time to think about it?" Tim asked.

Jonathon took another deep breath.

"What does it mean they'll guarantee our safety?"

"Well they pretty much control those areas. There are mines, but they laid them so they know where they are. And they're going to be hell-bent to make sure you guys have a nice experience because if anything goes wrong, they're the ones who'll be screwed. There's always a risk, but . . . maybe it's doable."

Jonathon looked at Tim. They had worked closely together. He trusted him. Images of his parents and of Maria flashed through his mind.

"I'll do it." The words escaped from Jonathon's mouth like birds from a cage whose door had momentarily swung open. He fought the synapse of panic urging him to call them back. Purity, he was learning, was an elusive goal. Morality was about difficult choices.

"Are you sure?"

"Yeah," Jonathon said with a slow, almost hesitant nod, "I am."

"I'll let them know. But Jonathon . . ."

"Yeah?"

"Don't tell anyone about this. We've got to keep it quiet."

24

Power, the tool of possibility, swirled with its uneven, shifting current around the annual awards dinner of the Asia Society.

The ballroom of the St. Regis hotel had rarely looked finer. Crystal goblets glistened even in the subdued light. Flowers bloomed from the round tables. Waiters in tuxedoes traversed tight figure eights around the room catering to the needs of the distinguished guests. It was a scene to which Tom Dillon had become accustomed.

Dillon's eyes fixed appreciatively on Witkowski, whose deep, barreling voice filled the room with a jovial austerity. Though not particularly tall, Witkowski's confidence dominated the room. Witkowski was telling an opening joke about a man who bets on a lame horse and then tells his incredulous companion that he knows he will win because he owns all the other horses in the race. Although not especially funny, the joke garnered an appreciative chuckle from the audience. Even humor, in Washington, was a function of power.

"Of course," Witkowski continued, "the man we are here to honor tonight owns the horses in the Washington foreign policy community—my friend, the deputy national security advisor, Thomas Dillon."

Dillon held his gaze on Witkowski as his boss, showered in the bright light of the television cameras, rattled off the basic facts of Dillon's career—former partner in the Dillon-Reed investment bank, foreign service officer with tours in Bangkok and Manila, deputy chief of mission in Saigon, national security council senior director and special assistant to the president for Asian affairs, and now deputy national security advisor.

Something in Witkowski's words made Dillon's rapid rise seem somehow celestially ordained. Success, Dillon knew, became inevitable only in retrospect. Going forward, it was a function of strategic thought and careful planning.

Dillon felt Meredith take his hand from his lap and gently lift it to the table for others to see.

"It is a tribute to the high esteem with which Tom Dillon is held in Washington that we are also joined tonight by my good friend, Secretary of State Perseus Bohlen."

The senators, lobbyists, current and former government officials, and others in the crowd stood and clapped for the secretary of state. Bohlen lifted momentarily from his seat and raised his hand slightly.

It always amazed Dillon that all you had to do in Washington to negate an obvious truth was to emphatically state its opposite. Relations between Witkowski and Bohlen had continued to nose-dive as each struggled to win control of the president's ring. Dillon wondered if he now detected a certain resentment in Bohlen's face at this humiliation through overenthusiastic praise.

"The man we are here to honor tonight has done so much for United States relations with Asia and with the rest of the world. He has become among the brightest in a sky of stars . . ."

Dillon wondered if Witkowski was hinting that Bohlen was a dimming star, if one-upping the secretary of state was becoming something of a sport for the fiercely competitive national security advisor.

"It is with great honor that on behalf of the Asia Society I present to Deputy National Security Advisor Thomas Dillon the Asia Society's Leadership Award for 1980, recognizing an outstanding contribution to relations between the United States and the Asian world. Tom."

Dillon released his wife's hand and trotted to the podium. He shook hands with Witkowski, then smiled at the applauding crowd. It was almost possible, for a moment, to see himself as those assembled saw him. He nodded at Bohlen, then briefly locked eyes with Meredith. Her blond hair pulled back tightly into a bun brought her studied smile and carefully primed features into sharp relief. The camera lights focusing on him made Dillon feel like an actor performing his own life.

As he gestured to the crowd to please stop clapping and began to speak, Dillon recognized, yet again, how much power established his place in the vast ecosystem of Washington. Power, as flawed as it sometimes seemed, was the seed of possibility. It was the seed of hope.

25

Of all the feelings Morgan had anticipated upon arriving in his first Cambodian refugee camp, excitement had not been one.

The Thai guard examined his pass, then waved Morgan through the barbed wire barricade.

As he began to wander the camp, Morgan was struck by the utter wretchedness of the refugees. Their clothes were old and torn. Children with bloated bellies wandered aimlessly and played in the filth. Women's clothes hung from their emaciated bodies as if clinging to scarecrows. An air of sickness hovered over the camp. But he had seen all of this before. They were traits most refugee camps shared. Morgan felt torn between the sorrow of what he was seeing and the excitement of being back in a world where he had once felt so alive.

For nearly five years he had completely separated himself from a culture he had once almost thought his own. He had retreated to his cabin in the forest to get away from the memories, from the tapestry of his experiences of the war. He had tried to free himself from everything, to find some pared down, minimal self from where he might rebuild.

After almost five years of trying, he now recognized his failure. The nightmares still haunted him, still followed him through the day. Perhaps had he succeeded, he never would have accepted Dillon's offer. Perhaps had he succeeded, Dillon's offer would have truly destroyed any peace he had found in that other world. But the structure of that world, that search for peace in the forests of Virginia, had been far from complete. He could leave Virginia, he now realized, because he had never fully arrived there, because he had never fully left here. Maybe the only way to complete his journey was to come back and to face this life.

Those same smells that had haunted him over these past four years, the motion, the energy of the camp, the Cambodian people speaking the language he knew so intimately, conversing with hand and facial gestures he had studied so carefully a decade before, led him back to this world.

But the tapestry was not complete there. The final strand was his unit, his children. Most of them were certainly dead. But if there could be even one, one person he could save, one person whom he could set on a new course, to whom he could apologize, maybe he might have a future, maybe he might have peace.

Sophal was the key. Sophal was on a deep-cover mission. It was odd that he wouldn't report in for three months, but certainly not impossible. Death was not the only possible explanation.

This hope could only live if Morgan found Sophal. If Sophal was the key to the others, perhaps the others, if they lived, were the key to Sophal. He had to find somebody. In this camp, this mass of humanity, there were clues. There were thousands of clues, millions perhaps. There were so many clues it was impossible to know where to find any one of them. Sophal had been to the camps, that much he knew. But which ones? What had Sophal found?

Phnom Chat was as good a place to start as any. A few soldiers from the old Lon Nol army had turned up there. Maybe kids from the unit had gone there as well. It wasn't much to go on, but it was worth a try. Perhaps Sophal had thought the same.

Morgan walked through the camp examining each face to see what five years of intense struggle and fast-forward maturation might do to somebody. The skin would be darker, the eyes more wrinkled. Maybe a nose would be broken or a face bruised. A youthful swagger might give way to a compliant shuffle.

Morgan knew these types of places intimately. They were where he had recruited Phim, Rithy, and Choeun. The kids in the camps outside of Phnom Penh during the war years had been hungry—for experience, for meaning, for a sense of belonging. They knew what it meant to fight for something. They weren't the sleazy tough guys in silk shirts, the general's kids who wove their fancy motorcycles up and down the boulevards of Phnom Penh. They knew the back alleys of life, where the people who suffered, who always suffered, lived.

But what shocked Morgan about this camp were the faces. There had always been, Morgan felt, a dreamlike quality to the Cambodian face. Some foreigners had interpreted the famous Cambodian smile as a mark of some kind of blissful happiness. Morgan knew this to be an absurdity. Even in the best of times the Cambodian people had suffered. They lived with an insecurity that would have debilitated many other people. The Cambodian smile, the Cambodian eyes, the faces of the Bayon temple at Angkor, these all belonged to dreamers, people who did not go on because they felt things would be better tomorrow, but because in their hearts they were dreaming of entire other worlds.

As Morgan traveled from face to face, he slowly realized that those dreams were gone. The wonderful Cambodian faces had hardened. Morgan remembered an elderly, wrinkled tofu maker who had lived in a small shop near his old apartment in Phnom Penh. Morgan would watch her work. After the beans were crushed, mixed, and cured, she would put the mixture over cheesecloth with a weight on top to push the water through. The dreams had dripped from the Cambodian faces like this water, leaving the parched, hopeless faces behind.

Was that Rithy there? It looks like him, but a chin doesn't change shape no matter what someone experiences. Is that Phim? Can proud, defiant eyes turn to that in four years? Was his mind playing tricks? Maybe he wouldn't find the clues by looking, Morgan thought. Maybe he needed to let the clues find him.

Morgan saw a small restaurant in a ramshackle hut. The Cambodians were incredible, he reflected. Even here in the camp people were opening businesses. He went in.

"Sousdey bong. Knyom klien baay, nas." Hello brother, I'm starving.

The restaurateur showed not the slightest excitement that a strange white man was speaking fluent Khmer, then ran to get everyone he knew. A small crowd filled the tiny restaurant as they gathered around Morgan.

"Bang ches niyay piesar Khmai, ter?" Do you speak Cambodian?

"Baat, knyom ches niyay bantec bantouc." Yes, I can speak it a little, Morgan said.

"Aht, ter, aht, ter. Lok pouker nas." No, your Khmer is great, the man replied.

"Oh, you are very kind."

"Where did you learn it?"

"I used to live in Phnom Penh."

"Where?"

"Street 242."

"I lived on street 260!" the man exclaimed.

"Two sixty? Isn't that where Kambudja Bot School used to be?"

"I used to be the groundskeeper there." The excited look on the man's face shifted to sadness. "We've been through so much. I lost my wife and my three children."

"Where did the Khmer Rouge send you?" Morgan asked.

"They separated us. I went to Siem Reap. I don't really know where the others went. I think to Prey Veng, but I'm not sure."

"Yeah, I'm missing people too. That's what I'm doing here."

"Have you had any luck finding them?"

"No, but I'm not really sure where to look."

"Some of the people are listing their names with the Red Cross. Have you tried that?"

"I went there, but they didn't seem to know much."

"Did you try putting up a sign?"

"No, I haven't."

"Lots of people know somebody who knows somebody who knows somebody. It's worth a try."

It is a good idea, Morgan thought to himself, but if I put all their names down, anybody who knows something about one of them might learn too much about them all. Something about that just didn't seem right.

"Maybe we know them," the restaurateur suggested.

Morgan hesitated for a moment. Was it safe? They hadn't sought him out, so they were probably genuine. He had just randomly picked the place. Maybe if a plan wasn't working he'd just have to throw in his lot with chance. He began reciting the names.

"Heng Sophal?"

The men looked at each other. "No."

"Hu Vuth?"

"No."

"Keo Phim?"

"No."

"Sok Rithy?"

"Sok Rithy, Sok Rithy! Knyom skual Sok Rithy!" I know Sok Rithy, a small man shrieked from the back.

"Sok Rithy?"

"Baat, baat, Sok Rithy. Cham muey pleht bong." Yes, yes, Sok Rithy. Wait one moment, brother. The man dashed out the door to get Sok Rithy. This was every refugee's dream, a foreigner coming in knowing your name. Maybe he could get you money, maybe he could get you things. Maybe he could get you *out*. Maybe even to America. Morgan's heart was pounding. Rithy had grown up on the river. He was an expert swimmer. Was it possible that he had not drowned in the impossible current?

Five minutes later the man came rushing in out of breath, as if he had been sprinting the entire time. A squat man in his mid forties huffed and puffed behind him. His back hunched. He had wide, expectant eyes.

"Sok Rithy, Sok Rithy, knyom Sok Rithy!" I am Sok Rithy.

They all recognized from Morgan's disappointed face that this was not the one. Four years could do a lot to a person, but they couldn't make a twenty-year-old forty.

"Knyom som tos, bong. Knyom rok Sok Rithy muey pseng tiet." I am sorry, brother. I am looking for another Sok Rithy.

The man's face fell.

Morgan still wanted to try with the rest of the list, but as he reached the last name he knew that it had come to nothing.

"I'm sorry," the restaurant owner said, "we don't know any of them. Can we ask you a question, brother? How can we get to America?"

"Has the embassy come here to do interviews?"

"They have, but right now all they're looking for is old Lon Nol officers and people who worked in the American embassy."

"How often do they come?"

"Just once a week. Actually they're here today."

"Where do they interview?"

"There's a special hut up near the entrance."

Morgan nodded.

"I'm sorry. I don't know how you can get to America. Maybe just go interview with the Americans." Morgan felt disgusted with his words. "Maybe if you have family in the United States . . ."

"Family? Our families are dead."

"I know," Morgan said quietly. "I know."

He placed his hands together before his forehead in an honorific greeting. *"Som au khun bong paon teang os. Som leah sen haey."* Thank you brothers. Now I must go.

He paid for everyone's drink with a five-hundred-baht note, ten times what the check would have been, and walked out.

As he walked toward the gate, two thoughts swirled in his mind. The first was that putting up a sign wasn't such a bad idea after all. He couldn't put the names, but how about a code that they all would recognize? But what?

The scene flooded back into his mind. It was Christmas, and the whole crew was together in the Takmau railroad car. Morgan had tried to explain to them the difference between the name Chris, Jesus Christ, and the holiday of Christmas, all of which had the same Cambodian translation—*Krih.*

"So what I'm saying is that Private Chris Harwood, the nurse at the base, is not exactly the same as Jesus Christ, who burns on the cross for our sins."

The half-drunk Cambodians loved the idea of the long-legged Private Harwood burning for their sins.

"There's not enough firewood in all of Cambodia for that," Vanny squealed.

"And today is Christmas, the day when Christ came back from the dead."

"Private Harwood can come back from anywhere. I'm ready." Rithy moved his hands back and forth like a sprinter as his head tipped back in laughter.

"So Chris is a person's name and Christ is the one who burns for our sins." As this was said in Cambodian, the distinctions made little sense to the unit.

Vuth had chimed in, "Well you're our leader, always getting us out of trouble, why don't you be Christ?" Or was it Chris or Christmas? "That way you get laid, you always have a fire for cooking, and you get us presents every time you show up."

The unit had exploded with laughter. Despite his constant protests, Morgan had been dubbed Brother *Krih,* *"Bong krih."*

BONG KRIH FROM TAKMAU LOOKING FOR OLD FRIENDS. CONTACT RED CROSS FILE NUMBER 23576. Morgan asked the Red Cross representative visiting Phnom Chat to put the sign in all the camps.

And if the Americans were looking for old soldiers, maybe some clue would come to them. He found three interviewers sitting behind a long wooden desk in a bamboo hut near the front gate. Long, orderly lines extended out the door.

They were a bit surprised to see Morgan, but there were lots of aid types coming and going.

"How you guys doin'?" Morgan said.

None of them could have been more than in their early twenties. They seemed relieved to see a white face.

"Same ole, same ole," a balding young man in an alligator shirt said with a southern drawl.

"I'm Morgan O'Reilly with Catholic Missions International. I'm looking for some friends and I was wondering if you guys could do me a favor. I think they might have worked for the Americans back during the war. If you come across them, could you give me a holler?"

"Yeah sure. That's no problem. We visit five camps a week. We can keep an eye out for ya."

"If you find anything, I'm staying at the Klong Luk hotel in Aran."

Morgan scribbled out the six names. "Here's the list. I really appreciate it."

"Hey, no problem. But if we find them we can't promise anything. We're having a tough time getting people out. It seems nobody back home wants too many refugees comin' in. They'd just as soon forget the whole thing, you know, the war."

"Yeah, I know," Morgan said. "I know."

26

The Cambodian porters were waiting when the Thai military trucks arrived at the border. It was four o'clock in the morning, and Jonathon should have felt exhausted. Saying good-bye to Maria, even if it was only for two and a half days, and the excitement and nervousness of entering Cambodia kept Jonathon wide awake.

Jonathon and the two others, a ponytailed Swiss from the Red Cross named Balard and a Belgian UNICEF doctor named Siefert, had met at the WFP warehouse at two in the morning. The Thai trucks arrived just on time. Thai soldiers loaded the bags of rice onto the trucks with an ease bred of familiarity.

Each of the three foreigners rode in a different truck, sitting between a driver and another soldier in the passenger seat. Three or four heavily armed soldiers perched themselves atop the bags of rice on each of the trucks. They drove into the black void. There were few signs of life where they were going, just darkness enveloping the convoy. For two hours, Jonathon's thoughts had drifted as he had tried to instruct himself to rest.

He thought of his parents. It was three in the afternoon in Chicago, and his father was hustling down the aisles of the family store, finding the perfect outfit or toy for the stream of perfect babies strolling through. His mother was in the back checking the accounts. They were probably thinking of him. How could they imagine where he was, where he was going, what he was doing? Was it fair of him to worry them so much?

He thought back to the day he'd told his parents he was going to the border. "How can you possibly know?" his mother had desperately asked when he'd told her he was going to the border. His mind lingered for a moment on the question. Jonathon smiled inwardly as he thought of his room, of all the layers of junk he had passed through on the path to his present identity. It was also three at the law school, advanced contracts was just getting out. What was the holding in *Chandelor v. Lopus* anyway? he almost joked with himself. The juxtaposition seemed absurd.

Parting with Maria that morning had been more difficult than either of them had expected. It would be the first time in the three months they'd known each other that the two would be so far apart. Had their lives become so intertwined? The Sunny Garden guest house was not especially nice, nor Aran a particularly welcoming town. But something about Maria felt so soothing. Maria made the border somehow seem less far away and more like a home. Yet he had felt surprised at the level of anxiety he'd registered in Maria's eye's the night before.

"It's only for two and a half days. I'll be right back," he'd said, speaking to himself as much as to her.

They kissed and held each other. Jonathon's mind conjured the image of two stones pushed together holding up an arch. He tried to put Maria at ease.

"It'll be fine. I'm just going to visit other camps."

Jonathon wondered if Maria had sensed there was something more he wasn't telling her. He closed his eyes and tried to send her his thoughts.

Then there was Nong Chan, the chaotic hell. The riots, Rongrit's men, the dishonesty.

He looked out the front window to watch the darkness illuminated before him in a ten-meter arc of light. What was out there?

The trucks slowed and a group of about two hundred teenage Cambodians, all dressed in worn black pajamas and plastic sandals, appeared in the light. The convoy stopped and Jonathon followed the soldiers out.

Climbing up the sides of the trucks, the Cambodian soldiers passed the bags one to the other down from the trucks and placed them on the back of each individual porter at the end of the chain. The porters filed into a steady line heading out into the darkness.

The Thai captain approached Jonathon and the others.

"This Mr. Sim, he take you Cambodia. Stay close him. First part through minefield. You come back two days. We meet here forty-eight hours."

The Cambodian leader made a hand signal, and the three followed him, merging into the file of porters. It was like an army of ants, Jonathon thought to himself, careful to remain exactly in Sim's footsteps. As they marched, the sun slowly rose to reveal the majesty of their surroundings. Palm trees and lush vegetation lined the hills around them. Jonathon had never known so many different shades of green existed.

As the row filed forward, Mr. Sim took them to an area just beside the path where two elephants were waiting. Another Cambodian man bent down and signaled for Jonathon to put his foot on his shoulder and lean against the elephant. The man stood and hoisted Jonathon and then the others onto the elephants' backs. Mr. Sim shouted to the elephants and they moved out, marching alongside the white line of rice bags flowing like a wave into Cambodia.

After an hour, they came to a clearing on top of a hill. Its flat dirt base contrasted with the thick trees and undergrowth beside it. Groupings each of a dozen or so people in black pajamas huddled at six different areas in the clearing. There was little noise but the pounding of the rice bags being hurled into orderly stacks of alternating direction. The situation seemed very much in control. Sim signaled for them to get down.

"Mr. Cohane, Mr. Balard, Dr. Siefert." The French-accented English was only slightly off.

Who could this possibly be? Here? Jonathon wondered.

A graying thin Asian man approached them. He wore a short-sleeve ox-ford shirt, a ball-point pen sticking from his pocket, haggard pants that looked as if they had once been part of a poorly tailored suit, and rubber sandals.

"I am Cham Piseth. Welcome to the Liberated Zone of Democratic Kampuchea."

Jonathon looked at the man, the surprise overtaking his face.

"How did I learn my English? Actually, my good man," he said, now with a mock English accent, "I have a doctorate in English literature from the Sorbonne. *A votre servis.*"

He bowed with a laugh, then became more serious.

"My task is to show to you the terrible conditions under which we are living in the liberated zone. Things are very difficult for us. We have very little food. You will see there is much disease. What we do have is will. Will to liberate our country from foreign invaders. Will to make our people whole again. We mustn't waste any time. First, you must see how our distribution works. Follow me."

Jonathon and the others followed, almost in shock at the oddity of this curious little man. It was as if he had stepped in from the set of a different movie.

They walked to one side of the clearing where a group of teens circled around a pile of rice bags. They stood erect with impassive faces. Small flags attached to sticks dangled over their shoulders.

"Each of these flags, as you see, is different," Piseth stated. "Each represents a commune, and there are twelve communes in Khao Dinh camp. When the rice, for which we are eternally grateful, comes in, we divide it between the twelve communes."

"Do you divide it equally?"

"*Mais non,* Monsieur Balard. The communes are roughly the same size but not exactly. On top of that, certain people have need for extra food. The sick, expectant and nursing mothers, for example, sometimes need more food than the men, so we calculate exactly how much each commune needs and give them a percentage. If commune six has eight percent of the camp population, they might get ten percent of the rice if they have a lot of nursing mothers. Or they might get seven percent if their population is healthier than average. We are nursing our people back to life and sometimes people need to make sacrifices for each other."

Dr. Siefert nodded, expressing his appreciation for the system's logic.

"As you see, behind each commune leader are the porters who will take the rice back to their respective communities."

Piseth gave an order in Cambodian, and one of the commune leaders came rushing over with a disintegrating ledger.

"Each commune keeps its own books, and the central distribution site also has its own accounting procedures. Here are the names of all the section leaders and the requirements for each. You see, here. Commune three has many sick people, so today they are getting an extra allocation."

Jonathon could not help but feel impressed. This was beyond anything he had ever dreamed of in Nong Chan.

As if anticipating Jonathon's thoughts, Piseth continued. "Now, I'd like to take you to visit the camp itself."

Jonathon had anticipated a large, flat enclosure similar to Nong Chan. The Khmer Rouge camp, he soon found, wasn't so much a camp as a grouping of inhabited areas built right into the jungle. Lean-to huts of bamboo sticks covered with palm leaves connected directly into the bases of trees. Freestanding wooden structures with straw walls seemed designed more for mobility than for protection from the elements. The only marks of anything less than perfect cohabitation with the jungle were the neat vegetable gardens, the defoliated, rectangular clearings, and the two large black plastic tarp awnings suspended from trees.

"We'll spend the day in commune eleven."

The group arrived just as the rice was being distributed. The inhabitants of the commune sat in perfect rows. Three men stood in front with the rice. As they read each name off a list, a different black-clad woman would come up to claim her allotment. All of the women had similar short haircuts and red or blue Cambodian scarves around their necks. Each accepted the rice and then moved to other perfect rows in a clearing to the side.

This is what we were trying to do in Nong Chan, Jonathon thought in amazement. They don't need a red marker here. People are just taking their rice and leaving, as if they trust that the aid is here to help them. The system seemed so impressively efficient.

Jonathon and the others stood watching for a peaceful hour, waiting for Piseth to give them new instructions.

"These are the strong ones," Piseth said. "The women are the leaders of our movement. They sustain us. But our people are suffering. We don't have enough food and we are dying of disease. Next I'd like to take you to our field hospital."

The hospital was also perfectly organized. Mats were laid in perfect rows, with folded pajamas, two feet between each. The Khmer Rouge hospital didn't even have the paltry medicines or rustic equipment as in Nong Chan, but it did have a calm that contrasted with the chaos of the other site. But if the infirmary appeared more organized, the patients seemed more sick. Their coughs were deeper, their eyes more sunken. They looked thin and frail, as if about to break into pieces. A few writhed on the ground scratching themselves.

Piseth paused to let the full impact of the horrific sight sink in before speaking.

"Our people are dying. Cholera, typhoid fever, dysentery—diseases we know how to treat, but we don't have the medicine. We don't ask for much from you, just the medicines to let us nurse ourselves back to health."

Siefert handed a large backpack he had been carrying to the man who seemed to be in charge of the infirmary.

"These are medical supplies. It's not much, but I hope you'll find it useful."

The man bowed his head. *"Merci, mis-yuh,"* he said. He looked down at a young girl lying on one of the mats. Her foot was deformed and the festering rash on her stomach was exposed to the open air. He nodded at her.

"Tenk you, suh," she said in a hesitant and neutral voice.

"If you will please follow me, over here is the garden. You have been very generous giving us rice, but our goal is to become self-sufficient. The vegetable garden is very important to us. We want to grow what we eat, even in these hills where it is impossible to grow rice. What is it you say in the West—give a man a fish he will eat for one meal. If you teach him how to fish, he will eat forever. We know how to fish and are only asking for a hook and a line. We thank you for your rice, but what would really help us would be vegetable seeds we could use to grow our own food."

"Je comprends, je comprends," Balard said.

"I hope you will not think it presumptuous, but we have prepared a list of the type of seeds we would most like to have."

Piseth nodded at an assistant who scurried up with a piece of paper. The words had been handwritten in an elegant French pen. Balard took the list with an understanding nod.

"I hope you will understand that we need these tools to begin rebuilding our country. The Vietnamese have seized control of our land. The Vietnamese are killing our people. They are starving us. They are making up stories to turn the world against us."

They followed Piseth to another area.

"This is our nursery. It's hard for women to give birth with so little food. Yet we are committed to rebuilding our population."

Jonathon felt himself almost being convinced. But these are the Khmer Rouge. He shook his head.

"But you also have an army?"

"Yes, of course we do," Piseth said. "How else can we fight the Vietnamese who have tanks and American weapons, who are using chemical weapons against us?"

"But what are your soldiers eating?"

"They are out in the jungle. They are constantly moving. In the jungle there is life. They can hunt, they can pick berries. They are guerrillas, they know how to live. But these people, these civilians, they can't live like the fighters. They are helpless. We need to provide for them. That is why your help is so important to us. Why we are so grateful to you for it."

Piseth took them all around the camp. Jonathon noticed the same discipline in everything going on in the camp. In one section women wove straw mats. In another they stitched together the spent rice bags into large canopies. They tended the garden with a morose intensity. There were not the smiles Jonathon had seen in Nong Chan. There was no drunkenness, not the same sense of the unexpected waiting in the wings. There were no aimless wanderers, no groups of men and women chattering away to each other, no children selling ice cream, no spontaneous laughter, no grenade-laden transvestites, no ostentatious traders, no restaurants, no one peddled cigarettes, there were no TV antennas sticking out of huts. People seemed to be taking action, not loitering around waiting for handouts. It was as if each individual contributed to a single mechanism that was the commune. It was perfectly focused discipline, creating a perfectly efficient force to do single-mindedly what Jonathon had attempted and failed in Nong Chan.

Jonathon couldn't forget the stories he had heard of Khmer Rouge killings. But these children, these women, these old people, they couldn't be Khmer Rouge, not *that* Khmer Rouge.

"But now you have seen a lot. You must be hungry. Let us eat."

Piseth led the three visitors to an awning under which a table had been set.

"Our food is simple. How can we eat when our people are starving?"

The rice with a few vegetables was simple but it tasted good to Jonathon. A young boy approached the table with a plate of large frogs' legs.

"We don't have much, but the people of the commune are very grateful for your assistance. Today they caught these frogs in the forest, which they would like to present to you."

"We cannot accept this," Balard said. "They need it far more than we."

"Thank you, Monsieur Balard. No matter what the circumstance, the Cambodian people must honor their guests. Please, you do us honor sir."

Balard took a single frog's leg on his plate.

"Thank you Monsieur Piseth," he said sincerely.

After dinner, an old Cambodian man played folk tunes on a wooden flute. The three slept well in the mosquito net–covered cots prepared for them.

They spent the next day in long conversations with Piseth, who went into greater detail about the distribution system, about the plan to become self-sufficient, even in this remote area, and about his hope that Cambodia would be returned to the Cambodian people.

"We know we made mistakes. We tried to do too much too fast and our people have suffered. We were not perfect, but we've learned, and we are committed to building a new Cambodia for all its people. We welcome you to come back and assess the situation in the future. You can contact us through the same Thai unit."

They went to bed at eight that night, and Piseth woke them at one in the morning to begin their journey back. By four, they and their group of porters had assembled at the border. The Thais were there as promised, and Jonathan slept the two hours back to Aran.

He had a quick shower at the guest house and a bowl of hot noodles with chicken. He couldn't remember breakfast tasting so good.

Jonathon was surprised to see Maria almost in tears as she met him at the convoy meeting point in Aran.

"Oh Jonathon, thank God." She squeezed his hand tightly. "I'm so glad to see you."

"Me too, Maria," Jonathon said. "It wasn't so long, was it?"

She looked at him with a puzzled look on her face and then smiled. "Can we have dinner tonight?"

"Of course, Maria, of course."

The call came for the convoy to move out. Jonathon squeezed Maria's outstretched hand as he headed toward his truck. Maria watched him move away.

The Khmer Rouge camp was very much on Jonathon's mind as sprawling, chaotic, frustrating Nong Chan came into view. Jesus, he thought, things in this camp could be so much better.

27

Oh, the click.

A month of constant searching and Morgan was exhausted. Each day a new camp. Arrive in the morning to case out the food distributions. Work the tangled web of passageways between the dense groupings of huts. Search for the faces he knew. Hunt for clues, any clues.

Nine years earlier, he had cased the alleyways of Phnom Penh and the camps just outside it with a similar thoroughness. Then he had known what he was looking for and all he had to do was distill it—if he kept his eyes open he knew then that he'd eventually find the right children. Now he needed to find something that might not be there at all.

What was he looking for? The boys, clues on how to find them, a trace of somewhere Sophal had gone, something he had done that would give Morgan some information about where he was? The last courier to Aran had said "M-21." What did that mean? What was M-21? It was probably a code name of some sort, but for what?

If there were a million points to be searched, all Morgan could think of was to cover his bases one at a time. He walked the paths of the camps with an unflagging consistency, beginning casual conversations with refugees, piecing together histories of what happened to the Cambodian people. The tales came to him in bits and pieces of hardship and death, of overwork, execution, and disease, of the relentless Khmer Rouge witch-hunts for supporters of the defeated Lon Nol regime.

There were moments when Morgan felt as if he were close—when a familiar face, a feature, a gesture, a sound from the periphery, caught his attention, inspired a synapse of hope quickly overcome by the judgment of his analytical mind. Death hovered over Cambodia like a storm cloud. If the members of his unit had been enveloped in its rain, what chance did he have of finding them among the living?

Morgan passed a small, makeshift pagoda in the Klong Tlak camp and was tempted to ask the monk to contact the spirits of the deceased members of his unit. He turned away. He would not give up that easily. At the very least, Sophal was alive, period. Morgan would not rest until he found him. No other thought was acceptable. None was possible.

The ghosts followed Morgan back to Aran. They followed him to Madame Di's, where he kept his facade of "mateship" with Evan and the other "friends" whom Morgan despised but who, he hoped, might be able to offer him clues. The ghosts wove their way into Morgan's tortured sleep and chased him through his morning runs.

The click, the click. It now seemed almost a hopeless aspiration for harmony, for oneness, for peace. There was too much sorrow, too many memories in this place. There seemed no speed Morgan could run, no level of discipline that could overcome this single, haunting fact.

And yet every morning he ran, his mind filled with the same memories, the same feelings of guilt, of inadequacy, hoping for the click that never came. He wondered if it would ever come again.

28

A new sense of enthusiasm and purpose had inspired Jonathon ever since his return from the Khao Dinh camp. Tim had sent him across the border into Cambodia to set up systems making sure that those civilians were getting the rice. After seeing the Khmer Rouge camp leaders in action, Jonathon had realized that the assumption behind the systems they had tried in Nong Chan was that the Cambodians were liars and cheats.

But the Khmer Rouge camps seemed different. The people there were building a system to help themselves. They hadn't asked for just rice, but also seeds to grow themselves. Jonathon did not forget what the Khmer Rouge had done. But the killers weren't women and children. Women and children were the killed. There were so many moral question marks on the border—even reports of cannibalism at some of the worst times of starvation. Who knew what people had done to survive, what they had seen, what horrors they had internalized? If Jonathon and the others had set a moral test to qualify for aid, who would pass? How could they ever know who had done what in the decade of war that had plagued Cambodia?

Blame was not all equal, but was it so unequal that it could be sorted into broad and differentiable categories? Jonathon had tried to organize his world this way when he had first arrived in the camp, but soon found the categories extraneous. The Khmer Rouge were the Khmer Rouge, yes, but some of them were also children.

Setting up a system in the Khmer Rouge camp was not difficult. The same type of plan Jonathon had wanted to establish in Nong Chan seemed to already exist in Khao Dinh. There was no need to organize distributions in the Khmer Rouge camp, no need to set further criteria for who the recipients of aid would be. The Khmer Rouge camp officials were doing this themselves, even the UNICEF doctor had agreed. All the foreigners needed to do was to check the distribution books, to verify that the Khmer Rouge were doing what they said, to visit the Khmer Rouge camp and watch the work in action, and to make sure that seeds and medicines were being delivered.

Tim had been impressed with Jonathon's efficiency. Within two days of his return from the Khmer Rouge zone to Aranyaprathet, Jonathon had written a report outlining what he had seen and proposing a system for future monitoring. Once every two weeks, a representative of the Non-Governmental Organizations or the UNICEF/Red Cross joint mission would cross the border in the same way that Jonathon and the others had done. They would meet Mr. Sim who would take them to Piseth. They would examine the distribution books. They would watch the seeds being planted and the medicines administered. They would then be hand-delivered back across the border to the Thais. It was a simple plan, but after so many complicated plans had failed, its simplicity seemed to be its strength. Rice and seeds would get to where they were needed. Western donor countries would receive reassurance that aid was going where it was meant to go and that they were not feeding the Khmer Rouge army.

Writing this report was Jonathon's most meaningful experience yet on the border. His willingness to march through a minefield with the Khmer Rouge to the Cambodian jungle had opened a swath of light into the darkness. Jonathon had used his special analytical skills and his legal training to produce a report and establish a system that would turn this faint beam into a ray of hope.

Distributing rice in Nong Chan was a task anybody could fulfill. But this cross-border aid became something special to Jonathon. It was a constant reminder of what he had done, evidence that he was making a difference. Jonathon volunteered to join the future monitoring missions. He asked Tim to meet for dinner and quietly made his argument.

"I know the route, Tim. I've met Piseth. I set up the system. You said this thing is secret. The more people who know about it, the less secret it's going to be. I can do this job, Tim. I'd like to do this job."

Tim was hesitant. He had expected Jonathon to do a good job in his assessment, but was somewhat taken aback by Jonathon's enthusiasm. The Mercy Relief board in Atlanta knew what they were doing on the border, but had stressed that the cross-border activities be kept under wraps. Maybe Jonathon was right. The fewer people who knew, the more secret it would be. And the less Tim's ass would be on the line.

29

"Maria, we are so happy that you can be with us tonight," Father Pierre said in his deep, reassuring voice. "We've missed you."

Maria smiled half at the kind words, half in embarrassment.

"Donna, would you like to get us going?" the French Canadian priest asked.

"Thank you father. Maria, we are happy you are here. We love you and we pray for you even when you are away." Donna, like most of the others, could sense why Maria had missed so many of the prayer sessions. A few of them had been through it before. Donna knew that love, or infatuation, or whatever it was, needed to run its course. Love, faith, truth, happiness— each of us had to come to our own understanding. She had learned over time that you just have to let someone know you'll be there if they need you, and be there when they do.

The nine men and women sat in a circle on a large, red and green straw mat in the living room of the villa.

"Dear Lord, we pray that you give us strength to carry out your work. Although we don't always understand your ways, we know that you have instructed us to be here with the refugees. We know that you will help the refugees be strong and regain their lives through you. We pray for the strength to do your work. We pray for the health of the refugees. We pray for the people of Cambodia and the people of the world. We pray for our dear fiend, Maria . . ."

Donna looked up to catch Maria's eye. Maria was smiling, her thoughts elsewhere. Maria's mind registered her own name and her eyes refocused on Donna's. She slightly nodded her head in gratitude.

Maria appreciated their concern. She drifted slowly back toward Jonathon. Sometimes she felt surprised at the role he was beginning to play in her life. There were even moments when she worried she was letting go too much. But her feelings felt so natural to her—like water flowing from a deep spring. She wasn't completely sure of the source, but the water tasted so sweet. How could something be wrong, she asked herself, that felt so pure?

"I've chosen Ephesians 1 for tonight's passage." Father Pierre opened his tattered Bible. "Paul told the people of Ephesus 'Blessed be the God and Father of our Lord Jesus Christ, who has blessed us with every spiritual blessing in the heavenly places in Christ, just as He chose us in Him before the foundation of the world, that we should be holy and without blame before Him in love . . . In Him we have redemption, the forgiveness of sins, according to the riches of His grace.' "

Maria nibbled at her dinner after the prayer session. She updated Donna on how things were going in the infirmary, and described Neang's miraculous recovery. It seemed to take forever for Father Pierre to slice the papaya for dessert.

"Thank you, thank you," Maria said, finishing the dishwashing with the others. They seemed to almost circle around her with their smiles.

"Thank you," she said again as she glided past them out the door.

30

Evan Pritchard was on a descending path in life. His spark was slowly extinguishing. He was often drunk. He was not as sharp as he had once been. But it did not take a genius to realize that Jonathon Cohane was up to something suspicious.

Jonathon had been in bed by eleven every night. Now he'd been gone for two days and had returned with a new attitude and red clay on his shoes. Evan had immediately sensed Jonathon was hiding something. This made him curious. Even in his deteriorated state, Evan was still not such a bad journalist.

"Hey, Jonathon, how ya going, mate?"

"Fine."

"Where ya comin' from?"

"Oh, I was visiting another camp."

"Which one?"

"Hey, we had a deal, remember? If you're going to act like a journalist, I'm going to have to treat you like one."

"Hey mate, relax. Just making conversation."

Why would Jonathon be so testy? Evan mulled it over nursing a morning beer at Madame Di's. If he was visiting another noncommunist camp on the border, he'd have just told him. No reason to hide that. Nothing to hide about going west into Thailand or going to Bangkok. He wouldn't have gone just across the border from here—too many land mines and the situation's too chaotic. So what's left? Did he go into Cambodia? If he did, where could it have been? The only place where his safety could have been guaranteed—the Khmer Rouge zone. Could it be? It was hard to believe. It certainly would be an incredible story. How could he find out? He felt a distant spark kindling within him. He was on to something. He sipped his beer and thought.

31

Was it really worth it? Morgan wondered. Was he visiting all of these camps because he truly believed he had a chance of finding him, of finding them? Or was this some type of ascetic penance that would finally allow Morgan to let himself off the hook? He did not feel at all relieved by his relentless search for clues.

Sophal had uncovered the communist spy in Lon Nol's Department of Defense eight years before by following in turn every member of the military headquarters staff. Sophal had memorized every state capital, every governor, every senator, intricacies of the US Constitution, and, just to be safe, baseball statistics from the past five years, for his citizenship interview. Sophal would not have rested until he'd found the others. He would have kept going and going, turning over each rock until there were no rocks left to turn. Morgan could do no less.

Perhaps it was not penance, but Morgan had turned over so many rocks they were all starting to look the same. Another camp, another food distribution, more huts with the sick and the dying, more conversations at small noodle stands, more journeys through camp markets, more questions, more stories, more histories—and what did he have to show for this effort? Exhaustion, despair? Morgan was certainly not one to give up, but this only added to his frustration. No end seemed in sight.

What angle had he not yet covered? The camp visits turned up nothing, the Red Cross nothing, the embassy nothing, trying with a plan nothing, trying without a plan, nothing. The names of the camps were starting to merge in his mind. Where was he today? Was it Tap Prik? Nong Chan? Phnom Chat? What difference did it make? He would recheck the name on his way out and cross it off his map. He walked the streets looking at faces as if flipping through endless police profile books.

He sat for a cup of tea at a small, makeshift cafe in the camp.

"Som tik tai muey." Tea, please.

"Lok ches niyay piesar Khmai ter?" You speak Cambodian?

"I speak, I speak," Morgan answered in English. He was tired and wasn't sure if he wanted to relive this same conversation that had yielded such meager results. The man brought him his tea.

"Ooh, pibah nas," the man said.

"Yes, I know, very difficult," Morgan answered, again in English.

The man sensed Morgan's hesitation or, perhaps, surmised that the only words this foreigner knew were how to order tea, and walked back to his seat in the shade.

Morgan looked out at the camp. A small child defecated in a drainage ditch. Two girls played together, jumping over a small string. A man walked by with a few pieces of firewood slung over his shoulder. A long-haired Cambodian soldier sped by on an old motorcycle. It's the same god-damn scene, Morgan thought to himself sipping his tea.

But something in his mind had been activated, a tripwire triggered. What was it? Was there something he was supposed to do? Or was it something he had seen? What was it? The cafe? The children? The motor-cycle?

It hit Morgan like an exploding grenade. The motorcycle. The green motorcycle. It had a red fender. Morgan jolted up from his chair. He fumbled through his pockets for the five-baht coin he tossed to the cafe owner as he sprinted after the motorcycle.

The motorcycle was long gone. Where was it? He could see the barbed wire fence to his left. This was one edge of the camp. If he worked each street from here all the way around, he would have the camp covered. The camp was big and to cover it he would have to move fast.

Morgan ran frantically up and down each street. His feet burned from the hot ground beneath his shoes. Sweat poured from his body. Up and down each street, back and forth, back and forth. He lost track of time. His entire life, it seemed, rested on this motorcycle, this first clue.

"Who has a green motorcycle?" he shouted as he passed groupings of refugees.

"I don't know, I don't know."

It wasn't as if so many people had them. Maybe they just didn't want to say anything to a stranger. Maybe he looked suspicious, running up and down the streets of the camp like a madman.

He finally saw it in front of a small hut in a dense cluster of bamboo dwellings. A blue scarf was draped over its seat.

"Whose motorcycle is this, whose motorcycle is this?" Morgan shouted in Khmer.

An old woman seated on a small platform nearby made a hesitant motion, pointing her lips at one of the huts.

There was no door on which to bang, so Morgan rattled the platform floor. "Hey! Hey!"

A young man wearing only green military pants came out, a pistol tucked in his belt.

"Who the fuck are you?" he said in Cambodian.

"Is this your motorcycle? Is this your motorcycle?" Morgan asked.

"Yes it is."

"Where did you get it?"

"Why do you want to know?"

Morgan realized he was triggering the worst insecurities in a place where all ownership rights were tenuous and the powerful could take from the weak, but had better look out for the more powerful.

"Look, brother, I don't want to take this motorcycle from you. It's yours, that's fine. But it once belonged to a friend of mine. I need to find him. Can you just tell me where you got it?"

"I bought it from someone."

"From who?"

"I can't remember the name."

"Where did you buy it?"

"I can't remember."

"Look, brother, I believe you. I don't want the damn motorcycle. I just want to know where you got it. Here's fifty dollars. When you take me to the person who you bought the motorcycle from I'll give you fifty more and you can leave right away, with your motorcycle."

The man stared at Morgan for a second. A hundred dollars was a lot of money. He had stolen a lot of things, he thought to himself, but the motorcycle he'd happened to buy.

The man took the fifty dollars, held it up to check its authenticity, then stuck it in his front pocket. He nonchalantly grabbed his shirt and his sandals, got on the bike, and motioned for Morgan to sit behind him. They drove for two minutes to a hut slightly smaller than his.

"Mineang, mawk mawk nis pleam." Hey lady, come right now, the soldier yelled into the hut.

A young, dark-skinned woman with sharp features, her head completely shaved but for a thin layer of stubble, came out the door. She cradled a tiny infant to her breast.

"Her," the man said. The woman winced.

"Did you sell your motorcycle to this man?" Morgan asked.

The woman looked up, surprised at the odd question.

"Chaa," she said quietly, turning her eyes downward.

"OK." Morgan gave the man his second fifty. The man again held it in the air. Pleased, he tucked it away with the other bill and sped off with a sly smile. A cloud of dust hovered over his tracks.

Morgan caught his breath.

"May I speak with you, sister?" he asked in Cambodian.

"Speak," she said in an almost inaudible tone.

"I'm O'Reilly, Morgan O'Reilly."

The woman's face went pale. She seemed to stagger backward.

"O'Reilly, O'Reilly. Go away. You are not welcome here." She started to chant some type of incantation Morgan could not understand. It seemed almost like an exorcism.

"Sister, sister, it's OK, it's OK."

"O'Reilly, ghost, leave this place." She turned her child away from Morgan as if protecting the child from an evil spirit.

"Sister, sister, I am not a ghost. I'm a human being. I'm an American. Why do you think I'm a ghost?"

"You killed my husband!"

"What?"

"You took my husband."

"I don't understand, sister," Morgan pleaded.

"My husband had malaria. He was fighting it and getting better, but then he seemed to get worse. He became delirious. We called the monk to pray for him, but the monk told us that a spirit was taking hold of his body. We prayed and lit incense. Then he became delirious. The bad spirits were taking control of him, but he fought them. He was so hot his skin seemed to boil. He was halfway to the other world and he kept groaning 'O'Reilly, O'Reilly.' We knew that O'Reilly was the name of the spirit dragging him into the underworld."

"Sister, sister, what was your husband's name?"

"His name was Ton."

Morgan didn't know anyone named Ton, but Cambodians often had many names.

"Did he have any other names?"

"Yes, he had another name I only discovered recently."

"What was that, sister?"

"Rithy, Sok Rithy."

Morgan took a breath to the depth of his being, as if this information was so immense that his mind was not enough to take it in. It required the entire vessel of his body.

"Sok Rithy," Morgan said in a quiet voice.

"Chaa."

"Sok Rithy, he was twenty years old."

"Chaa."

"He had a cut on his right arm below the elbow."

"Chaa, chaa," she said.

"Sister, Sok Rithy is my friend. Where is he?"

The second Morgan asked that question, he realized that he already knew the answer. There was only one reason this woman would have shaved her head. She was in mourning.

The woman looked down.

"I'm sorry," Morgan said. "I'm so sorry. When did he die?"

"Two months ago."

"Is this his son?"

"Chaa."

"What's his name?"

"Phally."

He had, Morgan now noticed, Rithy's eyes.

"How long have you been married?"

"Just for two years, sir."

"Uncle. Please call me uncle," Morgan said. "Where did you meet?"

"In Pursat province. I was on a Khmer Rouge work crew digging an irrigation canal. Ton was sent there from Kampot."

"Where had Ton lived before the Khmer Rouge time?" Morgan asked.

"He said he was a farmer from Kampong Speu."

Jesus, Morgan thought to himself, he hadn't even told his wife where he had come from, what he had done.

"The *Angkaa,* the Khmer Rouge, chose for us to marry. They lined up forty men and forty women and we were across from each other. They married us all at the same time."

"How did you get here?"

"When the Vietnamese invaded, *Angkaa* swept us all with them. Many people died. We got to the border zone and there was nothing. The Khmer

Rouge soldiers took the little rice for themselves. We ate bark from the trees and bugs we found in the ground. Ton caught malaria, but he insisted that we had to get out of there right away. One night we sneaked away with a group of four other people, trying to make it to the border. Ton wanted to get away from the Khmer Rouge, so we headed north. He was sick, but he was so determined to get here. Three of the people stepped on mines and died on the way. One woman drowned when we crossed a river. We were all so weak, especially Ton, but we made it."

"How did you get the motorcycle?"

"There was a man, a Cambodian like us. He came riding through checking every hut. He came into ours. When he saw my husband, they both started crying. Ton told me that the man was part of his family, that he would help us."

Morgan tried to control the emotions overpowering him. "And what happened?"

"Ton sent me out. He didn't want me to hear what they were talking about. But the man came back every day. He brought us drugs for Ton."

She reached for a small basket lying beside her house and took out a spent plastic wrapper. The word "Fansidar" was imprinted in thick blue letters on the foil backing.

"What did they talk about?"

"I don't know, uncle, but Ton said that the man was going to get us out, that he was going to take us to America."

"And?"

"The man had to go do something first."

"What was it?"

"I don't know."

"Do you know anything about it?"

"I think the man wanted to go someplace. Ton was feeling very weak, but he drew many maps. I saw them when Ton was sleeping."

"Are the maps here?"

"No, the man took them."

"Do you know what the maps were of?"

"Yes, uncle."

"What?"

"They were the path we took to get here from the Khmer Rouge zone."

Holy shit, Morgan thought. It was the Khmer Rouge zone. What the fuck was Sophal doing sneaking into Cambodia, to the KR zone? He had no time to think. He needed answers.

"And what happened?"

"The man came to the camp on his motorcycle, then he changed into Ton's clothes. A boy from the camp showed him how to sneak across the border. He said he'd be back in a week. He left his motorcycle with us."

"Yes, sister."

"We waited. One week, two weeks, three weeks, a month. Ton's medicine was running out and we didn't have any money for more. I couldn't do any trading because I had to be home taking care of him. We had no money for food or medicine."

"And so you sold the motorcycle?"

"Yes, uncle. We sold the motorcycle. We couldn't get the same drugs, but we got something else in the market. It didn't seem to work. Ton got worse and worse. He started groaning 'O'Reilly, O'Reilly.' Then he died."

The woman's voice resonated with sorrow but also with a quiet strength and acceptance of fate. Death seemed part of her world. She must have seen it so many times, Morgan thought. They all had.

"Do you remember those maps?" Morgan asked.

"A little."

"Do you remember the route?"

"Ton was leading us. He planned everything. I remember a little."

"Can you write it for me?"

Morgan pulled a small notebook and a pen from his backpack. The woman gripped the pen with a fist and began to draw in an unsteady hand. As she began to recount her memories of the voyage, it soon became clear to Morgan that her information would be all but useless to him.

"First we crossed a mountain and there was a river with a shape like an eight. We went over a field . . ."

Morgan tried to remember everything she said. When she handed him back the paper, all he saw were scribbles.

"Thank you, sister. Where was the camp you started from?"

"The Khmer Rouge camp? It was Pnum Malay."

Pnum Malay didn't mean anything to Morgan.

"And did you ever come across anything called M-21?"

"No, uncle."

"Have you heard anything from Sophal, from the man who came on the motorcycle?"

"No, nothing."

"Thank you sister. Will you write me down your name and your child's name?"

The woman hesitated. Morgan realized the problem and took the notebook and pen from her. She told him the names.

"I will come back," he said.

She tried to refuse his offer of all the money in his wallet even though she knew she needed it.

"Please. It's not much. Please take it, for the baby."

It was more money than she had ever seen in her life. She took it and folded it into the tie of her pants.

As Morgan walked away, he tried to control the whizzing sensation in his mind. Rithy, the expert swimmer, had braved the Khmer Rouge rapids and almost made it. Morgan felt the intense pain of simultaneously resurrecting and reburying his dear friend. He did not allow his mind to languish. Sophal's fate was still unknown. Sophal was lost in the Khmer Rouge zone.

One clue was so little. It was everything. Yes, Sophal was out of contact, but wasn't that to be expected once he'd crossed the border? The KR zone was hell itself, and Sophal had promised he'd be back in a week. No contact in the KR zone did not mean that Sophal was dead. It certainly meant that he was in trouble. Morgan needed to find out why.

Why had Sophal gone to the Khmer Rouge zone? Were his orders to assess, or was there something more? Had Dillon told him to go? Morgan had read the cables, but the cables were going straight to Dillon. Morgan wondered if he had been shown all the cables. What was it in the Khmer Rouge zone he was looking for? Was it M-21? So many questions, so many unanswered questions.

The twinge of fear checked the glimmer of hope in Morgan's mind. So many questions. There was only one place where they could be answered. He had to get to the Khmer Rouge zone.

3 2

Although Maria fought the realization, she was beginning to sense that Jonathon's newfound enthusiasm for his work was drawing him away from her. Jonathon had tried in vain to keep his experiences secret when he had first returned from the Khmer Rouge zone. He was bursting with energy and just waiting for Maria to ask a second time where he had been.

"I know you won't tell anyone, Maria, but I have to be careful."

On a long walk, he told her everything—the ride to the border, the fantastic journey to the camp. He described the details of camp life, his discussions with Piseth. He contrasted life in the Khmer Rouge camp with life in Nong Chan. Maria hung on his every word, trying to picture it in her own mind, to make his experiences her own.

Maria watched Jonathon's new demeanor with amazement. She had first seen Jonathon when he was witnessing the sick and dying in the infirmary for the first time. They had first spoken when he had just come through the orphans' mad rush for the bread, and their relationship had emerged, developed, and strengthened around Jonathon's painful experiences in Nong Chan. Jonathon had struggled with the ambiguities of the border. Amid those ambiguities, Maria knew, he had found calm, peace, and acceptance in her.

Maria loved Jonathon's troubled vulnerability. It was her entry to the depths of his soul. She prayed for Jonathon to find what he was looking for, for him to find strength through himself, through God, through her. She had shared his troubles. His pain had been hers. And if that pain was relieved, her pain was relieved, her prayers were answered.

But she had always imagined that those prayers would be answered with her. But now Jonathon had found meaning in a place she didn't know, a place he had left her to reach. He had returned from the Khmer Rouge zone changed by experiences unknown to her. She'd had to ask twice for his description. And if she was happy that his suffering had eased, she subconsciously feared that part of her relationship with him may have vanished together with it.

Though she didn't trust her intuition enough to say so, she worried that Jonathon might be getting in over his head in the Khmer Rouge camp. Although Maria didn't claim to have any deep knowledge of border politics, she knew enough to know that going into the Khmer Rouge zone was a dangerous thing to do. She wanted to share Jonathon's enthusiasm for helping set up a rice distribution system in the Khmer Rouge camp, but the one thing she'd learned from Sister Susan and from her limited experience in Nong Chan was that people only truly help each other one person at a time.

Her conscious mind fought against these conflicted feelings with the only weapon it had, the only weapon she had trained it to have. If she had doubts about God and the dying refugees, she would only believe more strongly. She would add wood to the flame of her faith. And when the faint odor of Maria's subconscious fears wafted toward her consciousness, her only response was to believe even more. The wings of her faith spread to cover the gulf of her creeping doubt. If she sensed that Jonathon was becoming more distant from her, her mind fought against the realization through faith in him and in them.

But even her faith was beginning to confuse her. Jesus taught us to love, but Maria felt her feelings for Jonathon crowding out all else. Did the love of God feel the same as the love of man? Maybe we need flesh and blood, touch and sense? Why else did God send us his son?

Maria's love for Jonathon at times empowered her, at times made her feel weak. She struggled to understand whether her faith was opening her to love or condemning her to blindness. She knelt before Sister Susan's crucifix. Jonathon was so deeply woven into her prayers and her thoughts. He was becoming her prayers and her thoughts.

The struggle within Maria was working its way toward the surface. A file went missing at the Nong Chan infirmary and Maria had to go through all the files to find it where she had mistakenly placed it out of alphabetical order. It was only brought to her attention that she had forgotten to add a refugee's penicillin shot to the chart when the refugee asked the doctor to give the shot in his left arm because his right was sore already. She prayed harder and harder for the refugees, for Jonathon, as if the manifestation of her commitment would itself overcome the conflicts brewing within her, as if the wings of her faith could fly without her.

She would sit in her office in the infirmary hoping that Jonathon would stop by to say hello. She ached for their walks, for their embraces in the moonlight, for the feel of Jonathon's lips on hers, his hands pressing her back closer and closer toward him until they were one.

And then, he was there. It was his second trip into the Khmer Rouge zone. He was in that strange, frightening world where he had found sustenance, a world that Maria would give everything to know, and out of which she was frozen. She felt afraid, alone. What is happening to me? she asked herself. Is this what love can do?

Her subconscious mind sensed that doubt would take her somewhere she dared not go, back to the lonely child waiting for the bells to ring. The bells had called her to her faith, which had changed everything. And if her faith was inadequate, she would have to believe even more. If her mind was telling her to slow down, to be cautious, to give less, then she must give more, she must give, perhaps, everything.

3 3

Morgan had followed Sophal's thoughts through to Sophal's actions. Now Morgan needed to think. The sun was rising on another perfect day. His mind was processing his options as he ran along the dirt road leading out of Aran without even a faint hope of the click. Sophal had wanted to find the unit. Morgan knew that and had followed those thoughts to the Red Cross. Sophal would have looked in the camps, and Morgan knew how thorough he would be. Again, his connection with Sophal had led him to the clues he had sought.

But now Sophal had entered a world where Morgan could not follow the same way. In the camp, Sophal had taken Rithy's clothes and in so doing had returned from Morgan's world to a place where there was no room for foreigners, no matter how well they spoke Cambodian nor how Cambodian their hearts. Whatever was in his heart, Morgan could no longer follow Sophal in the same way. To find Sophal, Morgan would have to project him, to anticipate where Sophal's path would have led him and arrive at that place by another route.

Morgan's mind weighed each fact, each hypothesis and its implications. Why had Sophal taken Rithy's clothes and crossed the border from Rithy's camp? There were other ways he could have done it. He could have gone to the Thais. They dealt with the Khmer Rouge all the time. He could have even gone to the Khmer Rouge themselves. He could have had the embassy arrange a meeting with the Khmer Rouge representatives in Bangkok. But why didn't he? Was he doing something that they couldn't know about? If the Thais or the Khmer Rouge were helping him, he wouldn't have gone in the way he did. That was certain.

And what about Dillon? Was Dillon in the loop? If he was, would Sophal have asked him for permission to cross the border? If he had, if Dillon had said yes, he would have arranged support for Sophal. But wouldn't Dillon have told me? Morgan wondered. If Morgan's job was to find Sophal, Dillon would have said something. It didn't make sense.

If Sophal had decided to go it alone, he would have just found his own way in. He wouldn't have told anybody, and he'd cover his tracks in case he were caught. That would explain why he sent the M-21 message. Maybe he was sending his coded cables to Dillon but knew he was doing something risky. Maybe M-21 was a clue for Conley. If nobody could know where he was going except for one man dying of malaria in a refugee camp, maybe Sophal wanted the CIA to know something. It wasn't much to go on, but Morgan knew Sophal. If Rithy had told him that a member of the unit was alive, Sophal would have gone no matter what his orders.

And what about Rithy's wife and son? Morgan had returned to their camp three times since his first meeting. At first, he'd pressed Rithy's wife for the few useful details she could provide. But he soon began to feel a strange comfort just sitting with this sincere, practical woman and her quiet child. She had been through so much devastation yet seemed to face the world with equanimity. Morgan guessed that Nat was too young to have ever known that life could be filled with other than slave labor, war, and death. Maybe, he wondered, there was a certain peace that comes with accepting one's fate. But now that he's found them, Morgan knew that he could not leave them to theirs. Sophal had wanted to get Nat and Phally out of the camp. Maybe Morgan could do it for them, for Sophal, for himself.

What if he reported to Dillon? Not a lot, but just enough to see how Dillon might respond. Maybe he could get a clue of how much Dillon knew. He went to his room and wrote meticulously:

*GATHERING CLUES ON SOPHAL. MAY FOLLOW TO NEW AREA.
DO YOU KNOW ANYTHING OF M-21? FOUND SON AND WIFE
OF DECEASED COLLEAGUE. WANT TO GET THEM TO USA. PLS
RESPOND IMMEDIATELY.*

He took a card of numbers and letters from a hidden compartment of his toiletries kit and translated the message into a seemingly random code. He lit a match and burned the original. So that covers Dillon, what about the Thais?

He wrote out another message, this one to Hutchins in Bangkok.

*PLEASE CONTACT US MILITARY ATTACHÉ BANGKOK. ASK TO
CONTACT THAI MILITARY EASTERN DIVISION. SEE IF THEY
KNOW ANYTHING OF M-21, LIKELY RELATED TO CAMBODIA.
ALSO SEE IF ANY CONTACT WITH AMCIT HENG SOPHAL IN
JUNE OR JULY THIS YEAR. PLEASE SUPPLY DETAILED MAPS OF
THE THAI-CAMBODIAN BORDER AREA ADJACENT TO BURI-
RAM AND SURIN PROVINCES.*

Morgan sealed the two letters in an envelope and rushed them over to Conley at Catholic Missions International. No matter what the answers to his questions, Morgan knew he still needed to figure out how he'd get to the Khmer Rouge zone. Could he go to the Thais? Could something be arranged through the Khmer Rouge in Bangkok? Sophal must have had a reason for not doing so. Morgan couldn't figure it out.

Morgan's temples throbbed with anguished impatience. Sophal was somewhere in the Khmer Rouge zone. Perhaps he was in trouble. Every moment now counted more than ever.

34

Maria seemed to be almost trembling at the convoy meeting place in Aran. She rushed over to hug Jonathon.

"I'm so happy you're back," she said, tears welling in her eyes. Over dinner at the noodle stand that night, he described his meeting with Piseth, the second tour through the camp, how he checked all the figures in the distribution log books, how Piseth had taken him to help plant the vegetable seeds in the garden. He told her of the sick children who had thanked him for the medicine he had brought.

He plied her for details of events at the infirmary and at the mission home. Her answers, however, were short. She steered the conversation back toward him. What happened in the infirmary? What was Piseth wearing? Maria seemed to be trying to implant an exact memory in her mind of where he had been and what he had done. As they walked, Maria placed two hands against his arm. She rested her head gently on his shoulder.

There was only a small slice of the moon, but enough light reflected off the rice paddies to illuminate the tears in Maria's eyes. Jonathon gently rubbed them with the back of his finger. He slowly turned to face her.

"Why are you crying?" he asked in an aching voice. He felt Maria moving at the same time closer and further away.

She looked at him with wide eyes. Her worry about Jonathon in the dangerous Khmer Rouge zone merged with the feelings she had so acutely felt when he was away.

"Because I love you so much."

He stood to absorb the powerful words. No woman had ever spoken them to him. He had never guessed he might find them here. He touched her cheek with the tip of his fingers and traced a small curve down her cheekbone. Was this what he had sought? Their kiss deepened like an electric current melting them into one. Jonathon closed his eyes to give way to the sensual perfection of the moment. He wanted to wrap his shoulders around her, to protect her, to envelop her like a warm blanket. He kissed the gentle tears on the side of her face.

Maria pushed up on the balls of her feet to drive deeper into him. Jonathon's hands explored the contours of her back, the curves of her buttocks. Maria clung to Jonathon's shoulders. After what seemed at the same time an eternity and an instant, they pulled their heads hesitatingly apart and looked into each other's eyes. Maria lifted Jonathon's hand to her face. Slowly disengaging, she led him back toward her villa. He followed her through a side door. Neither of them spoke.

When they entered her dark room, he felt her soft body again pushing into his. She crossed his arms behind her lower back and pulled him ever closer. Their hands interlocked, they unbuttoned her shirt and then his. He could feel her breasts pressing against his chest. His hands drifted down the contours of her back. She took his other hand and placed it on the clasp of her skirt. The skirt dropped to the floor. She unbuckled his pants. He stepped out to feel his full body pressing against hers. He thought he felt a slight trembling as she reached around him, through him.

He lifted her up and entered her as he laid her back on the bed. She wrapped her legs and arms around him as he pushed as if toward the core of her very being. The rhythmic movement of their bodies pulled to a climax expressed through a long, harmonious sigh that seemed to escape from a place neither of them had ever known. They lay back on the bed locked in their embrace.

"Maria," he whispered in her ear. She was so beautiful, part of this universe opening itself to him. She was this feeling he had never before known.

"Maria," yet again in an aching whisper. He felt her tears again falling on his shoulder.

"I love you. I love you so much," she cried softly.

Jonathon squeezed her closer to him. They drifted to a state halfway between wakefulness and sleep, their conscious minds clinging to their perfect connection.

Maria was the first to break the long silence.

"Did you hear the bells?" she whispered.

3 5

When it finally arrived, the information Morgan had awaited so impatiently produced discouragingly little. Dillon's response, which Morgan painstakingly decoded, was nondescript.

> *NOTHING ON M-21. CONTACT AGAIN AT END OF MISSION.*
> *WILL ARRANGE PERSONALLY AND IMMEDIATELY ALL VISAS*
> *THEN.*

That seemed standard enough. He hadn't said not to go to a new area, or what new area. Pressing further would tip Morgan's hand. Sophal was a renegade, and to hold on to him, Morgan needed to be a renegade too.

Hutchins's note was also short and useless.

> *THAIS NOTHING ON M-21 OR SOPHAL*

was all it said. The maps were good maps, but Morgan found at least nine small lakes that were roughly the shape of eights. On top of that, there were still bomb craters filled with water. The lake Rithy's wife had seen could have been anywhere.

There wasn't much to go on. Maybe, he thought to himself, there were no more clues left in Thailand. The clues lay across the border. But still the same questions nagged at him. How do I get there?

He struck up conversations at Ki Ki's and sat thinking at a noodle stand. He watched the trucks coming in from Nong Chan and aid workers getting off. But still nothing. Where were the clues?

"Hey, how ya doin'." The smile was back on Morgan's face as he swaggered up to the bar at Madame Di's.

"Hey there, mate," Evan said with a cheery stress on the last word.

"I think I owe you a drink from the last time," Morgan said.

"Well I'm never one to argue with that logic, mate."

"How's your career in the wonderful world of investigative journalism coming along?"

A momentary look of sadness came across Evan's face.

"Not so great, but I'm piecing things together. There's a lot of stories here, and I'm looking for a big one."

"Really, what on?"

"This. Everything. The border."

"What do you mean?"

"I'm piecing things together. Just need some more information."

"Do you know anything about the KR?"

"A little. What did you say you were doing here?"

"Looking for a friend."

"Is your friend a foreigner or a Cambodian?"

"Cambodian."

"Are they Khmer Rouge or do the Khmer Rouge have them?"

Evan's prescient questions seemed to sneak through his drunkenness.

"Either way, would you have something for me? Something I could use?"

"Maybe, but why would I wanna do that?"

"Well you tell me what you're looking for and maybe we can help each other."

"I'm looking for something on the Khmer Rouge also."

"Yeah, what?"

Evan knew that a good journalist doesn't give away the only good lead he's got.

"Sorry mate, can't say. Confidential."

Morgan could feel Sophal's trail slipping away. His gut told him to take a risk.

"All right. I'll level with you. This friend of mine disappeared. I think he's in the Khmer Rouge zone. I need to get there. Can you help me?"

Go to the Khmer Rouge zone? A white guy in the Khmer Rouge zone? This bloke's got to be crazy, Evan thought to himself. Evan shook his head with an incredulous chuckle.

"Yeah, I can help you, but you gotta tell me this. If you go, you gotta tell me everything about the trip and what you find."

"That's a deal. Can you get me there?"

"No, I can't get you there. I can't even get you close. I just know one thing. I'm pretty sure somebody I know is going over into the Khmer Rouge zone."

"How are they doing it?"

"My guess is that it's a secret aid mission."

Morgan could feel the energy surge through his body.

"Do you know who is going?"

"Just one person."

"Where can I find this guy?" Morgan asked calmly.

"Do we have a deal?" Evan looked him in the eye.

This guy is such a scumbag, Morgan thought to himself, trading for information on Sophal's life. He winked with a slight nod.

"We do, mate. Where can I find the guy?"

"Well I think I've got a pretty decent idea where to find him."

"Yeah?"

"Yeah . . . He's my roommate."

36

The clichés were entirely wrong. Power did not come from the barrel of a gun. It did not flow from the tip of a pen. Power, Tom Dillon knew, emerged gently from silence. Dillon had been in noisy places. He had sat at his desk in the American embassy in Saigon and heard the errant bombs exploding nearby. He had felt the thunder of artillery shells and carpet bombs in the Vietnamese countryside. These were not the core of power, they were simply a manifestation of its result. After returning to Washington, Dillon had endured the clatter of government agency representatives bickering over policies. The further from the core of power, the louder you had to yell to make the echo of your distant voice heard. At the very center, Dillon understood, was silence. It was the silence of deep thoughts of life and death, hard choices and decisive action nestled away in the gray matter of great men.

There was something very peaceful about the Old Executive Office Building at six-thirty in the morning. Only the whisper of the air conditioner and the soft hum of fluorescent lights demarcated the deep silence. In the daily hour of silence before Washington came to life with a vengeance at seven-thirty, Tom Dillon held court in his own mind. The strategic decisions that would play out over the following thirteen hours of noise were hatched in this brief, perfect hour.

Life, Dillon knew, was about making hard choices in a world of compromise. All men live their lives with multiple motivations. The man of action chooses between them and uses the tools available to him to transform the silent dictates of his mind into new realities of the noisy world around him.

He reminisced, but for a fleeting moment, about what life had felt like in Saigon. There is something so primordial about war, he thought. It creates an intensity of life, dangerous but addictive, surreal yet so intensely real. He had not fully realized when in Vietnam how much the war had touched him. For the first time in Dillon's life, he'd felt the ground literally shaking under his feet. By 1973 the Americans were on their way out. The brief American period in Vietnam had been a mirage. By the end of that year he was back ensconced in the solid rock of his stable home. He had then thought it would be possible to file all that he'd felt in Vietnam away, a momentary excursion along the forward march of his life. He threw himself into his Washington life with a newfound intensity, rising through the White House ranks despite the change of administration. The rest of the story was always in the papers—the brilliant boy wonder, the understated heir with the unlimited future. He'd read it so many times he almost believed it. But still he fought for more.

Dillon cut off his momentary reverie. Now was the time to think, to plan. He sunk into the meditative silence. O'Reilly's cable had intrigued him.

MAY FOLLOW TO NEW AREA . . . FOUND SON AND WIFE OF DECEASED COLLEAGUE.

Life, Dillon reflected, was a game of chess. Silence flowing through him, he charted his next move.

37

The two elephants worked their way toward the Cambodian hinterland. The crunch of sticks and grass under the elephants' heavy feet, the steady shuffle of hundreds of marching footsteps bringing the white bags of rice toward the Khmer Rouge camp, the sporadic call of birds and the chirping of crickets punctuated the solitude of dawn. Morgan sat transfixed atop the elephant. His life for the past four years had centered around the synthetic creation of borders. For four years he had struggled to build a fence around himself, to keep his tortured mind at bay, to carve out a space in which he could live. Dillon's blue Mercury parked outside his cabin had begun to erode these boundaries. Now, they were collapsing.

For four years he had built this border to try to keep Cambodia out. Now, somewhere along this path he had traveled since being dropped off by the Thai military trucks, he had already crossed the border back in. The trees seemed the same, the ground the same under him, and yet he knew that at some point in these past two hours, he had crossed back to that world he had left. Boundaries no longer existed. Two territories, two people, peace and war, hope and despair, merged as one. Any demarcation where one ended and another began seemed altogether arbitrary.

Once Evan had supplied him with the essential clue, getting to the Khmer Rouge zone had been easy. He told Conley about the secret mission, about a certain Jonathon Cohane who had crossed the border into Cambodia. The fit couldn't have been more perfect.

Catholic Missions International and Mercy Relief had worked closely together on the Thai-Cambodian border. Though one group was Catholic and the other evangelical, the two organizations had both served in Biafra and in Vietnam. Conley knew Tim Anderson well.

"We understand that people in the Khmer Rouge zone are having a tough time. Things are easing up here. We want to get aid to the refugees who need it the most, but want to see things for ourselves. Can you help me, Tim?" Conley had asked.

Tim had taken the bait hook, line, and sinker. Within five days the necessary arrangements had been made. Morgan O'Reilly, a senior official from the Catholic Missions International Baltimore office, would accompany Jonathon Cohane of Mercy Relief on a one-day oversight tour into the Khmer Rouge zone. Logistics and meeting times would be according to the routine schedule.

Jonathon liked the idea of bringing someone along on his assessment mission. He understood the need for secrecy, but what he had seen seemed so important to him that he was aching to share it. Sure he had told Maria, it would have been hard to hide it from her. She had asked for every detail and traced his every word. But Maria would never be able to physically join him crossing the border, to see with her own eyes all that he had done.

Jonathon could still feel her touch on his skin. They'd snuck into her room to make love one last time before he left. Maria pulled Jonathon toward her with all the strength in her thin arms. When it was time for Jonathon to leave for the WFP warehouse, she buried her fingers deep into his ribs. She squeezed her face against his chest and wrapped her leg around his.

"Stay with me," she whispered.

Jonathon loved the feel of her body. He loved the idea of their closeness. He felt the minutes ticking away. Images of the children in the Khmer Rouge camp and of the vegetable garden entered his mind as he gently peeled her fingers from his body. He kissed each one as he told Maria good-bye.

"I'll be back soon, Maria." He could still hear her sniffles as he tiptoed into the night. He felt torn between his longing to stay with Maria, to sink into this passionate intimacy that surprised him, that he had never before known, and the excitement of all he was discovering and accomplishing in the Khmer Rouge zone.

The weight of these thoughts had eased when Jonathon had met the Cambodian porters along with the new American from Catholic Missions International on the Thai side of the border.

"Hey Morgan, I'm Jonathon Cohane. Nice to meet you. Was your ride here OK?"

"Yeah, no problem." Morgan felt slightly surprised that someone so fresh-faced and eager as Jonathon was involved in cross-border assistance.

"This guy over there is Mr. Sim. He's gonna lead us across the border. Make sure you stay in the line. They say there are lots of mines around here."

Sim approached and acknowledged the two. They headed out behind him.

"Have you been to Cambodia before, Morgan?"

"I was here a long time ago," Morgan answered. The less Jonathon knew the better.

"It's incredible how well run the whole thing is. Look at these guys— one after the other like an army of ants."

Morgan nodded.

"This is the way it's been every time. Walk a couple of hours, then travel through the swampy area by elephant. Meet Piseth at the distribution site."

"Piseth?"

"Cham Piseth's the official who helped arrange things for me."

"What's he like?"

"Seems like a decent guy, pretty committed. He's been incredibly helpful."

Morgan reflected for a moment on Jonathon's enthusiasm.

After an hour or so of walking, the group reached the small clearing where they were lifted onto two waiting elephants.

Morgan's mind flipped through his options as the elephants and the rest of the group entered the Khmer Rouge camp.

The elephants came to a stop at a small clearing.

"Mr. Piseth, so nice to see you again," Jonathon said.

"Welcome Mr. Jonathon. Ah, you must be Monsieur O'Reilly. Welcome to the Liberated Zone of Democratic Kampuchea," Piseth said jovially. "We're so glad to have you. Mr. Jonathon has helped us a great deal."

Jonathon suppressed the smile pushing at the edges of his mouth.

"But you have only one day. There is so much for you to see, Monsieur O'Reilly. Let us go."

On all of his previous visits, Jonathon had been the visitor and Piseth the guide. Now Jonathon felt an urge to initiate his new colleague. Jonathon pointed out the small girl at the infirmary with the deformed foot.

"When we first came here, this girl had rashes all over her body. Now look at her. She weighs a third more than she did. Her hair was orange. Now look, it's starting to turn black again."

"Yes," Piseth confirmed Jonathon's words, "the drugs and vitamins you have supplied have made a great difference."

Jonathon and Piseth led Morgan to the vegetable garden. They described the distribution system and showed Morgan the record books. It all seemed so perfect, so smooth, that Morgan knew immediately not to trust it.

How many congressional visits had he witnessed in Cambodia during the war? It was the same story. We were winning, a visit to a village where everybody had been freed from disease thanks to American food and medicine, a big dinner, then back to the airport to zoom off to the next stop. The same guided tour that would make the congresspeople experts when they returned to Washington. How many times had he seen his bosses telling the senators and representatives that all was well, that everything was as it seemed, as everyone had hoped. It had all been lies. The better the story, the deeper the mystery it was attempting to cover. And Jonathon Cohane, this enthusiastic, naïve young American, it was becoming clear to Morgan, had unwittingly become part of the show.

The tour had a beginning, a middle, and an end. It began with the long journey to the camp. That was over and still he had nothing. As the sun began to set, Morgan sensed that the middle would not last long. If he did nothing, the end would arrive and he would be ushered back across the same border with the organized efficiency with which he had come. Perhaps the clues were here, but Morgan knew that his chance to reconnect with the path of Sophal's thoughts was slowly vanishing.

How could he possibly find anything in the vast jungle? The clues were not physical, they were buried in the minds of people. Somehow Morgan had to draw them out.

The clues would come, Morgan knew, in the unexpected. But what? What could Morgan do to break the rhythm of the show? Should he confess to being CIA and ask Piseth to take him to his commander? How many stories had he heard of Cambodians being tortured until they confessed that they were CIA, then executed because of it? Maybe the Khmer Rouge had hoped that the CIA would help them fight the Vietnamese. But what would they think about an operative sneaking into the heart of their camp? Maybe not the whole truth but just a piece of it could get Morgan what he wanted. Morgan's outward calm betrayed the panic inside him. He'd been trained to plan, but here he was in the enemy camp with no plan at all. His mind raced as he attempted to think of options—nothing. All he could think of was the simplest, clumsiest plan of all.

After the frogs' legs had been presented at dinner, Morgan served himself a spoonful of rice and spoke as casually as he could.

"Mr. Piseth, I am very impressed by what your people have done here. How long have you been on the border?"

"Thank you, Monsieur O'Reilly," Piseth said with a smile. "It has been over a year now."

"Have many foreigners been here in that time?"

Piseth seemed slightly taken aback.

"Of course, the two of you, and Dr. Siefert and Monsieur Balard."

"Has there been anyone else?"

"Why no. Of course not."

"Well I'm looking for a friend of mine, Monsieur Piseth, and I was wondering if you'd seen him."

"A friend?" Piseth asked inquisitively.

"His name is Heng Sophal."

"Heng Sophal? That's a Cambodian name," Piseth said.

"He's a Cambodian-American, a friend from home."

"And you think he's here?" Jonathon chimed in incredulously.

"Have you seen him, Mr. Piseth?"

"No," Piseth said with a laugh. He poured more tea into Jonathon and Morgan's glasses before filling his own.

"He's missing and I can't seem to find him."

The uncomprehending look remained on Jonathon's face.

"He was involved with M-21. I thought you might know something about it," Morgan continued nonchalantly.

Piseth drank from his glass.

"Does that mean anything to you, Mr. Piseth?"

"No. I'm terribly sorry, Monsieur O'Reilly. It does not."

After dinner, Piseth excused himself as the old man stepped to the table to play his flute. He returned just as the last song was nearing completion and ushered Jonathon and Morgan to their small thatch hut.

"I'll wake you when it's time to go back," Piseth said with a smile as he opened the door for them to enter.

"What was that about at dinner, Morgan?" Jonathon asked when they were inside.

"Oh nothing. There are lots of places on the border. I just thought he might know something."

Jonathon didn't seem to understand but was happy to let it go as he lay down on his cot.

"Maybe it's best to get some sleep. It's amazing how early it feels when Piseth comes to wake us."

Morgan listened to Jonathon's breathing patterns change as Jonathon descended into sleep.

The ghosts he had fought off all day descended upon Morgan. He was in the Khmer Rouge zone, where Sophal had headed, where Sophal, perhaps, was. Was Sophal close? Morgan closed his eyes and tried to feel it. All he could feel was the throbbing of his temples. Think, Morgan, think, focus.

Piseth hadn't seemed to respond to his words. Maybe Sophal hadn't even made it here. Maybe M-21 was a worthless clue, a false lead that meant nothing, a chance misstatement of the Thai courier. And Piseth would wake them up and they would begin their journey back, back toward what? Toward a self to which Morgan knew he could not return? To Aran with no new clues? To Virginia, where even the briefest moments of peace, the harmony he had occasionally felt running in the woods, would no longer be possible?

Truth, his life, his future was here, somewhere. But as time passed he could feel that life slipping away. Think, there are clues everywhere, there always are clues. Sometimes you can see them, sometimes you have to draw them out like snakes from a basket. Maybe there were magic words to start the process. Heng Sophal, M-21—could these be such words? He had incanted them and nothing had come. Think, think. Should he go out and talk with Piseth? What would he say? It was pitch dark. *It's amazing how early it feels when Piseth comes to wake us.*

Noises. Footsteps. Had the time come so fast? Had the final stage of his tour begun? How long had it been that he had sat almost in a trance? Had it been five hours? It didn't feel like it. This charcoal darkness. Morgan couldn't see his watch. He fumbled in his backpack until he found a match. More footsteps. He struck the match and looked at his watch. It was eleven-thirty. It had been an hour and a half. The footsteps, the rustling seemed closer. It seemed to come from all directions around him. Then, suddenly, lights. The weak beams of flashlights transformed pure darkness into a world of shadow.

Focus, Morgan, focus. He opened the door and saw what he now almost expected. Ten feet away stood Piseth with a phalanx of machine gun–toting soldiers surrounding the hut. Piseth was not smiling. His icy stare sent a chill through even Morgan's hardened body. The dim flashlights shined in Morgan's face.

"Step out of the hut," Piseth said in a steady tone. "Mr. O'Reilly, Agent O'Reilly, do you think we are fools?"

Morgan heard the creaking of Jonathon's cot behind him.

"Mr. Piseth, good morning. Is it two already? What are all these . . ."

If Piseth's fierce scowl was not enough to tell Jonathon that something had changed, the solemn look on Morgan's face made that message abundantly clear. Jonathon's earlier experience in the Khmer Rouge camp had become the standard by which he judged what was happening around him, which kept him from understanding.

"Put your hands on your head."

Morgan had been in tough spots before. You don't argue in a place like this. He lifted his hands and rested them on his head.

Jonathon's conscious mind, however, was not yet prepared to accept this transformation.

"Mr. Piseth, I don't understand. What has he done?" Jonathon stammered.

Still not understanding, Jonathon walked over to confer with Piseth.

"Jonathon, dammit!" Morgan's words were too late. At Jonathon's second step, two soldiers jumped at Jonathon and yanked his arms behind him. They tied his hands together behind his back with twine. Jonathon felt a stabbing pain in his shoulder. His eyes and mouth opened widely. This sudden pain jolted Jonathon from the world he had known, the world of aid and vegetable gardens, of elephants leading toward new hope and resurgence.

But the pain was only a spark. As the black-clad Khmer Rouge soldiers led Jonathon and Morgan into the vast, mysterious jungle faintly illuminated by the soldiers' flashlights, this spark began to slowly catch fire in Jonathon's mind. These were the Khmer Rouge, not the determined farmers he had met in the camp who seemed to have only a tenuous connection to that infamous title, not the children in the infirmary—the real Khmer Rouge, the killers.

The stories came back to Jonathon like a flashback or, worse, a vision of the future, his future. Rathana, the former soldier he'd met in Nong Chan, marching with the other Lon Nol soldiers out into the jungle, hands tied behind their backs, the Khmer Rouge soldiers descending with axes and hoes. Left for dead. Rathana was the lucky one, the one who had survived. But the others, where were they? Jonathon's breathing escalated to a punctuated staccato. He felt engulfed by the fierce impersonal darkness into which people disappeared, where a million Cambodians had been lost, the darkness indifferent to good intentions. The children, the Khmer Rouge infirmary, the vegetable garden he had planted with his own hands. Why was he being led away by the people he had sacrificed so much to help? Fear gripped Jonathon like nothing he had ever known before.

Jonathon recalled the words he had heard from Piseth in the way station between sleep and wakefulness, when he had heard stirrings outside his hut that morning. *Step outside Mr. O'Reilly, Agent O'Reilly.* Jonathon's incomprehension, as if to protect the remaining good place in his heart, transformed into anger.

"You son of a bitch, O'Reilly. Are you CIA?"

Morgan was not about to answer that question. Piseth had not accompanied them into the jungle, but who knew if the others spoke English?

"Jonathon, quiet! Calm down."

"Are you a fucking CIA agent?" Jonathon's voice cracked.

"Jonathon, stop it. Now!" said Morgan, again in a harsh whisper. Morgan had seen it happen before, had seen fear gain momentum and crash through the protective walls of a person's mind. Jonathon seemed to be counting down on an emotional launching pad.

Morgan needed to halt the countdown, at least to slow it and give himself time to think.

"Calm down, Jonathon," Morgan again whispered, stressing the second word. "It's going to be fine. Just stay calm."

But it was not fear alone that was motivating Jonathon's thoughts. Fear was only the trigger.

Morgan heard Jonathon's breath escalating toward hyperventilation. "We're going to be fine, Jonathon. Think of something soothing. Just stop talking. Keep quiet."

Jonathon searched his mind for something to calm him as he was being marched out toward greater depths of nothingness, surrounded by soldiers with their fingers locked on the guns poised to end his history. His mind searched and searched and found the one image that could bring him comfort.

It was so simple, so very simple. His bed—his large, soft bed at home in Highland Park. He felt himself sinking into it, woven into the cocoon of his thick, down comforter, his head lost in the feather pillows. The smell of his mother's soup cooking in the kitchen below wafted up into his dreams, into this safe world. He could almost see his parents waiting for him downstairs.

But they became younger in his mind, younger and younger until they were two small frightened children waiting in a line. Their clothes were torn, they scratched their shorn heads, dark rings circled their eyes, and they waited in line at the gates of the Warsaw ghetto, waiting to be marched out to the trains, to Auschwitz. The order came and they marched out not knowing where they were going, but knowing it was to a place from where there was no return. This darkness Jonathon had challenged was a darkness he had never known, a darkness he never could have imagined. His stomach muscles pressed uncontrollably in and out.

Jonathon looked briefly up at the moon. The image of his mother staring desperately at the moon as a child in Auschwitz floated through his mind. "How can you possibly know," she had asked. He only now understood what she'd meant. How can you possibly know what darkness looks like?

"They're going to kill us," he muttered. The words were somewhere between a whisper, a surrender, and a primordial cry.

Morgan could feel Jonathon going. He had to keep him from breaking.

"We'll be fine, Jonathon. We'll be fine." But Morgan knew better than to believe this lie. How many people had the Khmer Rouge killed—one, two million? Cambodians, foreigners, everyone must have wondered until the last possible moment how it could have been possible. Hope was absurdly enduring. It was the last vestige of a world in which any rules, any order might possibly exist. At that moment when the hoe falls or the bullet enters a person's head, the realization comes all at once.

"No, Jonathon, we'll be fine." Morgan knew that he needed Jonathon to finish this unknown journey, to follow Sophal's trail. As the darkness seeped into his bones, he began to realize that maybe this search for Sophal was finally providing him with the ultimate clue of where he had gone. Perhaps Sophal was dead and this search was Morgan's journey into the death he had unfairly eluded by his act of betrayal five years earlier. Perhaps this unbearable darkness was truth itself.

Morgan realized that this was just how he had imagined the kids from the unit being marched in his nightmares, a string of angry soldiers around them, toward a death that would leave no trace, that would never appear on a Red Cross list.

Think, Morgan, think. The path to that truth is through the unexpected. Where are they taking us? Why? Why didn't they just escort us out the way we came, finish the show? Why didn't they just shoot us in our cots or thirty seconds into the forest? Think. The ghosts, the voices of Morgan's past, attacked him like a swarm of hungry mosquitoes. They sucked the blood of this rational, disciplined self. Were there answers? Perhaps that was the only world in which he could exist. Perhaps Rithy's wife had been correct.

And as Morgan and Jonathon drifted into their own worlds, fatigued by the long difficult march, uncertain of their fate, each struggling to find something to pull them out of depths of despair, they saw the first light of the rising sun transform the world around them from black to maroon to orange. And they saw the hill toward which they were marching. They had survived the night. But as light and proximity revealed this new world around them, they found themselves being marched into a Khmer Rouge military camp.

Soldiers with grenades strapped to their waists cleaned the insides of their motley collection of guns, women sat sharpening the ends of long bamboo sticks. It was the sight of the large hut filled to the brim with white bags of rice, the letters "WFP" clearly visible upon them, that finally erased the distant memory of goodness that had sustained Jonathon through the night. It was so clear. The children, the garden, the infirmary, all a ruse, a terrible, terrifying lie. He had come to the border because he believed, and now he realized that he had fed the murderers, the executioners. Jonathon felt the soil of his soul overturning. His breath seemed to leave him as the soldiers threw Jonathon and Morgan to the ground.

38

Stay focused, Morgan commanded himself. You are closer than ever. Concentrate. Think. He felt his legs quivering. He could almost feel the intense glare of the Khmer Rouge soldiers surrounding him. What was his strategy—to vanish like the others? Morgan was not ready for the ghosts to take him so long as he held to a scintilla of hope. He lifted his head from the ground and wriggled onto his knees.

Morgan could not compute the vision before him as he looked up. His eyes widened uncontrollably. His body tilted backward. The eyes? A child's look of uncomprehending wonder came across Morgan's face.

"Phim?" Morgan's words were a barely audible, disbelieving whisper.

The face stared at him coldly.

"Phim?" he asked again as if everything unknown in the world could be condensed into a single word.

The glasslike eyes continued their stare.

"Phim? Is that you?" The realization set in. The fierce eyes, the dark pajamas, the red scarf. The unclear became clear—painfully, horribly clear.

"You make me sick." The loathing words slithered from the Khmer Rouge commander's mouth. "Bong Krih, Brother Christ, who the fuck do you think you are?"

"But you, the others, the unit . . ." Morgan realized he was blabbering uncontrollably. He had nowhere to file these eyes, these words, this face.

"You think you can just sneak into our country, into our home?"

"But I was . . ." Morgan cut himself off again. Coming for you?

"Did you think you were saving us? That you were doing us a favor? Rescuing us from the camps in Phnom Penh? What the fuck did you think we were doing there? Because you dropped bombs on our homes, because you killed our parents—and then you come and act like you're our savior, like you're helping us, like you're giving us a future. Brother Christ, your great sacrifice, leaving us to die when you go home to your own world. Saving us? Saving us while making us slaves in our own home, beggars clinging to your legs! You should have saved us from you! And now you come slinking back, acting like you're doing us a favor with your few bags of rice, sneaking into our country, like a microbe spreading disease. But the *Angkaa* has eyes like a pineapple, the *Angkaa* knows that the Cambodian people don't need Brother Christ, the Cambodian people need themselves. You come as if this country wants you, as if we ever wanted you. Looking for M-21? Do you want to see M-21?"

Jonathon had tried to keep his eyes closed as his head rested on the ground. Perhaps if he closed them hard enough, he thought, it would all become a nightmare. He would awake in his own bed. He opened his eyes and saw Morgan's incredulity, the ferocity of the young Khmer Rouge commander waving his gun and whispering to Morgan in what seemed surely the icy tones of death.

Jonathon felt a chill emanating from deep inside of him. Everything he had held sacred was slowly becoming infused with this cold, vast empti- ness, with the loneliness of histories coming to an end. Fear pulled through his body. He couldn't breathe.

"M-21? Do you want to see M-21?" Phim pulled the pistol from behind his green, canvas belt and swung around to face Jonathon.

Peering into the barrel of the gun, Jonathon felt the last dam breaking within him. His stomach constricted, cutting off his intake of oxygen. His widening eyes almost overtook his blank face.

The burst of the gun reverberated through Jonathon's body. He crumpled like a fetus in the dirt.

Jonathon twitched his hand, his legs. He had not been hit. Should he lie there and play dead like Rathana? Should he sink into the earth and be away, far, far away?

"Did you think you could save us, that we wanted you to save us? Only *Angkaa* can save us!" Phim seemed to be both yelling and whispering simultaneously.

Morgan shifted his mind into focus like regaining control of a car after a wild hydroplane. Morgan had entered a world where the search for understanding overcame everything. His body straightened in focused determination.

"Can it save you like it saved Sophal, like it saved the others?" Phim hissed.

The others, the unit. Something about the way Phim said the words, about the loathing in his eyes, made Morgan finally realize that Phim had erased Morgan from his heart. This man he had once known as a boy, this man standing before him with fierce eyes, with a gun he had not hesitated to use, did not need to utter the specific words to tell Morgan everything. The Khmer Rouge had erased the cities, erased the teachers, erased the memory of Cambodia's history. It was suddenly so clear, so terribly, awfully clear. This man had erased Morgan's unit, his family, his children. Now Morgan himself would be erased.

"You killed them, didn't you?" Morgan whispered.

Morgan and Phim stared into each other's eyes with a loathing and a familiarity so deep they could only be expressed by the ultimate opposition.

Jonathon writhed up on his knees.

"Can't you understand?" Jonathon cried in a last stand of will, "I've come here to help your people."

Phim pulled the gun from the back of his belt and he slowly lifted it to face Jonathon once again. Jonathon's trembling head felt like a weight dragging him toward his final resting place. What difference did it make what he had intended to do? This man, the night, the moon, were indifferent.

Morgan could see it happening as if in slow motion. Think, Morgan, think. Why have they brought us here? Why didn't they just kill us? Do they think we're together? Is there something they want from us? His mind was working again—processing. It was a long shot, a gamble. Morgan spoke quietly, softly, his head straight. He stared forward with an almost military bearing. Maybe he could not control the world, but perhaps he could still control himself.

"You knew me once. You know that I speak the truth. You say I am a spy. You are correct. I am the one who came here to find you. I used him to get here. Look at him. Do you think that is CIA? He's an aid worker. If you kill him the world will know. It will be in the newspapers. What will that mean for your fight against the Vietnamese? What will it mean if an aid worker disappears in the Khmer Rouge zone? I am the one you need. I am the one who can help you. If he disappears here it will be a major story. Almost no one knows that I am here. I'm the one you want, not him. I am the one who can get you what you want."

Phim's steady hand held to the pistol still pointed at Jonathon's head. O'Reilly's words were sinking in. Slowly, he shifted his Chinese-made pistol toward Morgan, then replaced it in the back of his belt. Phim paused in a moment of indecision.

"Take this one back across the border." Phim ordered three of his men. As they grabbed Jonathon's arms to lift him, Jonathon's head slumped toward the ground. They propped him on his feet and marched his body back toward the border.

Jonathon's tired legs felt his comforter wrapped around them. His weary body lurched toward a home so desperately far away, yet closer with every step.

Morgan watched Jonathon being led away.

"You want to see M-21? So you can offer me what I need?" Phim said, his anger now transformed to fierce determination. "Maybe we can make a deal."

Morgan doubted the terms would be favorable as the soldiers locked him inside the stark bamboo cell.

39

The three Thai soldiers were waiting for Jonathon at the border. There was no convoy, no spectacle, no hubbub of a hundred porters, just three lone soldiers and a green pickup truck. They shepherded Jonathon into the truck and were gone. Jonathon felt a numb relief as he sat in the cab of the speeding truck. The memory of the gunburst reverberated in his mind like an echo in a bottomless well. He was out of the hands of the Khmer Rouge. He would live.

Jonathon wanted to vomit out his experience, to cast it from his memory and regain what he had lost. But the darkness had seeped too deep to be expelled. He had ingested it and the only way to live with this darkness was to swallow it and be changed forever. Jonathon could feel this weight pressing him into his seat, pushing him deeper and deeper into himself. The distant world of refugee camps and victims, of suffering people who needed his help suddenly seemed so foreign, so alienating. Jonathon had come to the border to find his truest self and instead found an empty void more frightening than anything he had ever known.

One tiny ray of hope cast a faint, dying light in the distant reaches of his being. A flicker of an image, one chance that someday he might be whole again. Home. Away from this border, away from the sickness and the death, away from the perfidy, from the ambiguity that attacked what strove to be pure.

Was it my fault? I was used by the Khmer Rouge, used by O'Reilly, used by the CIA. Did Tim know? Had Tim set me up? And these Thai soldiers— were they part of it all, too?

Jonathon thought back to his parents' description of Auschwitz and the rings of accomplice guilt, and he was the kapo, he was the apprentice to the ultimate evil he'd intended to fight. The rice paddies, the smells, the feel of the humidity on his skin had been so exciting when he had first arrived in Thailand. They were now haunting reminders of his alienation, of being in a place where he did not belong. Jonathon sunk deeper and deeper into his seat.

The truck rounded a corner on the outskirts of Aranyaprathet and he saw Maria running from in front of his guest house. He had never before seen such an anguished look on her face.

He knew the first moment he saw her. She was part of this world too.

40

Maria's panic had begun at exactly 7:00 A.M. Ever since Jonathon had peeled her fingers from his body little more than a day before, Maria had carried out her own private vigil. He was away, apart from her in that frightening world she did not know that had changed him in ways she did not recognize.

She had sought strength in her routine—the ride to Nong Chan, her work in the infirmary office. She almost envied Neang, who could sit sharpening pencils and cutting paper by the hour. The clock was her ally. With each tick, Jonathon's return came one second closer. Hadn't he always come back exactly when he'd said he would?

Maria thought of Sister Susan and Father Pierre. She closed her eyes and prayed, but in her devotion found Jonathon. The clock ticked. Second by second, the large hand carried Maria to seven o'clock where she waited for the answers to her prayers.

The large hand crawled past eleven and reached toward twelve. She tried to think of all the benign possibilities. Maybe they had a flat tire. Maybe an oxcart had blocked the road. Maybe, maybe, maybe. Maybe could cover five minutes. Maybe could cover ten minutes. But at fifteen minutes, the benign maybes were losing ground. The cancerous, destructive maybes were taking command. Twenty minutes. Where could he possibly be? Each second brought with it a more terrifying tale. Tick, tick, tick. Maria felt her heart pounding. She sprinted to the Mercy Relief office.

"Tim Anderson, I need Tim Anderson."

He was gone.

She ran to the convoy meeting place just as the trucks were pulling out of sight. What if Jonathon came when she was away? What if he'd already returned? She raced to his guest house but no Jonathon.

The terror worked its way through every joint of her body. She looked at her watch over and over. Her ally the clock had become her enemy. Jonathon had pulled her fingers from his body and now time was erasing their imprint. Tick, tick, tick. She ran back to the Mercy Relief office and found Suchinda.

"You have to get Tim! You have to call Tim!"

"I no understand. What the problem? What the problem, Maria?"

"You have to call Tim! Jonathon! Jonathon!" Maria was out of breath. "I don't know where he is. I don't know what happened. Please, please, call Tim."

Suchinda rushed to the Red Cross office to radio the camp. Maria was moving toward hysteria when Tim's truck pulled in front of Jonathon's house an hour later.

"He's not back yet, Maria?" Tim was clearly nervous.

"No!"

"Oh my god."

Tim's words startled Maria. She had hoped he'd have an answer.

"Maria, why don't you come back to the office. I need . . . I need to contact some people."

"Who, Tim? Who?"

"Maria, I'm sure that Jonathon's fine. I'll let you know as soon as I know anything. Please, come back to the office."

"No, no. I'm staying here."

Tim realized that he would not be able to convince her.

"Then let Suchinda stay here with you."

Tim jumped back in his truck and sped off.

Tick, tick, tick. Maria was so frighteningly alone. Tick, tick, tick. Where was he? Come to me, my Jonathon. Let me wrap myself around you. And then, as if in a dream, he pulled up in a truck with three Thai soldiers. She sensed immediately that something was wrong.

"Jonathon, Jonathon." Maria flung her body into his, rubbing her tears against his chest. Her hand groped his shoulders, his back, as if convincing herself this vision was a reality.

Maria touched Jonathon's face with her palm. He was back. She had peered over the edge of a precipice and now he was here.

"Jonathon." The tears streamed from Maria's eyes.

Jonathon instinctively folded his arms around Maria. He hugged her tight to himself. An embrace, warmth, Maria. He tightened his grip around her.

Could his instinct be wrong? he wondered. The aching inside Jonathon felt to him like evidence that in many ways he loved her. He now didn't feel sure he knew what love was. Her body was warm against his. He wanted to take her pain, her sorrow into him, to pass his pain, his exhaustion into her, to merge like their kiss and, for a moment, to lose everything and re-gain a world where hope could survive. Perhaps the humidity could again feel good on his skin.

Maria, Maria, this overpowering love. Jonathon could sink into Maria's frenzied embrace. He imagined what it would be like to stay in this world and be here forever. Maria and him, Highland Park and the Thai-Cambodian border, would become two worlds bound together by division like stones in an arch. Or could he bring her home, and with her bring everything home? He felt so little capacity to handle Maria's pain. It struck him that her love would be the incessant reminder of his failure. He felt nauseous.

"Oh Jonathon, I can't tell you how worried I was, how afraid when you weren't back this morning. Oh Jonathon."

Jonathon looked over her shoulder to see Tim standing ten feet away, a grave look on his face. Jonathon slowly pulled away from Maria as Tim approached.

"Hey, are you OK? What happened? Maria has been really scared. I've been trying to tell her that everything was OK, that you were probably just delayed."

Jonathon looked incredulously at Tim as if registering his surprise that the world had gone on despite all he had been through.

"Tim, they've got Morgan O'Reilly. I think he's CIA."

Tim's face went white.

"What?"

"I think O'Reilly's CIA. They marched us out of the camp to some kind of military headquarters. They had our rice there. It's going to the soldiers."

Tim was speechless.

"Where is the camp?" he said following a pause.

"I don't know."

"What's going to happen to O'Reilly?"

"I, I don't know."

"Oh my god," Tim said softly. "I've got to tell Conley. Stay here. You look terrible, Jonathon. I'll be back." Tim was already running.

"Oh, Jonathon." Maria locked her arms around Jonathon as if closing an unbreakable circle around him. She led him to his room, took off his clothes, and washed his dirty body with a cloth. She laid him on the bed and buried herself into him.

41

Morgan O'Reilly should have been exhausted but he was not. He should have been afraid but he was not. His mind focused as he sat motionless in his cell. The tiny bamboo hut was small, windowless, and dark. The sun beat down on the steel roof, transforming it into a sauna. He felt as if his body was cooking from the inside out.

It had been a full twenty-four hours since Morgan's confrontation with Phim. Morgan had been led to this structure on the edge of the Khmer Rouge camp and locked in with the nagging realization of all he had learned. Rithy's wife in the refugee camp had told him how her dying husband had wanted to flee the Khmer Rouge zone as soon as they'd arrived. Was Rithy being hunted?

It made so much sense. Phim had known them all. The *Angkaa* has eyes like a pineapple. The worst image of his nightmares had always been his children hunted down by the Khmer Rouge. Now he was facing something far worse—the image of one of his children hunting down the others. He felt an icicle in his spine. Phim had hunted Rithy, had hunted them all. Where could they have hidden from the eyes of the pineapple? Rithy was dead. Phim, the Phim he had once known, was dead. This Khmer Rouge killer with his fierce eyes was lost to Morgan forever.

And Sophal, where was Sophal? The obvious answer screamed through

Morgan's brain. But could brilliant, resourceful Sophal have marched straight to his death in the Khmer Rouge zone? If he had met Rithy on the border, Sophal must have known the dangers of facing Phim. But why had he wanted to come? Was someone else from their unit still alive and was Sophal coming to rescue him? Was Sophal following orders Morgan never knew about?

The Khmer Rouge military camp reeked of death. Morgan had gotten Jonathon back across the border, but his own fate seemed far from certain. They could have killed me yesterday, he thought. They could have killed me in my cot at the other camp. Morgan didn't know why he was still living, but he was. And if he was, if there were cells in which prisoners were held, perhaps Sophal was alive. Perhaps Sophal was being kept someplace, for some reason. And if that were the case and if this was where Sophal had been going, perhaps Sophal was near. Sophal's name, M-21, had pulled the snakes of truth from the basket. Once they had begun to slither out, it was no longer possible to send them back.

If it was death that faced him, so be it. But death or truth, perhaps they were one and the same, were his destination. Morgan heard the door rattling and the sound of the wooden latch being lifted. The door swung open and the powerful rays of the sun lit a pathway into the hut. Two soldiers stood at the door exhibiting a disdain bordering on disgust. They led Morgan though the camp to a wooden table where Phim was eating a small plate of rice with a tin spoon. Phim looked up. The look of hatred Morgan had expected was now replaced by cool indifference. Morgan held his gaze waiting for Phim to move.

Phim swallowed his mouthful of rice and then reached down to feed himself another. His eyes never left Morgan's.

"Morgan O'Reilly," Phim said slowly, "Brother Christ looking for old friends from Takmau. I've been expecting you. Sit down please."

Dumbfounded, Morgan sat. Phim's hatred had tortured him through the night. Now, this indifferent politeness made little sense. Phim scooped some rice onto a small plate and placed it in front of Morgan on the table. Famished, Morgan did not eat.

"Morgan O'Reilly, I hope you now are beginning to understand who controls this country, our country."

The politeness began to make sense to Morgan. Morgan had been the father when he'd recruited Phim nine years before, and Phim, the hungry desperate orphan, had been the child. Now Morgan was alone, weak, hungry. He was the child at Phim's table in Phim's camp in Phim's country.

"I hope you understand what it means to control your own destiny, to not be a beggar, to not be humiliated and brought to your knees. This is our country. Your aid cannot buy our souls. Your bombs cannot force our submission. You cannot sneak into our country acting like you are helping us. You were once so big, so powerful, Brother Christ. You asked us to sacrifice for you, for our country. It was not for our country, it was for your country. And then you left us to die."

The words pierced Morgan's heart.

"Not for me," Morgan, the child, stammered. "For"—he paused—"us."

"For us?" Phim's anger began to show. "For us? For us to betray ourselves and our people, to give away our country? For us?"

"But . . ." Morgan realized he could not argue. Phim himself was proof that us did not exist. But what had happened to the others? Had they loved him or was everything a lie? Morgan had to know definitively what had happened. "The others?"

"The others were traitors to their people."

"You killed them," Morgan said softly, staring into Phim's eyes.

"Yeung trov ter kat smour chas cheagn dambey oy smour tmey dos." We cut old grass so the new grass will grow.

There was just one more question to ask, one more question to close the door on Morgan's mission, on his life. That final question fought to stay buried inside Morgan as if the answer was too much for him to bear. Morgan's need to ask clashed with his instinct not to know.

"But this is all the past," Morgan heard Phim stating. "What concerns me now is the future liberation of our country, the creation of a pure, free Cambodian homeland. You, O'Reilly, have what we need, and we have what you need. You have been sent to trade and trade you will. There will be no tricks this time."

No tricks? Trade? Morgan did not have the slightest idea what Phim was talking about, but sensed that this was the key to Sophal's mission. His guess the day before had been correct. Phim's words triggered, almost instinctively, the response that had been drilled into him in his CIA training sessions. When faced with the unknown you should know, act like you do know. Act like you do know, think Morgan, concentrate, focus.

"How can I be sure you have what we want?" Morgan asked.

"Because I will show it to you."

Morgan lifted his eyes as if waiting for an invitation.

"No, not this time," Phim answered. "This, for the second and last time, is the list of what we need. You will stay here until we get it."

Phim pulled a piece of paper from his pocket and handed it to Morgan. Morgan read the detailed list. It was the perfect arsenal for a small, highly mobile guerilla army—one hundred stinger antiaircraft missiles, three hundred antitank mines, an assortment of high-tech weapons and small portable explosives. The list was hardly surprising.

"I'll need to cross back to make the arrangements."

"As I said," Phim repeated, "you will stay here until these materials arrive. We will follow the same protocol."

The same protocol? What did he mean? Morgan was not about to lose this chance by revealing his ignorance.

"You will write out your request and the Thais will deliver it to your associate—Mr. Conley, I believe." Phim seemed to bask in the quality of his intelligence and his close relationship with the Thais. "You have one hour to write your message, and we will take care of getting it to Conley."

So they knew Conley. If they knew the identity of the Agency's secret rep in Aran then they knew everything. They had the Thais delivering messages for them, spying on our operations in Aran. There was still only one remaining question to ask. But was Sophal what they had to trade? Phim seemed to suggest that Sophal had come to get what they already had. Was it a hundred stinger missiles for Sophal's life? For Morgan's life? Could he ask? He needed to know, but it was too early to show his cards.

"OK," Morgan said, pulling himself together. "Now I need to make sure you have what you say."

"Mit," Phim ordered at a soldier standing nearby. "Take him to M-21."

Morgan stood before the soldier had reached him. The soldier led him away. Morgan's feet could not move him fast enough across the parched earth. He needed to stay calm, in control. He walked patiently behind the soldier. They approached a prison hut much like his but on the opposite side of the encampment. Morgan's heart pounded with expectation, with his last remaining hope, as the soldier lifted the latch and ushered Morgan through the door. The light caught hold of a foot. Morgan traced it up a leg as light gradually illuminated the room.

As the shadows transformed into a figure, Morgan saw not the powerful leg of a man, but the thin, long, smooth leg of a woman, not Sophal's broad shoulders, but delicate, thin shoulders. The light slowly revealed the woman's wild, disheveled hair, the dirt caked on her body, the bruise on the side of her face.

Morgan stood facing her with two overpowering emotions. The first was the intense pain that this was not Sophal. The second the shocking realization that dirt and all, she was the most beautiful woman he had ever seen.

42

Five quick knocks on Jonathon's door woke him from his deep sleep. Maria got up from the bed where she had been standing guard over Jonathon. She straightened her wrinkled shirt before opening the door. Tim Anderson and Kevin Conley rushed in. Tim's face was ashen.

"Jonathon, are you OK?"

Jonathon tried to shake the heaviness from his head.

"Jonathon, I know you've been through a lot, but I want you to hear what Kevin has to say."

"Hey Jonathon, how ya doin'?" Conley didn't wait for Jonathon's response. "Jonathon, what happened?"

The thoughts surfaced from Jonathon's dreamless sleep like floating wreckage from a sinking ship.

"Morgan asked for something, there, with Piseth. That night they came and took us by gunpoint. They marched us out into the jungle. I thought they would kill us."

"And then?"

"They took us to a Khmer Rouge military camp." Jonathon spoke as if recounting the travels of another person. "The rice, our rice, was there. There were thousands of bags, our white WFP bags." The thought that he had helped the Khmer Rouge army added to Jonathon's nausea.

"And Morgan?" Conley asked.

"They said Morgan is CIA. They're keeping him."

"Jonathon, I know you've been through a lot. I know that these events have been traumatic ones for you. Tim's told me how much you've done in the camps," Conley said.

The praise seemed ultimately hollow to Jonathon.

"We've all done good work on the border," Conley continued. "Things have gotten better. You've learned a lot on this last trip, a lot of things that maybe you never needed to know. But now you do know them, and because of that you have a great responsibility." Conley paused to let his words sink in.

"All the aid to the border, it's not coming from nowhere. People are giving it, people from all around the world who have seen the pictures are now learning about what's going on here, and it's making a difference. Morgan was working for people who are trying to help Cambodia, to get the rice through to the Cambodians by doing what it takes. Do you understand?" Again, Conley did not wait for an answer.

"Jonathon, think of what it would do if more people learned what you know. All the money that people are giving, that countries are giving, what would happen to that if everyone found out? Sure, maybe strange things are happening on the border, but look around you, Jonathon, you've seen it. This is not a normal place. It's a strange place with its own rules. The people on the outside don't understand that. They don't know what it takes to feed people here. And if they find out what you know, who is it going to hurt? It's going to hurt the people in the camps, the children, the civilians. Sure, it'll hurt the others, but they'll all be thrown in together. They'll all suffer if the well dries up. The soldiers will always eat, but the others will certainly starve again if there's no food. Jonathon, we have contacts with the Khmer Rouge through the Thais," Conley lied. General Prem had been little help and Morgan, for all he knew, was no longer living. "We have guarantees of Morgan's safety. What we need from you is your promise not to share what you know, not to put the whole border relief operation at risk, as tempting as it might feel to do so."

It wasn't, in fact, tempting to Jonathon. He hadn't processed that far ahead. The burden of what he had seen and the chaos that had destroyed the order within him were too powerful for such long-term thinking. After all this, the CIA was telling him to shut up, to help the refugees by recognizing how rotten everything was, how deeply, inexorably rotten. After everything, this would be his contribution—silence to protect an immoral system from the alternative that was worse. Jonathon's memory of the purity of his intentions felt like a cruel joke. And Tim, with his ashen face, was he part of it too? It didn't matter.

The image popped into Jonathon's mind of standing with his parents by the stream on *Rosh Hashanah* emptying their pockets to seek atonement for their sins. He had then been so disdainful, as if atonement accepted failure and imperfection while a life of goodness was simply a matter of choice.

Jonathon felt the hollow space within him where that naïve vision of truth had once resided. All that was left was this nausea of deep imperfection. He had come to the end of the road. To stay was to become stultified in his failure. Going home, emptying his pockets, starting over, *Taschlich* was his last remaining hope.

43

"Som tos . . . neah srey." Morgan's Cambodian seemed to fail him as he stammered to find words with which to address her.

"You can speak English." The woman's voice cracked from disuse but still maintained a certain strength.

Morgan's mind could not process fast enough. *"Som toh, neah srey . . ."* English?

"I not speak Cambodian," she said.

Morgan's lips moved as if to speak, but his mind still was not telling him which language he should try. She looked Cambodian. Was she Thai?

"I'm . . . I'm looking . . . for Sophal."

An almost eager, hopeful look seemed to come across the woman's face.

"Thomas send you?" The question ascended from the woman like hope.

"Thomas?"

She anticipated his confusion and repeated her question.

"Thomas Dillon, Thomas Dillon send you?" The hope floated like helium.

"But?"

"Thomas Dillon send you for me?"

"For . . . for you?" Who was this woman? How did she know Dillon? "But . . ." But she was not Sophal. "Who . . . who are you? Where . . . is Sophal?" Morgan was at the end of all strategy. The void in his knowledge was now too great for pretense. Morgan's ignorance chipped away at the woman's hope.

"Thomas send you?" She pleaded desperately for an answer.

"Yes," Morgan whispered. It suddenly occurred to him. Dillon had sent him, but for what? "I . . . I don't understand. I'm sorry. I'm here for Sophal," Morgan stammered.

The woman looked at him incredulously. "You really not understand?"

"No."

"But Thomas send you, yes?"

"He . . . he . . . how did you know that?" Who was this woman asking for his secrets? Somehow he trusted her. Somehow he sensed that she, like he, was searching for something she desperately needed to find, something separated from her by impenetrable boundaries. "Yes, Thomas sent me. He sent me for Sophal. Please tell me," he pleaded. "Who are you?"

"You not understand, do you?"

Morgan shook his head. "No. Please, please tell me."

Morgan trembled as he sat on the wooden plank beside her. He had come so far, he had risked everything for whatever it was he was about to learn. This woman, somehow he knew, was his destination. And the truth shall set you free. Morgan remembered the inscription at the CIA headquarters in Langley.

"My name is Tanh Li Ai Hoa. You know that?"

"No." So she was Vietnamese.

"Thomas tell you about me?" The hope again returned to her question.

"No. I'm sorry."

A sad look crossed the woman's face. She continued. "Thomas and I loved each other. Maybe still love each other. We live together two years in Saigon." The memory seemed to carry happiness. "In 1973, Thomas go back to Washington. He had work there, and I not want to stop him. I knew in my heart our love will pull him back, that he come back because he know what we shared." A tear formed in the corner of her eye. "I knew he come back, but I not want to force him. I know in my heart and proof of our love growing in my body. But I not tell Thomas. His love bring him back, not his baby, not his obligation."

Morgan dared not ask what happened to the child he didn't see. He knew he had to press forward, that the story had to be told, that his path had somehow merged with the path of this unknown woman. He nodded for her to continue.

"I waited. And then communists take control and I know he not come back." The tears rolled slowly from her eyes. She wiped them with a determination to keep going. "Four years I hide our baby. I wrap him in cloth and never let him outside. I keep him covered in dirt so they not find him, so they not take him away from me, so we have hope of being together again." She sniffled. "I didn't know what happened Thomas, but I have small radio and listen secret to VOA just to hear noises from his world. And one year ago, I hear his name. I hear him speak. It was Thomas, my Thomas. Interviewing him. They say he is deputy national security advisor. I know I have to be with him, that we must to be with him."

Morgan nodded his understanding.

"How I get to him? Then Vietnam army invade Cambodia and some refugees from Vietnam walk through Cambodia to Thai border, to freedom. And I know that I, that we, must go. It was our only chance. Thomas, Jr.—I call him in my heart—I know I have to get him away. If they find out he half American, we both in terrible danger. We sneak out of Saigon and ride with farmer to Tay Ninh province. We find three other people, Vietnamese people who want to take the same chance, and we start walking. Walking and walking. The jungle so dark. We had to hide. Many bodies of people killed, stepped on mines or eaten by animals. We walk and walk. We keep going, following setting sun, hoping that if we walk only far enough we walk to new life."

"And the boy?"

"It was very difficult. But what choice did we have? If we stay, it horrible. We walk and walk. The people we passed didn't know who we were because so many people coming and going after invasion. So many people returning from where Khmer Rouge put them, crossing the country, heading like us to homes they dreamed. Every day we walk, we hoped we getting closer."

"And then?"

"Then we come to . . . them." The hatred seethed out of the last word.

"The Khmer Rouge?"

"Yes. *'Yuan, yuan,'* they yell. They pull us by our hair. I held my boy with all my might. They drag us down and wait for commander to arrive. I no understand what he say. Commander took pistol from behind his belt and shoot one Vietnamese in head. Another soldier smashed one Vietnamese man's head to pieces with back of his gun. They pull plastic bag over head of another. I watch him suffocate. I tremble with fear. We were the only ones left. They pull bag from other man's head and approached me. I think they put the bag on my head, but they grab my son. I hold with all my might, with everything. I trembling but I know I have to save him. 'Please sir, please,' I say in English. The man with the pistol turn. I realize he understand. 'Please sir. Look at boy, look.' I rub dirt from crying boy's face. 'Look sir, look! This American boy. His father deputy national security advisor to president of the United States. Please sir, believe me.'

"The man pull his pistol from the back of his belt and point it at me. 'What is name of deputy national security advisor of the United States?' he ask in English. I almost die from fear. But the boy, Thomas, Jr., give me strength. 'It's Th . . . Th . . . ' The words not come out. 'Th . . . Th . . . Thomas . . . Thomas Dillon, sir.' He stare at me then say something to soldiers in Cambodian. They put bag away and pull me to my feet. They lead me here, to this camp. They lock us in this cell." The tears were now streaming down her cheeks.

"And?" Morgan asked eagerly.

"They question me five days. They take my son then give him back, they feed me nothing then bring rice. They want to know everything, everything about Thomas, about me, about our son. I speak to save us all."

"And?"

"The camp leader, the man with pistol, seemed to mock me. 'So you think he love you? You think your son is his? You think he want you? You whore! You beggar! We'll see what he will do for you.' "

"What did he do?"

"I only find out later. And . . . So . . ." She watched his response and lowered her voice. "Sophal came."

The intersection. Morgan felt his entire identity welling up in a single breath. He had crossed every border he knew, traveled to the dark core of the Khmer Rouge zone to find this point. Morgan felt, for a moment, paralyzed. He exhaled with a newfound determination to push forward.

"Sophal tell me that they want guns."

"I don't understand. How did Sophal get here?"

"The man with the pistol make me write letter."

"A letter?"

"To . . ."—her voice cracked—"to Thomas."

"What did you say?"

"That they have me, that they have his s . . ." The tears streaked from her eyes. "That they have Thomas, Jr., that they going to kill us both unless he get them what they want."

"And what happened?"

"I didn't know how they would get the letter to Thomas, but Sophal tell me they sent it through Thais."

"And, and?" Morgan was impatient to learn everything.

"We wait and wait. He say he kill us in thirty days. Every day Khmer Rouge commander shout the same joke into my hut. 'He save you yet today?' There not enough food. I gave everything I had to Thomas, Jr. But he become sick. He had dysentery that not stop. No medicine, no water." She was now sobbing uncontrollably. "I would have given my blood to save him, everything."

Morgan desperately needed her to go on. "I'm sorry. I'm so sorry."

She began to fight back the tears pouring from her eyes.

"But I still have one hope which keep me going despite everything. And they open the door, just like with you, and Cambodian in torn clothes come in. I thought this the end. My time run out."

"Sophal?" Here it was, this ultimate destination.

"Yes. He so confident. He smile. He tell me Thomas send him for me, for baby, and I know I need to live, to get to my new home."

"And what happened?"

"Sophal tell Khmer Rouge commander that guns ready, that they pass them to Thais to deliver as soon as I across border into Thailand."

"And?"

"Khmer Rouge commander say no. He hate Sophal. He say we wait until guns arrive. He make Sophal send letter to get guns first. Sophal write it, but I no think he ever mean to do it. He hate Khmer Rouge so much. He tell me what happened to his country."

"And, and? What happened?" Morgan was pulling the rope of her words closer and closer to him. Was it a noose or could he grab it to pull him back into his life?

"We wait for guns to arrive. And then, one night, in middle of the night, I hear the latch on my door lifting. I so afraid. I don't dare move. 'Hoa, Hoa,' he whisper, 'come with me, come. We get out of here.' Get out of here, to Thomas. He take my hand and I follow Sophal. We walk as fast as we can through dark jungle. It so thick we can barely move, but we keep going. I cut my arm, I bleeding. But we keep going and going. We hear gunshots in air. We know Khmer Rouge find us missing. The gunshots get closer. We try to run but it too difficult. The jungle so thick. They move through jungle like snakes. Closer and closer. We get almost to Thai border, but they moving faster than we are. The sun rising and they can see us. The bullets fly past our heads into trees. They surround us. No place to run, nowhere to go. Khmer Rouge closing in." She was now in a frenzy. "And they tie our hands behind our backs and pull us back to the camp."

"What happened? What happened Hoa?"

"I don't know."

"What do you mean?"

"They hit me in head and throw me back here."

"And Sophal, Sophal?"

"I saw Khmer Rouge commander and two others march him into the forest."

Morgan felt the last particle of hope departing from him. Hoa continued.

"I never see Sophal again. And there was screaming, terrible screaming I not understand when Khmer Rouge commander come back to camp. I think one of soldiers not come back."

The two sat crying on the wooden platform. He because she had finally delivered him to the prison from which he could never escape. She because Thomas had sent for her, because this wounded, exhausted, crying man was the only hope she had.

44

Evan Pritchard could hardly wait to reap the rewards of his gamble. There was a story out there, a major story, and he had to be ready to receive it. There would be no time to check the facts afterward. Afterward he would be in too great of a rush to reveal what he had learned, whatever it would be. He had to anticipate the contingencies, to gather all the clues, to prepare himself for the greatest clue of all, the keystone. He knew that Jonathon was taking periodic trips into the Khmer Rouge zone. He saw the red clay on the bottom of Jonathon's shoes. He watched the changes in Jonathon's behavior.

But now, something much bigger had happened to the young American. He had returned with the same clay on his shoes, but was now haggard and destroyed.

How had it happened to this young, idealistic American, this future of the world now sunk to his knees? Evan had seen the dead eyes before. He knew them. And because he knew them he knew he could record them. He could translate them into words. He could link them with whatever it was he had traded for. He had to be diligent, to gather his clues, to pile them one atop the other until he had built a scaffolding for whatever was to come.

Had he done this to Jonathon? No, he was a watcher, a recorder, a transmitter of information. Evan was not a spy, but a spy and a journalist both were dispassionate collectors of knowledge. I am not a spy, Evan thought to himself. A spy transforms information to action. I watch, I listen, I record.

And Evan was ready, ready for O'Reilly to return, ready for the story that would justify his career. And it was close. He could feel it was close.

45

From the moment he stepped from the truck Maria had sensed something enormous had happened. Jonathon's enthusiasm had given way to exhaustion. His light seemed to have dimmed. He seemed so heavy, almost grieving. She hugged him tighter and tighter. This was when he needed her to understand him, to forgive him, to make him whole again just like Sister Susan had done to her. She knew as she took his wounded body into hers that they would always be connected.

Jonathon and Maria walked out to their noodle shop. Maria's hand rested on his shoulder.

"Maria," he said in a soft, sorrowful voice. "I'm so sorry." Maria had once uttered the same words to Sister Susan. Whatever it was, she understood, she forgave.

"Maria, I'm sorry, you're so . . . special . . . to me, but . . . so much has happened . . . so much has changed." Jonathon felt a momentary panic. Was he making a mistake?

Maria's eyes pled desperate confusion.

Jonathon felt so little left to give.

"No, Maria. I'm so sorry. What I mean . . . I have to go, to leave, to not come back."

She understood. He had seen something. He had to go, they had to go, to a new place where they could be together, where they could make each other whole.

"OK Jonathon, OK. I'll go with you."

Jonathon looked down wishing he could cry.

Could he go without her? It seemed unthinkable to Maria. All of the fear she had felt, all of the terror she had ever known was insignificant compared with the paralyzing bolt traversing her body. She felt as if a part of her body was seceding from the rest. Maria did not understand, she could not understand.

"What?" The word slipped from her mouth uncontrollably. She felt a vast gulf opening within her. It was enormous, endless, dark. "You can't go," the words a primordial defense powered by her survival instinct. "You can't leave." Maria felt as if someone else were talking.

And then her voice returned to her.

"You can't," she said firmly.

The intensity of Maria's words frightened Jonathon. He looked at Maria then looked down at his noodles.

46

"I hope you see, Brother Christ," Phim said with a sly smile, "that we have what we say we have. The National Army of Democratic Kampuchea keeps its commitments. Sophal thought he would cheat us, that he would steal from us, would break our deal. He learned his lesson. I hope you will not make the same mistake. Maybe we should have just killed them both, but, you see, we need what you have almost as much as you seem to need what we have. We have been very patient, but our patience is running out. If you want her to live, you will now complete your instructions to Conley. Don't act surprised at what we know. We have many friends."

Prem. The fucking Thais are telling them everything, Morgan thought to himself.

"Here is your paper and here is your pen. Here is our list." Phim removed it once again from his pocket. "You will now write."

Morgan was still reeling from the shock of all he had learned from Hoa. Should he write? Should he refuse? He had but an instant to decide and so much clouding his mind. If I don't write, what happens? They kill me. They kill her. Sophal is dead. End of the story. If I write, at least I have time to think. The arguments did not seem clear, but Morgan realized he had little choice. He wrote out the letter to Conley, following to the letter Phim's instructions as to where the weapons should be delivered.

"It's going to take some time to get these here," Morgan said to Phim.

"We have been waiting long enough, and now they have two strong reasons to hurry. You are not our prisoner here, but our guest. Sophal did not understand that. Because of what he did, you will remain in your present quarters until the weapons arrive." With a slight flick of his head, he motioned to the soldiers who escorted Morgan back to his cell and locked the latch on the outside of the door.

For the first time since leaving Hoa, Morgan was alone. The weight of all he had learned closed in on him like darkness. He pictured Sophal the boy living on the street, the brilliant spy in Phnom Penh, the frightened refugee, the green CIA recruit, the cocky field officer, the cowboy, the believer, the friend. Sophal, his friend, his son, his believer in a world of despair, gone, lost, murdered.

Perhaps somehow, somewhere in his subconscious he had known that Sophal was dead the moment Dillon had come to his house six months earlier, and had merely been frantically running away from that realization since then. But here, in this smoldering, dank cell in the heart of the Khmer Rouge zone, the inescapable, terrible truth cornered Morgan.

Morgan felt the blood draining from his face, his heart stultifying. Tears streamed from his eyes.

Hoa entered Morgan's mind. This dignified, courageous woman was not what he had expected he might find at the end of his journey. She had lost almost everything and still risked, still fought for life, for a future, for love. It was love for a man who had left her but not forgotten her, who had sent for her. The marine in Morgan almost appreciated Dillon's obscene act. But despite Morgan's shock, despite the chaos of his mind, he could feel the anger growing.

Yes, Dillon had sent for her and for his son, but whom had he sent? Couldn't he have risked his own life, his own career? But Dillon was the master chess player and little people like Sophal, like Morgan, were his pawns to be moved toward victory and sacrificed when necessary. Dillon sent Sophal on a personal errand to the deadly Khmer Rouge zone.

An image came back to Morgan. It was Phnom Penh in April 1975 and

Morgan was standing in Colonel Bauer's office, the anger rising to his head like flame, the colonel was telling Morgan that the unit could not be saved, that they all had to be sacrificed, and Morgan was dying inside, slowly dying. The kids were expendable pawns in a chess game controlled by bigger pieces.

And now again, the little people were so expendable. Sophal was used, sacrificed, killed, for what? To get Hoa and Dillon's son? To arm the Khmer Rouge against US policy? The anger and the betrayal consumed Morgan. Had Dillon known everything? He must have. Dillon must have known that sending Sophal was an abuse of his authority. He knew that he was using Sophal, using Morgan. He probably knew even that Sophal was dead. Morgan could feel an uncontrollable anger welling within him. The bastard! The fucking bastard, Morgan thought. Dillon knew that Sophal's mission had gone wrong, and I was sent to do his coward's work, to carry out Sophal's mission or, if that failed, to leave no trace behind, to vanish.

Morgan's head felt swollen.

But why? Why was Dillon so sure that everyone would do just what he wanted them to do? Morgan's mind replayed the words over and over. "I've read your file, Morgan"—of course, of course, the personnel file. Dillon knew everything. The tests, the routine interviews, the sessions with the therapist to whom he'd been sent when he'd returned from the war, everything was in the file. Dillon the chess master had read it all. Marines get their people out, he had said. Dillon was pulling the levers on Morgan the puppet. Morgan realized that Dillon knew that if he got here he would get her out, that he couldn't leave other innocent people behind. But how could Dillon have been so sure that I wouldn't turn on him? Morgan wondered. How had he known?

The words of Dillon's last cable drifted into Morgan's mind. "Contact again at end of mission. Will arrange personally and immediately all visas then." The realization hit Morgan. He was being blackmailed. Rithy's wife and child—Sophal had promised he would get them out. Morgan thought of Nat and Phally sitting helplessly alone in the refugee camp. Sophal must have sent the same cable back to Dillon, and Dillon knew and hadn't said anything. Dillon knew that if I were to get Hoa and his son out he would control whether Nat and Phally came with her to America, Morgan now understood, and that I would do everything I could to help them.

Tears welled in Morgan's eyes. The discipline that had sustained his existence in these past years had delivered him to the hands of his puppeteer, the chess master Dillon.

"Fuck him!" Morgan's anger cried through his tears. I'll leave the goddamn girl. I'll give them their fucking arms. I'm gonna get back there and I'm going to kill that son of a bitch, he thought. The anger was grabbing hold of him, transporting him toward a world he had never seen, a world in which all control was gone and pure unbridled emotion took hold. Morgan sobbed uncontrollably, as if everything he had kept inside for so many years was gushing out. Deep gasps for air rocked his torso. This was what it meant to truly feel. It was terrifying.

From somewhere within him, Morgan received a message he already knew subconsciously. No matter what he was feeling—no matter how angry, alone, powerless, and empty—he could not abandon Hoa. He had no choice. He could not reject his one remaining chance; he had to give himself a last chance. And this misdirected, desperate, hopeful, isolated, imprisoned woman who was dead without him, what had she done to deserve her fate? She had loved, she had believed. It struck Morgan that he and Hoa were in some ways in the same position. They had each believed with all their hearts in something false. Phim had shown Morgan how false it all had been. Hoa still believed.

Morgan had no idea what Hoa would find if she made it to America. Perhaps only death would allow Hoa's dream to live on. Maybe, Morgan wondered, his one mistake was to have gone to the French embassy in Phnom Penh in 1975, to have lived. But despite everything, something told Morgan that though Hoa's dreams might die, he could not be their executioner.

Morgan had followed Sophal to this corner of the earth, but he had also followed the only part of himself in which he could believe. To hang on to the slightest glimmer of that hope, he knew he would have to take a piece of Sophal with him. Sophal had known what he was being sent to do. And he had done it like the cowboy he was. After everything, he had still tried to pick Phim's pocket. Morgan could not betray that memory. Morgan knew that his only hope of ever living again was to do the same.

Morgan took a deep breath, filling his lungs with the humid air. He gathered the shards of his mind and began piecing them together. Sophal was dead. The kids from the unit were dead. And Hoa was Morgan's last chance to become Sophal, to remember that somewhere deep inside his blackened heart was someone who never left the innocent behind, someone who, underneath all he had become, still longed to believe. Morgan the puppet pulled himself up by his own strings and handed them back to the puppeteer. He would do what Dillon had known he would do. He would get this beautiful woman out. He would get Nat and Phally out, and maybe he would live. His analytical mind kicked into gear.

How many days would it take to get the guns, Morgan thought to himself. If they're passing the letter to the Thais, that would take at least five hours. They'll give it to Conley and he'll send it on to Bangkok. That would be a day. To get the weapons from Okinawa, to fly them over, that would take three more. From there to the Khmer Rouge at least two. He had a week to somehow get out, to get her out, to stop the weapons from arriving. But the horror of it all, the betrayal.

Focus, Morgan, focus. The key to everything is getting out, is getting her out.

As quietly as he could, Morgan pressed at the walls of his cell looking for a loose board. Land mines and booby traps, he knew, filled the jungle all the way to the border. He searched the darkness for his only hope for salvation.

47

"You can work in the office, Jonathon, let things settle down, see how you feel," Tim said.

A part of Jonathon was not ready to admit defeat. He decided to accept Tim's offer. It was the same offer, Jonathon recognized, that Tim had made to the British woman on Jonathon's first day in Aran.

As Jonathon watched the convoy pull out for the camps and returned with Suchinda to the Mercy Relief office, he knew that even this gesture had been a terrible mistake. What am I doing? he asked himself, trying to focus his mind on adding the distribution quotas. It was all numbers. Was he so unable to face the complexities of life that he had become an accountant of abstractions?

By eleven, he was certain that he had no choice but to go back to the world where he could start over, where every moment was not another painful reminder of his failure, where he could empty his pockets into the river of atonement and renewal. He had begun translating this realization into concrete plans to go when Maria arrived with Tim. She came running into the office. Jonathon felt both comforted and disturbed by seeing her.

"Jonathon, I couldn't be away. I, I had Tim bring me back. Please, I need to talk with you." She led him back to her house.

"Jonathon, I've been thinking. I understand. You have to go. I know. Go. Go to Chicago. I'll stay here. I'll work in the camp. I've saved up my money. I just want to visit you."

Jonathon could see the image of Chicago reflecting in her eyes. He almost saw her walking with his parents, carrying their prayer books to the river. He almost pictured her in his other life, almost pictured her as part of his other world. He had come so far, experienced so much with her that these almosts almost challenged the instinctual imperative he was feeling to flee. They almost did, even as he increasingly realized that ultimately they did not.

A visit. It seemed so humble a request after all that had happened. He could go home, go away . . . and see. Jonathon stared at Maria, this woman who loved him so religiously. She was weaving him back into her life thread by thread. Each stitch would turn for another until the bonds became tighter and tighter, binding him into this life he so desperately needed to flee. He could bring her home, and with her, the germ of whatever he had seen in the heart of the Cambodian jungle.

Jonathon felt as if balanced atop the apex of a steep mountain with no path leading down. He had to choose the direction in which he would fall. On one side there was Maria, this life. On the other, home, the flowing river, starting over. It was a full retreat, a declaration of failure. He felt he had no other choice.

Jonathon's body stiffened.

"Please, Jonathon, please!"

Maria sunk to the bed and crossed her arms covering her face.

"You are taking ev . . . everything," she cried. "What, what do I have left?"

The words stabbed Jonathon. He wanted to vanish. He looked down at Maria. Words that had once dissolved into the silence of beauty and sense came to Jonathon, meaningless lawyer's words.

"Maria, don't you see? It's not you. It's me. Something happened."

There must be something to say, something to help her understand that

he had no choice. Jonathon stammered on. "What we have is so special."
Jonathon felt his words betraying him, felt himself with them betraying her.

Maria lifted her head from the bed and the first glimmering of hope
diffused through her tears.

"It is, Jonathon. It is. Don't you see it? Don't you have faith in it?"

Jonathon imagined himself holding Maria by a stick over the precipice.
He was slowly being pulled over with her. He could hold on only to go
down with her. He could save her for a moment by sacrificing himself, only
to tumble down with her once the dream was destroyed by the realities in
his heart. And then what? He who had walked with her, who had kissed
her, who had held her. He was responsible for her and all he could do was
to let her fall and hope that she would find another branch to grab as she
fell. He let go. A piece of him tumbled with her. The rest lurched in the
opposite direction toward what he now fully realized was his only hope.

48

Morgan waited for even the faintest sounds of human activity to die down before moving. For two days he had silently and methodically rubbed a small rock against a weak point on the back wall of his cell. He had felt it almost give way that afternoon and knew that the longer he waited the greater the chance he would be found out. He paused for a moment as he placed his hand on the weakened board. The image of Sophal the cowboy flashed across Morgan's mind. It seemed to guide his hand as he pushed gently. He felt the opening exposed to the night air.

Morgan slithered through snakelike, inch by inch, until he was out. He leaned the half piece of wooden plank against the back of the cell. He had developed a good enough idea of the layout of the camp to know that the path straight across would be filled with sleeping soldiers. One move, one soldier up for a drink, to relieve himself, and that would be the end of the story.

Should he trace an arc around the camp through the jungle? The idea was appealing, but Morgan guessed that the Khmer Rouge soldiers would only have been sleeping if they had booby trapped the perimeter. How deep into the jungle had the traps been set? Morgan would have to take his chances. He skirted the outside of the camp following the first line of trees. He lifted each foot slowly and deliberately, trying to match his movements to gusts of wind. Breathe evenly, calmly, he told himself. Morgan's heart was pounding. The Thai border was far. There were so many mines, so many soldiers. Focus on each step. One, two, three. Each step taking him closer.

It took him almost an hour, he estimated, to get to the other side of the camp. Though the huts all looked similar, he knew exactly where he was going. He crept ever so slowly, quietly, around the corner of the hut and lifted himself to a crouched position. Placing his hand on the outer latch, praying it would not squeak, he lifted it with a touch so gentle it almost felt as if the wood was not moving at all and slowly pulled the door open. Which way was her head pointing? If he guessed wrong, if she yelled, if she moved, that could be it. He held his hands over her body, following the faint sound of her breath, tracking it first with his ears and then with his hands. With a quick and gentle movement he fastened his hand on her mouth and held. Her body jumped and squirmed. He stuck his mouth almost into her ear.

"Hoa, Hoa, it's me, O'Reilly, Morgan. Don't move, stop moving," he whispered. Her squirming stopped, her body released, her head rested in the care of his strong hands. "Hoa, don't say anything. Don't speak. I'm going to remove my hand. Do you understand?"

He felt her head nodding and he pulled his hand away. He took her hand and led her to the ground.

"Crawl on your stomach. Hold on to my feet and follow me," he whispered.

He crawled on his stomach out the door feeling her hand on his heels as they moved into the jungle inch by inch, not making a sound. When they were thirty feet away, Morgan stood and pulled Hoa to her feet.

"Hoa, do you see that star? That is west. That is where we are going. If anything happens to me, keep going. Don't stop. Do you understand?"

"Yes," she whispered, "but . . . "

"Come Hoa, I want you to follow directly in my footsteps. Every step I take, I want you to be in that step behind me. Do you understand?"

"Yes, but . . ." Hoa whispered silently.

"Hoa, there are mines. If something happens to me, you go on. It's the only chance we have."

The thought occurred to Morgan that perhaps Sophal had said these same things, had warned her in just the same way—and led her where? Focus, Morgan, focus, he thought. The jungle was impossibly dense. Morgan could feel the thick, dewy moisture on his body. Insects climbed on him. Each step was his death awaiting him, waiting to leave her alone in this dense, dark jungle. He turned to check on Hoa and sensed her nervousness.

"Hoa, what is it?"

"This where I was with Sophal. They found us. They find us."

"How long did it take before they found out?"

"I don't know. Maybe one hour, maybe two hour. We hear gunshots."

"We have to move fast, Hoa. Follow me. Stay in my footsteps."

Morgan tried to push through the jungle but the thick undergrowth held him back like the arms of the earth pulling him into the darkness.

"Come Hoa, come. Stay with me." He tried to run, but there was no space to run. They drove deeper and deeper into the jungle following the star.

"Come, Hoa," Morgan repeated.

He took her hand behind him and pulled. He could feel her weariness. How long had it been? How much time did they have? He didn't know. All they could do was move, as fast as they could yet so painfully slow. The slight moon was disappearing. They pushed and pushed and then the gunshots—far away, but not nearly far enough.

"This how it was. This how it was! They are coming. They can move through jungle."

Morgan knew that she was right. He knew that the Khmer Rouge soldiers were of the jungle. They were trackers and mountain people. Morgan drove his body through the jungle, ever conscious of Hoa's delicate breath behind him.

"Ahhh." Morgan heard the yell before his brain registered that it was he yelling. The sharp, piercing pain throbbed through his leg. He reached down to feel blood trickling down. He muttered a soft moan.

"What happen?"

"I'm, I'm, I'm OK." Morgan pulled the sharpened bamboo stick from the side of his leg. Pain surged through his body.

"Come, Hoa." He felt the energy draining from him. The spirits of the dark forest were taking him for their own. He was the runner in the forest, Morgan reminded himself, ordered himself, pushing on with every ounce of his energy that remained.

He pulled on Hoa's hand.

The gunshots seemed closer and closer. How long would it take to get to the border? Three hours, maybe four? The hint of dawn was waking the jungle. The sounds of night giving way to the cries of the morning. The birds and the insects chirped the next cycle of life into being.

"Morgan!"

He turned to face Hoa. He had not yet seen her with his eyes. The look of terror on her face pierced him. She was pointing down at his leg. Morgan followed the path of her finger. His entire leg was drenched in blood. His shoes were covered with a thick, red film. But this was not his leg, this was not his body, he was a single idea—survival, salvation. He pulled on Hoa's hand with a newfound strength. He would not leave her. He would not run to the French embassy like in 1975. He would stay with her. This time he would get her out.

The orange morning sun was rising. The sounds of shots grew louder and louder. Morgan pulled Hoa. He lurched forward with all his might away from the rising sun. He thought he heard voices from behind. He pushed on. "Come, Hoa." A bullet whizzed over their heads. Morgan realized that the soldiers knew where they were. The sound of them was so near.

They came to a clearing. It seemed to Morgan to stretch about a hundred yards across. The land had been bulldozed or bombed and was now filled with dead trees and broken branches. On the other side, Morgan saw a rice paddy surrounded by a dirt wall. The paddy was green, a deep green that Morgan knew meant Thailand, a green that Morgan knew came from a country that imported fertilizer and chemicals. And all that

Morgan had to do was take Hoa across this space and she would be saved and, because of that, entirely because of that, he could live. A look of hope emerged through Hoa's fear. Morgan almost smiled as he looked deeply into her eyes.

At his first step into the clearing, Morgan suddenly realized what was before him. He jumped back into the jungle, pulling Hoa toward him with a fierce, determined jerk. What had appeared to be the fallen branches of dead trees, he now saw, were skeletons, human skeletons picked apart by birds as they lay rotting under the fierce, rising sun. The bones were everywhere. The voices of death, the spirits of the dead descended upon Morgan.

"It's a minefield." The words sucked the hope from Hoa's face. Her look of determination remained.

Morgan felt her soft, trusting hand in his. He was back in CIA field school in a thirty-minute course on mines. He remembered the instruction— crouch down, poke ahead with a stick. He looked deep into Hoa's brown eyes. Her eyes seemed to place everything she was, everything she hoped to be, in his hands. He paused for a brief, perfect moment.

"Hoa, we're going through there. Follow me exactly. Do not move until I say so. Step only into my footprints. Do you understand?"

She nodded.

Morgan needed to be sure. "Do you understand, Hoa?" He almost shouted.

"Yes, yes. I understand."

"And if something happens to me, you pick up this stick and you do exactly what I'm doing—poke in front, keep your head low."

She looked at him as deeply as anyone had ever looked at him before.

"Thank you," she said.

Morgan forced himself to stop looking into her eyes. He grabbed a stick from the ground and crouched as low as he could. He poked it far in front of him then took a single step into exactly where he had poked. He then poked a new spot and moved into that. One step, a series of pokes, then another. He turned to be sure that Hoa was in his footsteps.

"Stay behind me, Hoa," he shouted. He was poking as fast as he could. Moving one step, then another. The gun bursts were getting louder. Their cautious steps were not fast enough.

"Come, Hoa. Come!" He had to move faster. He could see the rice paddy. If they could be on the other side of that wall they would be safe. They would be in Thailand. Closer and closer, one step at a time. Now he was certain he could hear shouts. They were coming and Morgan and Hoa would be easy targets in the middle of an open field.

Morgan moved faster and faster, poking with his stick four times at first before taking a step, but as the shouts and gun bursts grew closer, he only had time for three, then two.

"Stay behind me, Hoa. Move, come! Let's go, Hoa!" The Khmer Rouge soldiers were rapidly approaching. How long did they have? One minute, maybe two?

"Move! Come Hoa!" The bullets were now whizzing by. Morgan poked furiously in front of him as he and Hoa moved ever faster across the minefield.

"Come Hoa, faster!" There was no hope in this clearing and so little time to get across. He poked wildly, ever conscious of her breath on his back.

The sound exploded into Morgan's soul. He knew before he turned around, before he saw that everything was over.

She lay face down in the earth. The entire bottom half of her body was gone, blown in pieces on Morgan's back, strewn waiting for the birds to come. Her hands had fallen forward, as if praying to Thailand. Her hair scattered over her head and fell to the ground.

Morgan felt his entire life escaping from him. He took a step back and stroked Hoa's hair. It was more than tears that burst from Morgan's body. It was everything he had ever been, everything he had ever known. It was the ghosts that had become him, that he had become. Morgan fell to the earth like a corpse, as if cursing the fate that had denied him what it had offered her. He was beyond tears, beyond life itself. He was nothing.

The bullets came closer and closer. Morgan saw one strike the earth thirty feet away. Where was there to go? Why was there any reason to be anywhere but here, with her, returning to the earth? The blood on his leg was merging with hers in communion, the stream of death flowing to the indifferent ground. Morgan curled up like a fetus. The bullets hit the ground closer and closer.

From somewhere below his deepest level of consciousness, Morgan felt an instinctual command. His body curled around from his fetal position and stretched back like a sprinter at the blocks. Morgan lifted his leg from its crouch and hurled himself into the open field. One, two, one, two. His arms and legs moved back and forth floating along the arc of his stride.

And the spirits, the ghosts, the death—everything vanished from him as the click took hold. He was in a world beyond the bullets whizzing by his head. His stride was unbroken, he was one with the wind. One, two, one, two. He no longer existed but for this single physical motion. The bullets flew by. He ran, straight, effortlessly, perfectly. Crashing over the dirt wall of the rice paddy, he felt the cool brown water covering his collapsed, sinking body.

The ghosts returned as darkness engulfed him.

49

The drive back to Bangkok in the Mercy Relief truck was entirely silent. Jonathon sat with the Thai driver watching the rice paddies slide by. There was nothing to say. The driver probably didn't speak much English anyway. He knew the word "airport." That was enough.

The memory of his arrival in Thailand now haunted Jonathon. So much hope, excitement, facing his heritage, the unknown. And he had found it— frightening, devastating, indifferent, random, brutal, overwhelming. He had found truth. He had dreamed of staring it down, of challenging iniquity with belief. But at that time belief had been real, iniquity an abstract concept. His experience in the Khmer Rouge zone had established the reverse. Now, the Khmer Rouge army, the CIA, the deception, the inhumanity, the cruelty—these were real. The idealism that had brought Jonathon to the border seemed far off, nebulous. The image of the white bags of rice piled in the Khmer Rouge military camp, of the Khmer Rouge commander's gunshot, floated painfully through Jonathon's mind. And what about O'Reilly, what would happen to him?

Jonathon had fought these realizations, fought to find some compromise to let him stay. And Maria? He had never felt such a connection to anyone before.

How could he leave what he had only just started? he wondered. How could he leave *her?* But he had reached a dead end. He had gambled every-thing for meaning and come up empty. Would his ideals, his hope, lie aban-doned on the Thai-Cambodia border, or could he somehow transform this painful knowledge into something more enduring? The question seemed too much to ask.

Maybe his only chance was to perform his own personal *Taschlich,* to throw his former self, his failed self "to the depths of the sea."

I'm sorry, Maria, he thought piercingly to himself. I'm so sorry.

What happens, he wondered, to the stones they throw into the river? Do they sink to the bottom and get buried ever deeper in the muck? Do they roll down the river and join the vast and open sea? Were they washed clean by the flowing water and eventually deposited on dry land? Jonathon didn't know, but not knowing somehow comforted him.

Somewhere, a soft bed waited for him. Jonathon ached to crawl into it.

50

The circle closed around Maria. Dark rings surrounded her eyes.

The twelve others could all feel it, but no one said a word. They held hands.

"We pray for strength, to share our love with each other through God . . ."

Donna's words seemed to float past Maria's ears.

"We pray for expressions of your love, like when you brought sight to the woman in the Nong Chan camp . . ."

Maria did not seem to notice the reference.

"We pray that you will grant each of us the power to find strength in ourselves . . ."

Maria almost heard Donna's voice.

"We pray that you will give us the strength to forgive others for their transgressions . . ."

The pain.

"And that you will give each of us the courage to forgive ourselves."

For a moment, the image of Sister Susan flashed in Maria's mind. Sister Susan had forgiven Maria for her imperfections. Maria could accept the

refugees, forgive them, forgive the world. Why was it so difficult to forgive herself?

As fast as it came, the thought was gone.

Maria could feel the two hands squeezing hers. She closed her eyes to
feel it more.

51

"O'Reilly, O'Reilly. I think he's waking."

Morgan sensed the noises dragging him from his dreams.

"O'Reilly. Look, his eyes are flickering."

His eyes fought to stay closed. He didn't want to wake to this world. He had dreamed that Hoa was alive, that Sophal was alive. He felt the touch of Hoa's hair on the tips of his fingers.

"O'Reilly, O'Reilly."

Stay, stay closed, sleep. Morgan's eyes were betraying him. Though he fought to keep them closed, his eyes opened to the world where he was alone—ultimately, completely. He wanted to drive his eyes shut forever, to sink back into those dreams, into the earth.

"O'Reilly." There was an enthusiasm in the words that reached for Morgan. He felt a hand resting on his shoulder. His eyes flickered open.

"How ya doin', pal?" Conley asked.

Morgan's eyes twitched, focusing on the two faces floating over him. They were faces he knew, faces that made him long ever stronger for sleep.

"You really scared us, O'Reilly."

Morgan's eyes focused on one face, then the other.

"A Thai farmer picked you up in his field, says he found you floating in a pool of blood. He called the local police and they brought you here. You lost a lot of blood, pal. We've been frantic."

Morgan's face remained passive, indifferent. His eyes drifted from the faces and observed the rustic Thai hospital room around him before drifting to a point on the ceiling. Another pat on his shoulder.

"The doctors say you're going to be all right, O'Reilly. The helicopter from Bangkok is on its way. Bangkok General is one of the best hospitals in Asia. You're gonna be fine," Dan Hutchins added.

The words meant nothing to Morgan. He closed his eyes and saw Hoa's trusting face, her mangled body strewn across the ground. He opened his mouth to speak but there was no air.

"Hey, you take it easy, pal. You've been through a lot. We'll do all the talking."

Morgan needed to speak. He tried to push the air up from his stomach. He pulled it toward his throat.

"Di . . ." The sound was faint and weak. He pulled harder and he felt his voice returning to him.

"Did you get . . . my letter, Conley?"

Conley nodded.

"I didn't mean . . . Don't send, don't send the guns, don't send the weapons."

Dan Hutchins patted Morgan's shoulder for the third time.

"Sure, pal. Sure." He smiled.

Morgan knew the smile.

"Where . . . where's the letter?"

"We passed it back to Langley."

"Are you sending the weapons?" Morgan said weakly. "Don't bullshit. Are you going to send them the weapons?"

The two visitors looked at each other. "That's out of our hands. We'll see what we get from Langley."

"But . . ." Morgan realized there was no point in arguing with these guys. For all of the bravado they had shown on his way in, he knew that they would do whatever they were told. They all would. None of it was in their own hands. They would all wait for the little scraps of autonomy that would make them believe they controlled their own destinies.

"You'll be back soon," Hutchins said, "maybe you can talk with them when you get there."

Morgan's body was weak from the exertion. He felt his voice receding to his stomach. He pushed on.

"I, I need something done, here."

"What is it O'Reilly?"

"I have a friend. Someone who worked with us during the war."

"A Cambodian?"

"Y-yes." Morgan paused to refuel. "He's dead. His wife and his son are in the Site Three camp. Her name is Sok Nat. The boy is Sok Phally. I . . . you need to get them out."

Morgan saw that Conley and Hutchins were waiting for some reason why they needed to do this.

"It's all authorized."

Their heads picked up.

"By . . ." It hit Morgan, hit whatever was left to hit. "By Thomas . . . by Thomas Dillon at the NSC."

"That's no problem," Hutchins said. "We just need authorization from him. You know how it is, O'Reilly. Congress is really letting us have it about the refugees. Getting our old Vietnamese officers over is hard enough . . . We just need the authorization and it's no problem."

Morgan's eyes closed. He tried to jam his lids into the top of his cheeks, to merge them forever. The tears broke the seal and slid out the corners of his eyes.

"Bastards." The words petered out like the voice leaving Morgan.

"He must be exhausted," Hutchins said to Conley. "You just relax, O'Reilly." He patted Morgan's shoulder. "That helicopter must almost be here."

The silence was broken by three quick knocks on the door. The two men saw a head peer around the corner.

"Hi there. I'm Evan Pritchard from Mercy Relief. I hear Morgan's here?"

Hutchins stepped toward Evan.

"O'Reilly's been through a lot. I don't think he's ready to see anyone yet."

Evan was not moving. He stood in the doorway waiting for something to happen. Hutchins stepped toward him.

"Hey, I'm sorry, pal. The guy's been through a lot," Hutchins said firmly.

"Let him in." The men were surprised at the strength of the voice coming from the bed. "Let him in," Morgan ordered again. "He's my friend."

Evan walked past the two men.

"Hey, how ya doin' mate?"

Morgan stared at Evan with a look Evan had never before seen on Morgan's face or anywhere. It was a look, Evan thought for a moment, of naïve wonder.

"Leave us alone." Morgan's eyes focused on Hutchins, then Conley. The two men, embarrassed, looked at each other.

"OK, but if you need us we'll be right outside." They moved hesitantly out the door.

"Jesus man, what the hell happened to you?"

Morgan focused on Evan's face. Maybe this was his only friend left. This reporter who had only set for himself the task of recording—not acting, not saving—recording, writing. Maybe after everything, Morgan realized, after the war, after all the death, after his search and everything he had learned, maybe the only way to do no harm was simply to bear witness and not interfere.

"Sit down Evan. Do you have a tape recorder?"

Evan took a small recorder from his shoulder bag and clicked it on. Morgan began to speak.

"My name is Morgan O'Reilly. I am an operations officer of the Central Intelligence Agency. I served in Cambodia from 1970 to 1975. From 1971 to 1973, Thomas Dillon, who is now the deputy national security advisor, served in the US embassy in Saigon. In that time, he had a Vietnamese girl-friend named Tanh Li Ai Hoa." The mention of her name felt like a stake in Morgan's heart. "He left her behind when he returned to the United States in 1973, not knowing she was pregnant with his child . . ."

Morgan told Evan everything. He told of the secret unit, of Hoa's journey, of her letter to Dillon. He told of Sophal's mission and Dillon's orders. He told of the Thai links with the Khmer Rouge, of the weapons, everything, every detail. The words flowed from Morgan like the blood had flowed from Hoa's body.

"And now Sophal is dead, Hoa is dead, and for what? The arms list is in Washington, and . . . and . . . I don't know." He wished he knew the end of the story, but the end was beyond him.

Conley poked his head around the corner before he and Hutchins walked back in.

"The helicopter's ready. We're going to take you out to the truck to get over to the helipad."

Two male Thai nurses entered with a stretcher. They lifted Morgan, placed him on it and carried him out the door. Hutchins and Conley followed.

Evan Pritchard sat in his chair breathing deeply, as if drawing in a sublime aroma. He touched his recorder to make sure it was real. As he heard the truck pull away, he picked up the recorder and held it to him. He sprinted the six blocks back to his guest house, where his Smith-Corona was waiting at the bottom of his suitcase.

52

Thomas Dillon sat alone at his desk waiting for the phone to ring. Silence permeated his corner of the Old Executive Office Building. It was 6:30 A.M., and most of Washington was just waking up. Bohlen was probably already on the tennis court. Dillon pictured him racing to the net for the smash.

On the desk in front of him was a copy of the *Boston Globe* opened to page 8a. Dillon stared at the article. It was not a major story. There were no pictures. The header was relatively small. His ears picked up the whisper of the air conditioner and the soft hum of fluorescent lights.

The calls will come, he thought. They love this. They love to take hold of somebody and stick him through the ringer. He had seen it happen before. He knew how big this story would be, the utter destruction it would cause. His position, his reputation, his future—his wife—he could see the dominoes beginning to fall. The ecosystem would unflinchingly regain order. The buzzards would swoop down to handle his carcass. He looked at the phone then back at the article.

He closed the newspaper and folded it on his desk. His mind laid out a defense.

There was no evidence for this. The whole article seemed to rely on a single source, a half-baked CIA operative who had cracked up after the war. Yes, he had met with O'Reilly, but there was no record of his orders. Nobody could ever find them. They didn't exist. There certainly were no orders for O'Reilly to cross into the Khmer Rouge zone.

There were all kinds of stories—old vets trying to sneak back in to save lost comrades. Who was to say that O'Reilly wasn't acting on his own? Dillon had authorization from the president and from the national security advisor of the United States. He had sent an officer out to assess the situation on the Thai-Cambodian border. Let anyone prove otherwise.

And who wrote the ridiculous thing? Who the hell is Evan Pritchard? Pacific Times News Service? What the hell is that, a telex machine in someone's basement? This has absolutely no credibility.

Dillon had scanned the major papers—the *New York Times,* the *Post,* even the *Chicago Tribune*—nothing. Nobody cared what Pacific Times News Service had to say. Nobody cared what was going on in a faraway place called Cambodia.

Tension permeated Dillon's head like a sinus infection. The silence around him felt oppressive, menacing. He opened the paper again. His eyes led him back to the same paragraph he had already read twenty-three times that morning.

> *According to O'Reilly, Deputy National Security Advisor Dillon sent CIA Operations Officer Heng Sophal into the Khmer Rouge zone in Cambodia to trade illegal sophisticated weaponry for the lives of Ms. Tanh Li Ai Hoa, the married Mr. Dillon's Vietnamese girlfriend from the war years, and their five-year-old son, both now deceased.*

How many times could he read it? It still read the same. Hoa, his son, "both now deceased." The image of Hoa fighting her way across Cambodia to reach him, of his son buried in the Cambodian jungle, of Hoa's bones rotting in a minefield, seared a place in Thomas's heart he had never fully known existed. He felt his life imploding, his hidden, sustaining hope constricting into nothingness. Thomas folded the newspaper again. Still no ring. The hum of the fluorescent lights.

His ears felt the sound waves a fraction of a second before he heard the noise. He picked up the phone after three rings.

"Dillon."

"Thomas, Witkowski here."

"Good morning, sir."

"Good morning, Thomas. I just got a call from Graves at the CIA. He told me about a story on the wire by a guy named Pritchard from Pacific Times News Service. Do you know anything about it?"

"Yes. I've seen the article, sir."

"He tells me the article says that you sent two CIA operatives into Cambodia to rescue your girlfriend. Is that true, Thomas?"

A pause.

"No, sir."

"Yes . . ." Another pause. "I'm sure it's not . . . Graves says Bohlen's going to bring it up at the eight o'clock cabinet meeting with the president. I'll be there in an hour. Meet me in my office."

A pause.

"Yes, sir. Seven-thirty."

Thomas heard the phone click. He sat motionless, wondering if he was still alive at all.

The Old Executive Office Building was silent. The lights hummed. The air conditioning whispered like an old librarian. Shhh.

EPILOGUE

UNITED STATES OF AMERICA

Immigration and Naturalization Service
Refugees, Asylum, and Parole
Washington, D.C.

Admittees under section 207(c)(1)
of the Immigration and Nationality Act of 1952:

Date of Admittance: 23 October 1985

NAME: LAST, FIRST	COUNTRY OF ORIGIN
Soegiarso, Edouardo	Cuba
Sogoba, Ahmed	Iran
Sok, Nat	Cambodia
Sok, Phally	Cambodia
Sokolovsky, Vladimir	USSR
Soleimani, Farrar	Sudan